MEGAN MULRY

Bound with Honor

AN EROTIC HISTORICAL NOVEL

RIPTIDE
PUBLISHING

Riptide Publishing
PO Box 6652
Hillsborough, NJ 08844
www.riptidepublishing.com

Bound With Honor

Cover art: L.C. Chase, lcchase.com/design.htm
Editor: Delphine Dryden
Layout: L.C. Chase, lcchase.com/design.htm

ISBN: 978-1-62649-317-9

First edition
August, 2015

Also available in ebook:
ISBN: 978-1-62649-316-2

MEGAN MULRY

Bound with Honor

AN EROTIC HISTORICAL NOVEL

RIPTIDE
PUBLISHING

Your task is not to seek for love, but merely to seek and find all the barriers within yourself that you have built against it.
-Rumi

TABLE OF *Contents*

Chapter 1

Camburton Castle, September 1810

"*D*amn it, Archie." The Marquess of Camburton pulled his eyes away from the microscope as he chastised himself. His laboratory was usually a place of guaranteed concentration and uninterrupted thought. Lately, however, he hadn't been able to focus his mind on anything but Selina Ashby's bright cheeks and slightly parted lips. Even as he'd stared at the latest cowpox variolation through the scope, he had imagined Selina's long, dark eyelashes instead of the menacing virus he was attempting to stabilize.

Archie looked out the partially open window at the afternoon sun as it shone across the deer park. Accomplishing as little as he was, he decided to give up for the day. He scrubbed his hands and dried them meticulously, then hung his apron on the hook near the door. Slipping his formal coat back on, he took one last glance around the lab and, satisfied that everything could wait until tomorrow, set off for a walk around Camburton Park.

All of the land technically belonged to him, but he had never thought of it that way. His mother had raised him and his sister to view their inheritance as a temporary gift of immense responsibility. He was a custodian for future generations. He was starting to become preoccupied with said future generations, since it fell to him to be their progenitor. He sighed at the weight of it all, of wanting very much to be correct in his decisions, to honor the memory of his dead father, and to support the ongoing work of his imaginative mother.

It was not by chance that he found himself walking near the cottages where many artists spent the summer months. Or rather, chance had turned to habit of late. For years, Archie's mother Vanessa Cambury and her partner, Nora White, had invited painters, writers, musicians, and all sorts of inventive souls to rusticate at the large country estate every summer. Throughout Archie's rather bohemian upbringing, he had been exposed to every manner of creativity. Perhaps that was why he had pursued a career in science, for its supposed *absence* of creativity. He liked order.

Unfortunately, he was now coming to realize that science held an infinite number of mysteries. Yes, there were some irrefutable scientific facts, but that was like saying all paintings were composed of paint or all books were written with words. Those facts were the barest beginnings. The study of infectious diseases had captured his imagination because of one very promising idea: a cure. It hadn't penetrated his youthful enthusiasm that a cure sometimes took hundreds or even thousands of years to grasp.

He looked at the leaves overhead as he walked, marveling at the variety and nuances of each branch, each cell.

"Ooofff!" he grunted, then realized he'd bumped into Selina, and quickly reached for her upper arms to prevent her from falling. She was warm from her walk in the sun, more alive to the touch than in even his most fervent imaginings.

"Oh!" she gasped. "I'm very sorry to be so careless!" She slipped a finger into her book to keep her place and then held it close to her chest. He released her arms with great reluctance. "It's such a terrible habit to be walking and reading," she continued breathlessly, "but I simply had to be outdoors when the air is so . . . so . . . *silky*, don't you agree? But I couldn't tear myself away from this scene either. The villain is about to be discovered . . . Oh dear, I'm rattling on again." She curtseyed formally. "Lord Camburton."

"Oh, Selina. Please call me Archie. I beg of you."

Wrong choice of words. He knew it immediately. When he said "beg" and she looked at him like that—quick and wise—he was quite sure his tailor had mismeasured all of his clothes and cut them too small. He refrained from tugging at his collar like a schoolboy, but the urge was pressing. He stood perfectly still.

"Well, since you beg so nicely . . . *Archie* . . ." Her voice wasn't singsongy exactly; more like Archie was a shiny new toy she was very eager to play with.

She was tormenting him. He knew it as well as she did. But she was so sweet about it, so honest.

"Shall we walk together for a spell?" He held out his arm in a formal, gentlemanly way.

"Yes, thank you." She looked quickly at her book, remarking her page, then shut it completely and slipped it under her other arm. When she rested her fingers on his proffered forearm, they both shivered slightly. She pressed her fingers harder, gripping his muscle. "That's better."

He exhaled. *Better* was debatable. *Unsettling* was more like it.

He'd spent the past few weeks alternately avoiding Selina and seeking her out. He'd felt rather listless and enervated when he failed to track her down, and then rather overexcited and agitated on the occasions when he'd found her. Neither state was at all familiar. Archie was what was commonly known as a steady, settled sort of man. He had seen all manner of debauchery in his days at university and later in London, and he'd neither judged nor desired to participate in anything of an extreme nature. Yes, he occasionally fulfilled his baser desires when he went into town, but it was merely a passing comfort—like a warm meal on a cold day—when he and his close friend Christopher Joseph would spend a few hours in Christopher's rooms at the Albany. He had never thought, never could have believed, a girl would overset him quite like this—on his blind side.

But this . . . this . . . girl. For dear God, that's all she was. A slip of a girl. Blonde hair and creamy skin and dark pink lips. An English lass like any other. But she was so completely *unlike* any other. Or at least he was unable to dismiss her or overlook her as he had overlooked every other young woman of his acquaintance. To wit, he now imagined her as a possible wife, despite knowing very little about her past—except that it was checkered.

"How is your writing coming along?" he asked politely as they strolled.

"Oh! Terrible."

"Well, you aim for terror, don't you?"

She laughed, a clear burst that startled a bird from the branches above them. "Very good, Archie. Very good." She sighed. "Alas, that's not the kind of *terrible* I meant. I can't get a word to come. Or rather,

I have many words that are of the most pedestrian, hackneyed variety. As if my only inspiration is akin to the latest medicinal ointment being purveyed by a passing charlatan: Get your satisfaction here! Buy me now!" She did a fair imitation of a circus barker.

Her profile was limned by the hazy sun, until she turned her animated face directly toward him and her glittering green eyes sparked with that challenging taunt that made his heart hammer so. He faced forward quickly. "It's difficult when we are trying to achieve subtlety, for quite often the very attempt only serves to make us that much more crass." He would know.

"That's it exactly!" She grabbed his forearm even more tightly. "The words whisper around me—the *good* words, the subtly delectable ones—and then I put quill to paper and all I'm left with are the awkward, bungling words. Stomping boots when I want a featherlight *pas de deux*." She sighed and leaned into his upper arm. "But you must not encounter anything of the sort in your work. You're more of a hunter, yes, stalking the crafty viruses? Going in for the kill."

Even the way she talked about his work scattered his thoughts. Stalking. Crafty. Why was she so free? Why was it so enchanting? "Quite the contrary," he replied. "The truth eludes me far more often than it presents itself. And then when I do catch a glimpse of it, I'm usually misreading the evidence or imagining something that is not even there."

"Oh! I think it sounds fabulously exciting!" She loosened her hold as she looked off into the distance, where a pair of riders crested the low hillock.

"That must be Mayson and Rushford come for supper," Archie offered.

"I believe you're correct." She kept staring. "They are a handsome couple."

He looked down at her again. Despite his mother's decidedly liberated approach to everyone's sexual freedom at Camburton Castle, he had never become entirely accustomed to that level of *openness*. When he visited Christopher in London, he didn't go shouting announcements from the rooftops. That sort of thing was *private*. Or at least he'd always thought so. His mother and sister often poked fun at him for the way he clung to his old-fashioned notions of propriety, of what should and shouldn't be said aloud, but cling he did.

Trevor Mayson was marrying Archie's beloved sister, Georgiana, in a week's time. Trevor also lived with James Rushford. Even this, Archie could get his mind around. Everything was fine . . . for other people. He merely had certain traditional notions when it came to his *own* future. He had no wish to judge.

Over the summer, he had seen Selina with her dear friend Beatrix Farnsworth often enough, and while some suspected the two of them were more intimate than mere friendship, he had never broached the subject directly. For some reason, now he felt the compunction to do so, to let Selina see he was not a moralizing man. Perhaps he also felt the courage to ask because deep down he was certain two such lovely women could not possibly be involved in anything sordid. "You and Beatrix are a handsome pair as well."

Her face clouded instantly. "We are, aren't we? The closest of friends." She spoke to herself more than she spoke to him. "*Were*, I mean. We still are—" Selina stumbled over the words and her brow furrowed "—friends, that is. It's just that Bea left this morning, as you must know?" Her face cleared somewhat.

"I'm sorry, Selina. I didn't know. I apologize for my carelessness—"

"Not at all. She's off to perform in Milan and Rome and Venice and everywhere, and it's all very glamorous and wonderful."

"Why didn't you go with her?"

She looked up at him boldly. "I didn't want to leave England."

And wasn't that proof enough that there was nothing more *intimate* than deep friendship between Miss Farnsworth and Miss Ashby? Surely Selina would've gone with Beatrix if they were indeed a couple. "Really?" He knew he was being childish, but he wanted more. He was greedy for her interest. And confirmation. "What is keeping you?"

She licked her lower lip, slowly, like a cat preparing to pounce. "Unfinished business . . ."

His heart felt too large for his chest. "What type of business?"

Trevor and James were nearing, and the sound of pounding hooves began to encroach on their conversation.

"Oh!" She broke the moment with a toss of her chin. "I've a book to deliver by December. A book that's all clumsy, inelegant words at the moment."

"Yes." He exhaled to get his pulse back to a normal rate. "Your work. Of course."

"And for you, Archie." Her words were barely audible. Perhaps he'd misheard, he must've misheard—and then Trevor and James were upon them, tipping their hats to the lovely Miss Ashby, who curtseyed prettily and dipped her chin with a polite, "Lord Mayson. Mr. Rushford." The horses were sweaty and breathing heavily from the brisk ride over from Mayfield House, and Archie had a forceful desire to protect Selina from their threatening presence. Wrong again.

She released his arm and reached for Trevor's horse, the larger of the two. "Well, now, who is this beautiful creature?"

Archie watched, enthralled, as her small delicate hand pressed into the gleaming fur of the horse's powerful neck. She rarely wore gloves—she said they were tedious when it came to turning pages, and since that was her primary occupation she'd had to decide between gloves and books. And of course she'd chosen books. So he was free to stare at the subtle turn of her bare wrist, the fine bones of her long, slender fingers, the ink stains on her right hand.

"Archie!" James called with a jovial lift of his chin. "How is this fine day treating you? Solving any mysteries in the laboratory?" Smiling when Archie caught his eye, James winked to let Archie know he'd caught him ogling the lady.

"Alas, no. The little creatures are still winning in some instances, and we are aiming for complete eradication. But Jenner's on it. We're close to having a stable enough vaccine to package and distribute on a wide scale."

"Good to hear, good to hear."

"Will you be joining us for supper?"

"Yes, with all the wedding plans, it's the only chance we get to see Georgie. And we wanted to ride before dinner—nothing surpasses Derbyshire at this time of year."

"Agreed."

Selina finished her conversation with Trevor while petting his horse, and then the two men continued on their way, trotting slowly across the park toward the castle.

Archie pulled a clean handkerchief out of his pocket. "Would you care to wipe the smell of horse sweat off your hands?"

Dear Lord, this man was put in her path to give her every sordid thought. The mere mention of "sweat" and "hands" and "wiping" coming out of his prim, delectable mouth made her want to—

"Selina?"

Her gaze flew from his lips to his eyes, those amber eyes that always appeared so brilliant and tentative and eager all at once. Men were supposed to be full of blustery conviction and arrogance and superior notions. Men were not supposed to be biddable. Men were not supposed to tempt her the way the Marquess of Camburton tempted her.

Damn it, Selina, you are not that sixteen-year-old miss with no control of your emotions! As her fingers rested on his forearm, she tried to steady the frantic beating of her heart, gripping harder onto him as if that would ground her somehow.

Falling in love with the Marquess of Camburton was absolutely *not* on her agenda! She had books to write. She had her own life to lead. Not to mention Beatrix had barely been gone a day! Even though Bea had given Selina her blessing should she decide to pursue her burgeoning feelings for the marquess, Selina had believed herself to be a bit more in control than this. She'd fancied it would be a lark, a safe male friend with whom to satisfy her curiosity about what it would be like to be with a man.

Yet.

Here she stood next to Archibald Cambury, attempting to be immune to his kind, gentlemanly ways, and instead her heart was pounding wildly . . . and not just with lust. She actually admired the man. The way he spoke about her relationship with Bea with such understanding and acceptance, the way he listened to her when she talked about her work, and the way he looked at her with such devotion. She wanted him, yes, to touch him and fulfill her own dreamy sensual desires, but she also felt the beginning of something far deeper—a desire to protect and nurture him and to be protected and nurtured by him in return. She wasn't just smitten.

In fact, Selina was beginning to entertain the previously preposterous notion that she might actually wish to *marry* the Marquess of Camburton.

She accepted the handkerchief out of polite habit, then, without thinking, brought it to her nose, wanting to inhale the warm scent of Archibald Cambury's pocket square . . . wanting to inhale Archibald Cambury.

"Thank you," she murmured through the fabric. He watched her hands; he always watched her hands. But her hands were so close to her eyes that he was forced to meet her gaze.

"Archie . . ."

When he licked his lips, she reached for him, and her book fell from between her arm and her ribs. "Damn it, Selina!" she chastised herself.

They both bent simultaneously to fetch the book and nearly banged heads. He got to it first, and they rose slowly at the same time. He was a good four or five inches taller than she was and, unaccountably, that made him even more precious—like one of those German boarhounds on the estate that, despite its size, still thought it fit on her lap.

He held out the book for her to take it back, but she ignored the gesture and reached for his face. She gripped the handkerchief in one hand and trailed the other along his slightly rough jaw. It was the first time she had really touched him, skin to skin, and the surge of power through her fingertips was even greater than she had dreamt it would be. "Archie . . ."

His eyes closed and a gentle moan escaped him as her fingertips continued to explore the planes of his cheeks, the turn of his jaw, the arch of his brow. She avoided his mouth, savoring the anticipation, watching him closely as his nostrils flared and the tip of his tongue touched the corner of his lips and then retreated. She toyed with his ear, lightly caressing the edge and wondering if the silky texture was similar to the sensitive skin of a man's cock.

Standing perfectly still, except for those stunningly desperate breaths, Archie resembled a statue, or a treasure—something awaiting discovery, or about to be pillaged. "I want you, Archie . . ." Words escaped her when she saw the color flood up his neck and cheeks. She had never seduced anyone, and the power of it was beginning to fill her with a throbbing energy. Not that she'd ever been passive—she'd been with three loving, attentive women over the past five years, with whom she had been exuberant and fearless—but she had never *initiated* any of those relationships. In the first two instances, they had found each other, a shared joining of equals. And Beatrix, well, Beatrix was like a force of nature; she had taken Selina with her sheer intensity, in a passionate night that had unfurled into three years of companionship and deep, abiding love.

And Beatrix had encouraged her over the past few months, egged her on even, when it came to the marquess. "Why don't we invite him over?" she'd taunted.

"He would never!" Selina had replied, knowing what Beatrix was suggesting. "Archibald Cambury is looking for a wife, not an orgy."

But Beatrix was gone for now. And it was just Archie and Selina standing here under this beautiful tree, with him holding her book and her touching his magnificent face.

"I'm going to kiss you now, so if you don't want me to, you must stop me."

His eyes opened slightly—amber shards burning with desire—but otherwise he remained perfectly still. She stood on the tips of her soft-soled summer shoes. When her lips touched his, they both pressed against each other, quivering. He dropped the book again, God bless him, and put his strong hands on her upper arms the way he'd done earlier when he was trying to stop her from falling. But now it felt like he was holding on, afraid he would be the one to fall.

"Selina . . ." His voice was thick and full of want, as he brushed his lips against hers. "Selina . . ." He pushed her away, but kept his hands on her in that firm, almost accusatory way. "It's not proper."

God, how she loved his propriety. She wanted to slink around it like a randy cat, rubbing herself against his upstanding self. "I don't want to be proper when I'm with you," she whispered.

He shook her slightly, then looked ashamed that he had manhandled her. The inner battle was divine. She wanted to push him to the edge of that conflict, force him to release all that inappropriate, violent lust despite himself. She adored his aristocratic ways, because unlike the airs and grasping of her own family, his devotion to his place in society was entirely authentic. In all their walks around the estate and quiet strolls across his lands, she had seen the depth of his commitment to a life that many would see as a burden of birth, or something to be leveraged for financial or social gain. Not Archie. Getting to know him over the past few months had proven to her that he was that rare creature: a true gentleman.

But beneath that, simmering just there where no one else could see it—or perhaps no one but she had ever been *permitted* to see it— resided a crouching animal, some part of him that he held in check. That was the part of him that she wanted to break free. Against his better judgment. To get him to unleash it on her.

He exhaled through his nose. "Please don't say such things. I don't want to do anything to compromise you, Selina."

She repressed a laugh at the idea she could be compromised. "Very well." She stepped back, and he was forced to release her. With Beatrix gone for at least three months, she had more than enough time to pursue Archibald Cambury. Three months? Three days would probably be enough to get him to his knees, where (quite certainly) he very much wanted to be. "I know *proper* matters to you."

"Does it not matter to you?" He bent to pick up the book from its second tumble, and handed it back to her.

They began walking again. "I suppose not. My parents were very strict, and I decided many years ago that I would not live my life in the same way, filled with fear of society or the opinions of some imaginary jury. Or God."

He held his forearm out again, defaulting to tradition. She went along, resting her hand easily on the fabric of his coat and walking in time with him. "Do you not feel the prick of your own conscience?" His voice held a hint of worry.

She let the silence spread easily around them while she thought about that, finally answering with a slight laugh. "Of course I *have* a conscience. I just— Oh, I don't know. I don't believe in sins of the flesh, I suppose." She paused again, and then blurted, "Did you know I was in hospital?"

"What? No. Were you ill? I'm so sorry to hear it."

"No, actually. I wasn't ill. But I was a *problem*. I wouldn't be quiet. My mind wouldn't settle. I didn't like embroidery." She laughed again. Without looking at him, she realized the truth of it. "I think my parents put me into a lunatic asylum because I refused to broider."

"How long were you . . . there?" The tenderness of his concern almost made her feel more sorry for him than she did for the injustice done to her. Almost.

"How long was I imprisoned, you mean?"

"No! Your family wasn't imprisoning you; they were caring for you. They must've thought they were doing what was best."

"Oh, but you have a generous heart." She remembered the daily ice baths and restraining devices, and suppressed a shiver of disgust. "My family does not care for me, not in the way you mean."

They walked on quietly, and she could tell the *unaccountability* of her parents not loving her was causing his brain to stutter. "Was it for a few weeks, then? They put you in someone else's care?"

"It was over a year. A full cycle of the seasons . . . so I have something to remind me . . . all year round."

"But they must've wanted you to be healthy."

"No, they wanted me to be *tamed*."

That silenced him completely. He was a brilliant man, she knew that from the way he looked at the world, from the walks they'd taken—the very proper walks—when he'd discussed his research, or the sonata that Beatrix had played, or Nora's latest painting. He saw things clearly. And those things that perplexed him, he was able to ponder at great length. He was patient.

"I can't imagine such a thing."

She burst out laughing again and pulled her hand from his arm. "I can see why!" She spun around, her arms wide and free, encompassing the seemingly infinite breadth of Camburton Park, with Camburton Castle shimmering in the distance. "You were raised here in paradise, and you were raised by Vanessa. Did she ever tell you no? Even once?"

His brow furrowed adorably. How a man of twenty-eight could have the innocence of a child, she knew not, but she never tired of his virtue. He looked as though he were quite methodically going through every interaction he'd had with his mother over those twenty-eight years, before he finally replied. "I can't think of . . .

Now that you ask . . . I think not. Of course there were matters of etiquette and behavior and that sort of thing, but when it came to our own ideas? No. In fact, I think she may have even encouraged us to disagree with her. She would laugh and throw up her hands when we would question her authority, and kiss us on our heads and tell us how beautiful we were." The realization appeared to strike him hard, perhaps the guilt of how lucky he was.

"See? Heavenly. Whereas . . ." She hated being glum. It was so tedious talking about her puritanical childhood. Beatrix had been a glorious remedy to all of that. Any time Selina even approached the dark edges of memory, Beatrix would laugh and tell her to celebrate her freedom, her escape from the clutches of those small, mean minds that had raised her. She would usually make love to her at times like that. "You are free now. Dwell in that," Beatrix always said.

Archie reached for her hand and, rather than the formally proffered forearm, he laced his gloved fingers through her bare ones. They walked hand in hand like that for another quarter hour or so. Eventually they ended up at her cottage as dusk fell. She looked appreciatively at the late summer wildflowers and riotous blooms that filled the small front garden. And she was lonely already.

And grateful. She sighed. Lonely and grateful.

The writing life had turned her into a walking conflict: she craved the peace and isolation that would allow her to write, but she loved the sounds and scents of another person nearby. She was selfish, and she knew it. About that, at least, her parents had been quite astute—Selina Ashby wanted things.

"Here we are." He stood away from her and clasped his hands behind him.

"Yes, here we are." She stared at the bright-red front door, then back into his eyes. "Would you like to come in?" She'd meant to ask it in a casual way, but her desire betrayed her, and she knew she sounded like some sort of throaty seductress.

He stepped back another pace. "Oh, I think not."

"Of course, yes. You need to get back to the house in time for supper." She turned toward the setting sun as if it held all the answers between them. "I'm going to stay here at home for dinner tonight. I think I need a bit of quiet."

"I'm going to London." He said it like a bark.

"Oh?" She looked back at him. "Yes, that's right. For your sister's wedding." She wasn't sure why he was telling her. Initially, his advances and withdrawals had amused her, but lately—today especially—she was feeling agitated and needy around him. She wanted to go into her cottage and pleasure herself before she did something stupid like beg him to touch her. When he failed to elaborate, she continued, "Very well. I hope you have a pleasant journey."

"Come with me."

"What?" Good God, when he spoke in that halting, desperate way, she wanted to tear off her clothes and pull his lips to her breasts. "To London?"

He settled somewhat, still with his hands clasped behind his back, which (unfortunately for his propriety), drew her attention to the bulge in his tight, revealing breeches. She forced her gaze back to his eyes.

He spoke softly. "Yes. Would you like to accompany me to London? In addition to my sister's marriage celebration, I have several appointments and a lecture to attend, so I am going to town for the week. With my prior obligations, I wouldn't be able to escort you anywhere, but I thought perhaps you would want to see your publisher, or might wish to visit a friend. I have room in my carriage. Mayhap it was a silly invitation. I regret—" He began to sketch a small bow of apology.

"Yes."

He startled. "Yes?"

"Yes." She smiled broadly through the word. "Yes, I would love to accompany you to London. And once there, I shan't inconvenience you. I shall stay with my father's sister, the one from whom my mother is certain I inherited all of my *worst* attributes—she is forward and brash and shameless. And wonderful. She designs sets for the theater and lives near Drury Lane, and she has been wishing for me to visit all this past year."

"Very well, then." He was pleased, she could tell, but he was keeping it all buttoned up in that riveted way of his. "We will leave Monday morning at first light."

"Very well. And thank you . . . Archie." Saying his name aloud felt like the greatest intimacy. She lifted herself up on tiptoes and kissed him quickly on the cheek, then turned and ran the last few steps into her small home. The door shut behind her, and she waited breathlessly until she heard his footsteps recede down the path and off into the park. Then she slid to the floor, set her book aside, and reached her hand between her legs, burrowing under the multilayered folds of her dress. She was swollen and wet, and it didn't take more than a minute—imagining Beatrix suckling at her breast while Archie pounded into her pussy—for her to come in a brilliant flare, right there on the floor.

Chapter 2

*I*n the misty dawn of Monday morning, Vanessa and Nora stood close by in the forecourt while the footmen hoisted Selina's bag onto the rack at the back of the carriage. Archie watched out of the corner of his eye as Selina waited slightly apart from the rest of them, in that observing way of hers, as if she could look and not look all at once.

Vanessa kindly included her. "Farewell, Selina. I'm sorry we won't see you in London. You know you are more than welcome to attend the wedding."

"You are too kind," Selina replied graciously. "But it is a family affair, and I will also have my own commitments. But thank you again. I look forward to hearing all about it when we return here in October."

"Yes," Nora agreed. "We will all be back in a few weeks, isn't that right, Archie?"

"Yes, Nora. We'll all be back." He opened the carriage door for Selina. "But now we must depart if I am to reach London in time for Jenner's lecture tomorrow evening."

"Yes, you must go." Nora hugged him and smiled. "We will see you in a few days, my dear."

As soon as the carriage door shut, the horses began trotting away at a steady pace. It was an excellent carriage, well sprung, comfortable, and amply stocked for the rigorous three-day-long trip ahead of them. He removed his hat and set it on the seat next to him. After checking to make sure everything was secured properly, he stared across at Selina and let himself look his fill. She happened to be peering out the window with a seemingly oblivious concentration, the edge of her poke obscuring part of her profile, yet accentuating the turn of her jaw and her delicate chin.

He loved observing the world; he especially loved observing Miss Selina Ashby. Archie was no artist himself, but even though Nora was not his mother by birth, she was still one of his parents. He had inherited her habit of seeing the world carefully, noting the hints and shadows of things.

"Archie?" Selina asked without turning from the window.

"Yes." He almost said, *Yes, love*, as he did to his mother or Nora or his sister, Georgie. Selina was beginning to reside in the same chamber in his heart.

"What do you think of me?"

He tried to laugh it off. "What a strange thing to ask, Selina. I think very highly of you. You must know that."

She turned slowly, and the way her hat framed her face made her look even more like a portrait, a perfect ivory cameo or immaculately painted miniature. "I mean, do you *think* of me? Do you . . . imagine me?"

He suddenly realized six hours spent in this confining manner would be an eternity. He might need to ride up on the box with the coachman if this sort of intimate conversation was the only alternative. "I think of you often. I think of you . . ." His throat was dry, so he reached for the hamper. "Would you care for some tea?" He took out the flask that had been wrapped in cotton wadding to hold in the heat, and held up a small cup. "Yes?"

She ignored his offer. "Am I being too forward?"

He unscrewed the top of the flask and poured it carefully into the cup. "Here. Have some."

As he handed it to her, the coach jostled and a bit of the hot liquid spilt onto her finger. She didn't flinch, and she was actually smiling when he looked up.

"I am so sorry for being so clumsy."

"It's not your fault." She took the cup in two hands and held it close to her chest, still with that lovely smile playing at the corner of her lips. She held his gaze as the warm liquid passed her lips and slid down her throat. He watched her swallow. The image of her taking his cock like that—lips taut, throat working—flashed in his mind like a pornographic firework. An impossibly inappropriate vision.

He blinked it away, cleared his throat, and sat back abruptly, then refastened the top of the flask.

"Aren't you going to have any?" she asked.

"No. I'm fine, thank you."

They rode in silence for nearly an hour after that. He spent most of the time wondering how he could appropriately distance himself from her in the current circumstances. It was much too close in the coach; perhaps at the first stop for the horses he could suggest that she might prefer privacy.

"Archie?" She tilted her head slightly.

"Yes, Selina?" He'd been working his way through the periodic table in his mind to pass the time, while she'd been reading a novel.

She'd removed her hat, and her hair was coming loose, a few blonde tendrils snaking down the side of her neck. It was much easier when he didn't have to focus on her, but she'd asked for his attention and it would be rude to look away. The silence lengthened and his heart rate increased. She just gazed at him like that, quietly taking him in. "Will you come sit next to me?"

His cock twitched, and even though the flaps of his coat concealed his lap, he suspected she somehow knew how his body reacted to her. "I don't know if that's a good idea."

"Why isn't it a good idea?" she asked, sounding a bit short-tempered.

"For obvious reasons." He exhaled. "When I get close to you, I . . ." He couldn't finish that thought. What could he say? *When I get close to you I want to touch you? When I get close to you I want to pull the pins out of your hair and burrow my face into your neck? And I want to make love to you? I want to put my face between your legs and swallow every ounce of what makes you who you are?*

"What happens when you get close to me?" She set her book down and came over to his side of the carriage. She moved his top hat and set it respectfully on the other bench, where she'd just been sitting. He wondered if the seat was still warm, if his hat was somehow enjoying the warmth of Selina Ashby's body. She was touching him, lightly caressing his hand. "Do you want to touch me, Archie?"

His heart was pounding so hard now; it was becoming difficult to hear her over the ferocious drum of blood in his ears. "We shouldn't..."

But she didn't stop. Her fingers traced his, skimming the sensitive skin between each one, then the flesh at the base of his thumb. "You have amazing hands. I love them." She brought his knuckles to her lips and began kissing her way across each ridge. "I imagine you touching my body."

He ripped his hand from hers and gasped. "Please go back to your seat, Selina. This is entirely improper."

She didn't move. In fact, she smiled. "It is, isn't it? Deliciously improper. The two of us in a closed carriage. The noise of the horses concealing my screams of passion. The clatter of wheels and springs muffling your moans."

He leapt away as she reached for his now-hard cock beneath his straining buckskins. Then he settled on the other seat, nearly crushing his hat. "Perhaps I should sit with the coachman—"

She didn't even try to stop him. He was about to pound on the ceiling of the carriage to alert his man that he wanted to stop—his arm extended for a seemingly infinite moment—yet still he hesitated. And she saw it. She saw him so clearly.

Selina looked at him, all tense and pulled in every direction, his strong arm reaching for escape, but his whole body yearning to stay. "You want this, Archie."

His arm fell, but he said nothing.

"Why else would you have asked me to join you?" She began to unbutton her spencer, and his eyes widened as her fingers worked at the tight fabric buttons over her breasts. "I kept thinking about it over the weekend. Why would he invite me? Does he want me as much as I want him?" She spoke casually, as if she were alone and musing aloud.

His breath caught when she said "want."

She tugged at the spencer after she'd undone the buttons. The rose velvet was close-fitted, the garment one of her best, so she had to arch her back to tug the sleeves free. He kept staring at the edge of her gown where the bodice skimmed across her straining bosom. After she'd managed to get one sleeve off, she breathed a sigh and reveled in the new freedom for her ribs and breasts.

"So confining." Her other arm finally slid free, and she smiled as if the marquess would understand her sartorial frustrations.

"Selina . . . you should . . . you should not . . ."

Her eyes caught his as they skimmed her arms, bare except for the short sleeves that capped her shoulders. It was cool in the carriage, but not uncomfortably so. The autumn air was beginning to whip across the hills and the morning was still brisk. "That is the problem, isn't it? I should. And I should not. That has always been my difficulty. I want things. And then I think about the things I want. I think and think. My imagination takes over. I imagine things in great detail. I imagine you."

He swallowed, the loud gulp echoing through the compartment.

"Have you imagined me, Archie?" He stayed silent. "That's fine, you don't have to answer. I know it's hard for you." She loosened the laces of her dress as she spoke, and felt the throbbing between her legs. God, the way he looked at her, paying attention to every detail, every movement of her fingers and arms, the way her legs shifted or her neck tilted. He almost didn't need to touch her, his gaze was so powerful. Almost. For now. She could live without his touch for now, but eventually . . .

Eventually she would have his skin against hers, even if it meant she had to tie him down to accomplish it. He would like that.

She smiled devilishly at the prospect. "I think about you while I touch myself."

He began to perspire, the sheen of sweat making his face—that perfect patrician face, usually all cool authority and solid planes— even more desperate, more eager.

"I'm going to touch myself now."

He grunted or moaned or something that might have constituted some form of resistance in the high court, but he didn't move. He sat there like a statue, a prisoner of what he so obviously wanted but could never actually ask for. She could see his cock pressing against his breeches.

She rolled her shoulders, first the right and then the left, enjoying the liberty of her loosened stays and her absent spencer. "If you don't care to watch, you should close your eyes." His eyes stayed open, and she felt it like the greatest victory—she almost tossed out a cavalier *I thought so*, then decided that would perhaps break the spell, and put him back on the side of propriety. She brought her fingers to her mouth. "I often think of kissing and licking your hands, like I started to do before . . ." She licked her fingers, then dipped her thumb and forefinger into the front of her gown, where she'd loosened the fabric enough to pinch one of her nipples. She bit down on her lower lip as she did so. "I think of your mouth on my breasts. I want that so much. I want that beautiful mouth of yours on me."

He moaned, and she saw his knuckles strain as he gripped the squabs on either side of his powerful thighs. Poor, beautiful man. So tight. So contained.

She squeezed her nipple hard and sighed at the bittersweet satisfaction of it. "I would beg you to be hard with me. Strict and strong. You would know how much I need that, for you to be strong for me. For us."

He ground out some unintelligible epithet or plea, and it was more than enough to prod her on. One day she would make this man scream out what he wanted.

"And I will be strong for you, as well. I will be able to take what you so obviously want to provide." She used her other hand to lift up her skirts, slowly revealing her stockings and the pretty rose-colored ribbons she'd used to tie them. "I thought of you while I dressed this morning. I wanted you to see me like this." She spread her legs and exposed her naked, swollen sex.

He rubbed both of his hands over his face, viciously scraping his palms against his eyes and cheeks. "Selina . . ." His voice was ragged and so deliciously conflicted.

"Yes, love. I'm right here." She began to stroke her pussy, lightly at first, trailing her finger along her slit while she kept toying with her nipple. "I do this while I think of you." She traced the shell of her opening. "I imagine you being tentative and curious at the beginning."

He whimpered and pressed his hand over his engorged cock, as if he could make it go away.

She slid her hips forward to get a better angle—better for her to see her hand working and better for him to see as she did. "But then I would want more, wouldn't I?" She began to circle her clit, to pinch and moan. "Because the way I want you . . ." She panted through the words. "There is nothing tentative about the way I want you, Archibald Cambury." Thrusting two fingers in, she kept up the pressure on her clit. Her ragged breath made it hard for her to speak. "I can make it last, when you finally come to me, I promise I will make it last . . ."

He pressed cruelly against his crotch, groaning in near pain. "Selina . . ."

"But right now I am going to take my pleasure fast and hard, picturing you thrusting into me—" She rode her hand for three or four harsh strokes and then exploded, crying out his name as she arched and quaked for him. For him to watch.

When she was once again able to focus, she saw his jaw was clenched, eyes murderous. Breathing in steady, controlled pants, he kept his lips in a firm line as he inhaled and exhaled through his nose. He looked so angry, so furious, because she had . . . what? Sullied his opinion of her?

She wasn't about to let him deny what was so obviously true for *both of them*—he wanted her as much as she wanted him; she was sure of it. Refusing to let his supposed irritation limit her lingering pleasure, she removed her hand from her breast, adjusted her bodice, then pulled back the fabric of her petticoats to get a better look at her hand pressed against her pussy. Her slick moisture was glistening against her inner thighs, and she spread it around, imagining a time his seed would be mixed with it. "God, what you do to me. I'm so wet—"

"Stop it! At once!"

She peered up with a slight smile. "Well, it's pretty much over at this point. For now. But fine. I'll stop." She dragged her hand away from the still quivering flesh between her legs and put her dress to rights.

The coachman called "Whoa," and the coach began to slow.

"Perfect timing." She adjusted her hair and tightened the laces of her dress. "I could do with a bit of fresh air and to stretch my legs."

He stared disapprovingly at her spread legs when she said that, and she couldn't help laughing at his furious censure. Surely he would admit his own desire at any moment. Wouldn't he?

"Do not laugh at me, Miss Ashby." His voice was cold and empty, as if she were a stranger, or a servant. Though she'd never heard him speak in quite that stony way to anyone, servant or otherwise.

She ceased giggling at once. Her heart was pounding, with a heady combination of fear and desire. "Yes, my lord. As you wish." She bowed her head slightly and put her knees primly together.

"I suspect you are mocking me, or mocking the formal show of respect you are now employing, but I shall take you at your word—that you will do as I wish—and you will permit me to ride the rest of the way with the coachman, outside the confines of the carriage."

"Oh, Archie—" She reached for him, and he withdrew as best he could. More like recoiled. "I'm very sorry," she whispered.

"So am I." He opened the carriage door before the horses had come to a complete stop. Unable to abandon his manners entirely, he waited patiently for her to exit the carriage, so he could aid her descent. She had to put her spencer back on, and the arms were too narrow and she almost cried in frustration. She refused to cry, damn it. He wanted her. She knew it. Just because he was ashamed or embarrassed by his desires, didn't mean she had to be ashamed of hers. She would never be ashamed of that. She slammed her stiff hat on her head and tied the satin ribbons tightly beneath her chin.

When she stepped from the carriage, she ignored his offered hand. "Thank you, Lord Camburton, but I'm quite capable of stepping out of a carriage—and accomplishing many other things—without your assistance." She walked toward the tavern across the stable yard where the carriage had stopped to water the horses. Selina entered the modest establishment in search of a privy, a bracing drink, and a secluded room where she could avoid the scathing, judgmental glare of the Marquess of Camburton.

Chapter 3

*A*rchie had so hoped Selina Ashby would prove to be the woman he had long imagined in his rather particular vision of what he wanted in a wife: a woman who would be an attentive, loving mother to his children; a woman with a keen intellect, who would perhaps share his interests in Camburton Castle and the responsibility of keeping it in high fettle for future generations; a woman, in short, he could respect.

As they approached London, he did his best to shove all those hopes aside. Selina was not that woman. She was a sexually precocious trollop. Well, maybe he didn't need to go as far as *trollop*. She was sexually precocious. And that simply did not coincide with his wishes for a happy, secure home life. She was too pressing, too forward. It was probably for the best that she had accosted him in that way, revealed herself, as it were. He groaned at the double meaning.

Of course he had responded physically! What man wouldn't? But he was not a beast. He could control those base desires. He didn't need to act on them. Why did she have to act on every careless impulse?

"Damn it," he mumbled to himself.

"I beg your pardon, sir?" The coachman turned to him. They were both sitting on the raised driving seat of the large carriage.

"Oh, I was just thinking aloud." Archie paused and looked around at the encroaching city. They would reach Mayfair within the hour. "Are you married, Granger?" He realized the coachman had worked for his family for as long as he could remember, and yet he had no idea about the man's personal life.

"I am indeed, my lord. Twenty-two years of wedded bliss." Granger turned and winked ironically, but Archie remained perplexed. The driver resumed his serious concentration on the crowded street ahead.

"I didn't mean to appear humorless. Congratulations on your domestic happiness."

"Thank you, my lord."

They rode in silence the rest of the way. Archie was in knots. Was he a hypocrite? He'd never thought so, but damned if he didn't resent Selina for what amounted to honesty. The entire situation was far too vexing. He eventually decided such vexation was yet another indication Selina Ashby was not the right woman for him. He did not wish to be vexed.

When the carriage finally pulled up in front of Camburton House on Grosvenor Square, Archie leapt from the high perch as if he'd been riding on a bed of hot coals for three months, rather than a mere three days.

And here came said hotbed. The footman held the carriage door open as Selina peered out. She smiled when she saw the glorious autumn leaves in the center of the square and then she beamed appreciatively when she scanned the sparkling mansions along the north side.

"Miss Ashby." Archie sounded especially formal, even to his own ears.

"Lord Camburton." She adopted the same cool tone, taking the tips of his fingers for support as she stepped down without making eye contact.

He had tried not to notice her appearance earlier in the day, but there was no avoiding it now that he was helping her from the carriage—she was gloriously dressed for town in another damnably tight spencer that pulled affectionately across her full bosom. Beneath, she wore a pale blue dress of some sort. Archie had never taken an interest in fashion, but the dress seemed to skim her body in the most distracting way.

She avoided looking at him. "Shall I hire a hackney to take me the rest of the way to my aunt's?"

They had stayed at two of his favorite inns during the journey, and he had originally envisioned private dinners with the pair of them chatting comfortably in front of a low fire. After the disastrous carriage ride on the first morning, he wasn't surprised when Selina chose to dine alone in her room both nights. He knew it was for the best. Of course it was. But *damn it*. Why couldn't she just behave like a *normal* young woman?

"Of course you will not hire a hack!" He sounded more exasperated than he intended, but he was at his wit's end with this woman. The least she could do was adhere to the last few threads of propriety until he deposited her at her aunt's townhouse. "I will drive you to your aunt's in my curricle as soon as your luggage is transferred. It is easier to navigate the smaller vehicle on the narrow lanes near Covent Garden."

"Very well." She removed her fingers from his and clasped both hands around her reticule.

"Won't you come in for refreshment before we go to your aunt's?" He gestured toward his grand home behind them.

She looked up at the imposing façade of Camburton House. "Thank you for your kind invitation, but I think not. I told my aunt I would be to her by five, and I have already gone far beyond the boundaries of your kind consideration. I also know you are eager to attend Mr. Jenner's lecture."

Everything she said was true, but he was irritated nonetheless. For some reason, it felt as if she were giving *him* a set down.

He spoke to one of the passing footmen. "Have my curricle brought round at once."

"Yes, my lord."

They stood silently for the next ten minutes, Archie refusing to engage Selina in conversation when she was in this icy mood. The curricle arrived at last and the matched bays pranced and snorted. He watched as Selina reached for one of the animals, about to stroke its shimmering russet coat.

"You do not wish to be late." His voice was overly stern, but he'd had quite enough of watching her *touch* things. "Let us not tarry, Miss Ashby."

She gasped at his obvious effort to prevent her movement, and withdrew her hand before she touched the animal. "Yes, my lord." She dipped her head in apology and accepted his hand with cool detachment when he assisted her up to the elevated seat. He double-checked that her luggage was attached to the back of the curricle, and then he took the long whip and reins out of the driver's hand. He leapt up to the high perch next to Selina and they were off in a trice.

He had very few vanities, but this vehicle was one. He'd redesigned the suspension system himself, and the flow and movement of the two wheels beneath them was smooth and exhilarating, especially after the large traveling carriage and team of four they'd used to come down from Derbyshire. Trying to ignore the close press of Selina's thigh against his, he focused on the horses and held the whip more as a gentle reminder than a form of discipline. His sister Georgiana had trained these two mares herself several years ago, before she'd left for Egypt the first time, and they were a perfect pair in both temperament and appearance.

He led the curricle down Audley Street, then turned onto Curzon, quickly reaching the bustle of Park Lane. The more he focused on the horses, the less he thought about his swirling, convoluted feelings for the woman next to him. He navigated them around Hyde Park Corner and, when they entered Green Park, he loosened his hold and gave an encouraging swish of the long whip. The two horses bounded forward, thrilled to be given free rein. Letting the autumn air swish past him, enjoying himself fully for the first time in three days, he risked a quick glance at Selina. He expected her to be gripping the low handle to her right, probably hoping to steady herself in the midst of a frightfully exhilarating ride. He was slightly ashamed to admit he *wanted* her to be afraid, to have to rely on him, but that was the truth of it.

He shouldn't have looked. He simply should *not* have looked. Her head was tilted back joyfully, her chin lifted in some sort of cosmic welcome, her partially open mouth revealing a blissful half smile, eyes nearly closed in communion with the wind and speed. She looked just like she had when she'd cried out his name—

He pulled at the reins far too abruptly. It was only due to excellent training that the two mares didn't break their traces altogether. As it was, the high wheels beneath them tilted at a precarious angle and one even came off the ground for a few dangerous seconds. Selina grabbed his right arm with both hands when they were in that suspended moment of unknowing, and their eyes locked. It couldn't have been more than a few seconds before the carriage righted itself and bounced slightly when it resettled. She stared into him a moment longer, then pulled her hands—and flaming green eyes—away from him.

"I am so sorry—"

"You should be!" she raged.

He'd never heard her angry, and it sent a shocking thrill of desire straight to his cock.

"You are angry at me for being wanton or forward or whatever you wish to call it," she cried, "but it is *you* who are reckless. You could have killed us!"

The way she clenched her hands into tight fists made him want to hand over the reins and the whip and let her mete out his punishment. He'd never gone in for that sort of thing, but something about the fury in her expression made him want to . . . receive it.

"I am utterly to blame."

She breathed in fast pants, like the horses in front of them who were trying to calm themselves, and stared at him. "You are. You are entirely to blame. I shan't forgive you for this anytime soon, Lord Camburton."

"I lost control of the curricle—"

"You do not lose control!" Her voice was raised to a high pitch, and he looked worriedly toward an approaching carriage that bore the family seal of the Duke of Devonshire.

"Selina—"

She caught the direction of his look. "Damn you," she hissed through clenched teeth. "You are more worried that I'll make a scene in front of Hartington? He's my cousin, you idiot. And unlike some people I know, he actually *respects* me." Despite her contentious tone, she smoothed her skirt politely and sat prettily as the other carriage neared.

"I respect you," he whispered.

She glared at him for a second, then shook her head in frustration and turned with a fake smile toward her cousin. Archie tried to appear calm; the Marquess of Hartington was an inquisitive, observant young man and the last thing Archie wanted was to be *perused* by the twenty-year-old William Cavendish.

Alas. He seemed to be getting the last thing he wanted on many occasions recently. Selina's smile appeared to be more genuine as the brilliant red phaeton slowed to a stop next to them.

"Well, if it isn't the reclusive marquess and my wild cousin." Hartington tipped his hat. "Camburton. Miss Selina." He looked from one to the other. "What brings you to the big bad city, Camburton? I thought you preferred life in Derbyshire."

"Nice to see you too, Hartington. My sister is to be married at the end of the week—"

"Ah yes! Yes, I will be there." He narrowed his eyes. "Will Rushford still reside at Mayfield House after Mayson and your sister are married?"

Damn him and his direct, invasive questions. It was none of Hartington's business how Georgie and Trevor and James chose to set up house. "I believe they will be visiting Egypt for several months after the wedding."

"Not the answer to the question I asked, but point taken. And you, Miss Selina?" He turned his imperious gaze on her, but there was a twinkle of affection beneath the haughtiness. "Enjoying your freedom, I see."

"Yes, my lord. Thank you."

"You're quite welcome, my dear." He tipped his hat again. "Enjoy your stay in town." With that, he clucked to his pair of horses from his high perch and set off at an elegant trot, his back as straight as his too-high starched collar.

Archie was irritated again. They spent the rest of the journey in silence—except for the most basic exchanges when Selina gave directions to their destination—until they parted ways at the door of Selina's aunt's house on Tavistock Street.

"He is so impossible! Such a hypocrite!" Selina was pacing furiously while her aunt poured tea and tracked her movements back and forth across the drawing room.

"So the marquess is very disagreeable, then?" Diana asked kindly.

"No! He is damnably agreeable. That's what makes him so infuriating."

"Hmm, really?" Her aunt had finished preparing the tea and was holding out a dainty pink porcelain cup and saucer for her to take.

Selina sighed and flopped down in the chair to her aunt's left. "Yes. Really." She reached for the tea and took it steadily into her own hands. "I know I sound ridiculous. I just thought . . . Oh, I don't know what I thought." Looking around the room, she took a moment to appreciate the world Lady Diana Ashby had created for herself. Deep-blue velvet curtains hung at either side of the large windows that faced out to the small, beautifully landscaped private garden at the back of the townhouse. The solid furniture was not new, but had been well made and well cared for. Here was a woman who had taken possession of her own life. "Oh, Aunt Diana, what was it like for you when you refused all those marriage proposals?"

Diana was now in her middle forties, and she was quite nearly as beautiful as the portrait that Angelica Kauffman had painted twenty years earlier, when Diana had had her season in London and caught the eye of every eligible aristocrat. The painting above the stone fire surround depicted a stunning young heiress in her prime, and also captured the simmering hint of rebellion in her sparkling green eyes.

Stirring her tea, Diana paused before speaking. "It was glorious." She placed the silver spoon on her saucer, and then looked at Selina.

"You weren't afraid of severing your family ties?"

"Were you?" Diana knew every detail of her difficulties with her parents.

"No." She sighed as she remembered the day her father had threatened to disown her, and she had finally laughed in his face and walked out of Ashdownly House for the last time. "It was sweet liberty."

"Precisely." Diana continued to peer at her, perhaps wondering if she was being told the full spectrum of emotion that had accompanied that decision to sever all ties with her past. "The alternative was so blatantly unacceptable," Diana continued. "I could never be a wife—I live for variety, I'm awful with children, I despise country houses—no, it never would have worked. A life in the theater suits me to a T."

Selina contemplated this reply. In her own case, yes, she welcomed new experiences and loved to write about them, but she certainly wouldn't describe herself as someone who *lived* for variety. She was most happy when she was in a routine: working in the morning, walking in the afternoon, wooing Beatrix in the evening. She sighed again. "Whereas I love a domestic life—as long as it is of my own devising—and Archibald Cambury is a wonderful man. So it must be me."

"If you don't mind my asking, what do you really want from him?"

Without Diana's help and guidance, Selina never would have survived the very real consequences of leaving her wealthy family. She owed her aunt a great deal, so telling the truth in this was the least she could do. She put her teacup on the table in front of her and leaned into the comfortable armchair. "I wish I knew." Letting her head fall back, she stared at the detailed plasterwork on the ceiling. "I'm twenty-six, but he makes me feel like a nervous schoolgirl."

"There will always be those people who cross your path only to vex you. Does he speak down to you? Treat you like a child? Men of that sort can be so tedious."

Selina wanted to cry. If only Archie were disrespectful in those ways, then perhaps she could dismiss him with ease. "No!" Her frustration escalated again. "He is interested in my work. He shares his own scientific investigations with me, respects my thoughts and opinions. In fact, I believe he admires me." She covered her face with her palms. "Ugh."

Diana pulled Selina's hands gently away from her face and held them in hers. "What is it, dear?"

"What if my parents were right? What if I am some sort of insatiable harlot?"

Diana erupted with laughter. "You are hardly a harlot, my dear. Simply look at you—" She tried to pull Selina's hands open wide, as if she were a puppet taking a bow. "You are the picture of respectability."

"No!" Selina tore her hands away and stood up to start pacing again. She had been confined in that despicable carriage for three days straight and she needed to move. "I don't know quite how to say this, perhaps it will come out sounding horribly gauche, but, well, what I'm trying to say is . . . I . . . I like certain . . . I . . . am very . . ."

"You enjoy sex?"

"Yes!" As soon as the word flew from her lips, she covered her mouth as if she could take it back.

"And you think that makes you a harlot?"

"Doesn't it? I mean of course my enthusiasm has never been a problem with Beatrix." She blushed slightly, but Diana knew all about her relationship with Beatrix, and there was no point in playing coy when they were this close to the raw truth. "She and I are equals. Obviously in our bodies, but it's more than that. It would never occur to Beatrix to see my enjoyment as *prurient*. Why do men see it that way?"

Diana smiled knowingly. "Not all men see it that way, my dear."

"I know, but Archie does."

"Then perhaps this Archibald Cambury is not the right man for you."

Selina sat down again, having tired herself sufficiently with her rapid marching about. "But he's the only man I've ever wanted."

Diana laughed softly, looked at her lap, and then met Selina's gaze when her humor faded. "So is it merely a childish case of you not getting what you want?"

"You are awful." But she smiled at her aunt. "And I fear you may be right. I thought men . . . welcomed this sort of thing."

"Oh dear. What sort of thing? Did you make an overture?"

Selina examined her fingernail. "You could call it that."

"What else could I call it?"

"It's too mortifying." She stood up again. "I can't relive it this soon. Eventually I will be able to laugh at myself, or even use it in a book of some sort, when I am eager to deflate a character's confidence to the full extent of my powers."

"Oh, sweet Selina. It can't have been that bad."

"It was that bad, Aunt. It was *that* bad."

They parted for a few hours after tea, then ate dinner at home that night, a delicious spread of French food, prepared by Diana's chef of many years. They spoke of Selina's father—Diana's brother—Viscount Ashdownly, who was declining into ill health. Diana also had news of Selina's younger sister, from whom Selina had been estranged for the past six years.

They had a pleasant discussion about the solicitor they both shared. It was only thanks to Diana's avid interest in her well-being that Selina had been able to secure her small bequest from her grandfather. Upon leaving her childhood home, she had prepared for the worst. She had a few jewels from her grandmother that she'd been going to pawn, but without Diana's influence, she could have ended up as a governess or far worse—a harlot in fact, rather than just in the eyes of Archibald Cambury.

They finished supper and retired to a small study where Diana spent her days working on set designs. There were watercolors of scenes and small clay models of different theaters. "Do you need to work?" Selina asked, looking around the cluttered space.

"No. I'm fine for now. But thank you for asking. Do you?"

She shrugged. She was mellow from the excellent wine and the delicious food they'd just shared. "I'm struggling with this story a bit. But I have several months until the first draft is due to my editor, so I'm not too worried about it. I've found that worrying rarely improves the manuscript, no matter how hard I try to worry."

Diana laughed as she poured them each a brandy. "It's the same in the theater. No matter how much I worry, the work gets done. So I try not to worry. But some worrying can't be helped." She handed Selina a snifter. "I had one set that involved a trapdoor, and every time the very famous lead actress stepped on that section of the stage I held my breath."

"There are certain scenes and characters in my books that make me feel that way. Worried and eager all at once."

"Yes, that's it exactly. I could have scrapped the trapdoor idea, but it was the highlight of the show. When the villain disappeared in a flash of smoke and lightning, the audience was thrilled."

"Yes. I think I will write well while I'm here, with the bustle and verve of the city. I've been too much in my own mind out there at Camburton Castle."

"But you have enjoyed the summer, yes?" Diana had helped her secure her place in Vanessa's creative program.

"So much. Everyone who was there added to the experience, but now that most of the artists and musicians have left, it is very quiet."

"Why, then, will you stay there through the winter?"

Selina groaned. "Isn't it obvious?"

"Archibald Cambury?"

"He's one reason." She looked into the snifter of brandy she held in both hands. "Probably the main reason. But I also work well there, despite my preoccupations of late. It's quiet, and I can think. I'm not distracted the way I am in the city. And with Beatrix gone . . ." She shrugged. "It seemed like a good opportunity for me *not* to be gallivanting, for once."

"I see." Diana swished her drink around. "And, again, I don't mean to press. Or maybe I do—" She smiled at Selina. "But, in a perfect world, what would you ultimately want from Archie? I think it's worth thinking about."

"Why should I bother with conjecture, when nothing will come of it?"

"I wouldn't be so sure, my dear. He sounds like he is a bundle of conflicting emotions when it comes to you."

"I think the conflict has been resolved. At this point, he is probably entirely certain I am a strumpet and he likely wishes he did not have to provide me with return transportation to Derbyshire."

"Perhaps."

Selina sighed and leaned back into the settee, enjoying the comfort of being warm and safe in her aunt's lovely home. She would spend the next week focusing on her manuscript and thoroughly quit any thought of the Marquess of Camburton.

Chapter 4

he problem is, I can't quit thinking about her."

"So then go ahead and think about her. Let your thoughts run their course." Christopher was sprawled on the Turkish carpet, his back leaning against the front of the green velvet sofa, between Archie's spread legs. "It's the same with any experiment. You know how it is: the harder you try to make it fit your hypothesis, the more likely you are to miss the obvious clues. Stop trying to manipulate the outcome, Archie."

Together, the two of them had attended the Jenner lecture—brilliant as always—and their animated conversation had buoyed them from the Royal Society, through Trafalgar Square and Leicester Square, along Piccadilly, until they ended up at Christopher's apartment at the Albany. Christopher Joseph was what was commonly known as a consummate bachelor. For several years he'd thought he would become a don at Cambridge, but it soon became clear, despite his extraordinary intelligence, that the academic life was not at all suited to him. Nor he to it. He was impatient and outspoken, neither attribute holding him in good stead with the older academics.

With his professors' best wishes, Christopher had moved to London and set up his chemistry laboratory at the University of London under the aegis of an anonymous nobleman.

"I've tried that too." Archie knew he was beginning to sound like one of those repetitive motion machines, speaking endlessly of Selina and how incomprehensible he found her. Christopher was obviously tiring of the constant blather.

"Would you like something to take your mind off the young miss?" Christopher turned his cheek so it pressed suggestively against Archie's inner thigh.

Archie narrowed his eyes and raked his free hand through Christopher's thick brown hair. "Would you mind? I'm wound up damnably tight."

"My pleasure." Christopher set his drink on the floor and shifted so he was facing Archie and kneeling between his spread thighs. Archie began to unbutton the placket of his trousers but Christopher put his hand over his to stay him. "Allow me. You know how much I enjoy opening presents."

Archie groaned in blessed relief as Christopher undid the buttons and released his stiff shaft, then took him into a familiar rough hold with his right hand.

"I feel like I've been hard for weeks." He gasped when Christopher licked the length of his erection.

"Tell me about her," Christopher said in a throaty voice while he continued licking and teasing.

"I shouldn't speak of her while you and I are . . . like this . . ."

Christopher kept up with those tantalizing licks and hints of suction, without ever taking him full into his mouth. "If you want me to suck you off, Archie, I want you to talk about her. Doctor's orders." He cupped Archie's balls with a firm hold. "Tell me about Selina's lips . . ."

Archie couldn't help it; he canted his hips toward Christopher and groaned at the mention of Selina's pouty, full lips.

"That's it . . . describe her mouth to me . . . or her other lips . . ."

Clenching both hands around Christopher's head, he tried to force the man's mouth onto his straining cock, but his friend was just as intent as he was, and his neck muscles resisted.

"Do you picture her doing this?" Christopher smiled devilishly, then curled his tongue around the bulging head of Archie's cock. He still refused to take him in.

"Oh God." The words spilled out. "Her lips are full and red as summer berries and slightly darker at the edges—" Archie gasped as Christopher dove at his cock, taking him full and deep with hard suction. Christopher moaned his encouragement. "She blushes when I compliment her hat." He spoke eagerly, the dam breaking. "But then she doesn't blush at all when she shows me her slick pussy—" He growled when Christopher deep-throated him to the hilt.

"Oh God, man, she is so raw and honest . . . so inappropriate . . ." His voice cracked and shredded over the words. "She wants to do this to me, I know she does . . ."

He bucked as Christopher began an in-and-out pace of slow, strong pulls. When the speed accelerated, he tried to disentangle all the threads of his desire—Selina's sweet mouth, Christopher's knowing tongue, his own physical cravings—until it all wove together and he cried out his release. Christopher swallowed every ounce of him, consumed every drop of his shameful lust for Miss Selina Ashby.

"Jesus, Archie. How long have you been holding that in? You nearly blew the back of my head off." With a suggestive smile, Christopher swiped the tip of his tongue to the edge of his mouth. "Not that I'm complaining."

"What the hell am I going to do?" Archie asked through halting breaths.

"Why don't you marry her?"

Archie sighed as he rubbed his face with both hands. "She's not at all what I had hoped for in a wife. In fact, she would be a terrible wife."

"Then don't marry her." Christopher laughed as he began to pull Archie's trousers the rest of the way off.

"What are you doing?"

"What do you think I'm doing?" He removed Archie's boots, and then yanked off his breeches and underwear in one swift tug. "I'm going to fuck you."

"Christopher . . ."

"You always have to be convinced, Archie. And you're always grateful after. If I had a mind to, I'd write Miss Ashby a letter and tell her so—"

"You wouldn't—"

Christopher laughed again, this time while he was removing his own trousers. "Maybe not right away, but if she continues to *vex* you, I'd be willing to risk your temporary ire for your long-term happiness." Christopher gestured for him to turn onto his stomach, which he did without question, as if they were having a picnic and Christopher had asked him to pass the wine. "God, you've got a fantastic arse." Christopher gave him a quick, appreciative slap on his bum, then continued speaking. "You've always needed a firm hand. Why shouldn't it belong to your wife?"

"Would you choose such a wife?" Archie asked, looking over his shoulder.

"I've no interest in a wife, you know that. The only things I like to do are fuck you and work on my experiments—and to go to sleep quite happily alone. And there's nothing matrimonial about any of those desires." Christopher rubbed his hand in provocative circles on Archie's arse. "I'd be a terrible husband, and an even worse father. But you, you've always wanted that sort of life—the spread in Derbyshire, lots of little Archies running around—not to mention the hot press of soft female flesh in your bed every night. You love consistency. Order." Christopher gave him another firm smack. "Maybe she's not precisely what you'd envisioned, but maybe that's because what you envisioned in a wife was wrong, not because Miss Ashby is wrong."

Archie tried to think about the words, but he was becoming too distracted by Christopher's hands on him. Christopher had removed Archie's shirt and was smoothing his hands along Archie's back and thighs. They were both naked now, and with his eyes closed and his face turned, he could easily imagine Christopher and Selina were both there, both caressing him in that preparatory way.

"Incredible specimen. Honestly, you should do Selina the great favor of letting her have the run of this body. She's probably frigging right now, picturing your muscled back and your firm thighs and your huge cock . . ."

Archie groaned and shoved his face harder into the sofa cushion.

Christopher began to rub liniment in and around Archie's eager, puckering arsehole. "Look at you, just begging for it." Archie hated when Christopher narrated like this, even though it got him rock hard after having come only a few minutes before.

"Yes, you despise when I recount all the salacious details while I fuck you, don't you? How good your balls felt when they slapped against my chin when you came in hot spurts against the back of my throat, how tight your arsehole is going to feel around my throbbing cock." Archie's whole body was gearing up for the invasion, his hips and arse tilting and rocking in silent entreaty. He could hear the slick sounds of more cream being spread onto Christopher's cock, and the other man's low moans as he prepared to enter him.

"You hate the talking—" The head of Christopher's cock breached his anus, and he felt the joy and relief shudder through him as his body welcomed the penetration. "But oh, how you love the doing." Christopher pushed his way home and held them both perfectly still, fingers digging deep into Archie's hips, both of them suspended in time. Very slowly, he withdrew almost entirely, and Archie was about to beg for his return, when Christopher thrust back in with a confident, powerful stroke. He maintained a steady rhythm after that, trailing up and down Archie's spine with his fingertips. "I won't make you talk."

His pace increased, every incursion a silken whip, the words reminding Archie of Selina. Christopher leaned down the length of his back, covering him like an animal, and began to nip at his shoulder where it met the straining muscles of his neck.

Reaching one hand around, Christopher took hold of Archie's cock and began working it in time with his thrusting. "I don't need you to speak, Archie, because you're so damned obvious." His voice was hot and low, close to his ear. Christopher bit on the soft lobe. "Your body was made to fuck and be fucked, Lord Camburton." His pace was becoming erratic, but he kept on with those taunting words and nips and bites. "And I bet the astute Miss Ashby sees how very *vigorous* you are—"

Archie moaned into the upholstery at the mention of Selina, his body peaking again, wanting all the sweat and filth, wanting Christopher to defile him in this powerful, mutual way. But not Selina. Not in this way. Not like this.

But yes Selina. Yes in this way. Yes like this.

"Think of Selina's hot pussy tight around your cock while I fuck you like this—" Christopher's incendiary words set him alight. *Not Selina!* his mind protested, as every muscle exploded and gripped and sighed and shuddered, as his body said *Yes Selina!* in every way except words.

Christopher eventually released his hold on Archie's softening cock, then pulled out of him and rolled off his back. They both breathed into the silence for a few minutes. "She's in you, Archie.

Have a care. You've never cried out anyone's name in all the years I've known you."

Archie turned slowly to face Christopher, who was across the room putting on a Japanese robe, his lean, tall body etched in candlelight. "I didn't cry out."

"You most certainly did." Christopher picked up his snifter of brandy where he'd left it on the carpet. "No hard feelings, old chap; I never thought we were exclusive." He winked lightheartedly.

Archie smiled at his friend's easy banter, then his face fell. He trailed the palm of his hand up and down his stomach, touching the sticky residue of his release as he made the pass. The image popped into his mind of Selina's lips, of Selina bent there, tasting him, cleaning him, wanting him again—

"Aw, fuck it." He sat up and began to put his clothes on.

"That's probably a good place to start with her," Christopher lobbed.

"Maybe you're right. Maybe I'll just *fuck* her. Maybe I've been utterly misguided in my foolish attempts to *respect* her."

Christopher paused before drinking, and then tilted his head slightly. "You fuck me and respect me. They're not mutually exclusive, you know."

Archie stared at him after he finished pulling his trousers up. "That's an absurd analogy. You're my friend. And you're a man."

"I'm a human being, Archie." Christopher's smile was bittersweet. "And perhaps this Selina Ashby is a human being too."

It's just a carriage ride. It's just a carriage ride. At least, that's what Selina kept telling herself. Her aunt had insisted on hiring a coach to take them from Tavistock Street to Mayfair early Monday morning, ostensibly to visit with Vanessa and Nora, with whom Diana had been well acquainted over the years. But Selina was certain Diana's accompaniment was mostly to provide her aunt with a closer inspection of the marquess.

"It's just a carriage ride, Selina," Diana echoed. "You'll be fine."

The coach came to a stop in front of the Grosvenor Square mansion, and Selina took a deep breath and pulled her gloves tighter.

"You look splendid. No need to fuss."

"I don't care how I look." She flushed at the lie.

Diana smiled and glanced out the window. "Apparently someone else does."

Selina turned quickly to see Archie walking down the shallow steps that led from the open front door. Two footmen in deep green finery stood behind him. "Why does he come out to greet us? He's supposed to be waiting in his drawing room with a bored expression on his face."

"He doesn't look at all bored to me." Diana turned as the door opened.

"Lady Ashby." Archie held his hand out to assist Diana. "My mother and Nora will also be very happy to see you."

"Thank you, Lord Camburton. It's been many years since I've seen you."

He smiled. "Yes. I believe I was still in short pants."

Selina watched as Diana looked into his sparkling amber eyes, and knew her aunt would see nothing but transparent good will. Selina was in such a load of trouble.

"Miss Ashby." Archie's voice was slightly deeper when he spoke this time, as he reached into the coach to assist her. She considered refusing his aid, as she had last week, but she decided she would not stoop to petty acts of rebellion.

"Thank you, my lord." She rested her gloved fingers in his and dipped her head as she stepped down to the pavement. She began to pull her hand away but he held firm, so she was forced to look up into his handsome face.

"Have you enjoyed your week in town?" He put her hand to rest on his forearm as he led them into his home.

"Yes. And you?" She was struck by his simmering confidence. Gone was the agitated companion she had endured for those endless three days the previous week.

"Very satisfying, yes," he replied easily.

If she didn't know better, she would have surmised he'd spent the past week in the arms of a mistress, but he couldn't have—

"Mother. Nora. Lady Ashby." They were all standing in the drawing room, and Archie turned to each of them as he spoke. "I'm afraid Selina and I really must be on our way if we are going to make Rockingham by nightfall."

"Rockingham?" Selina tried not to show her dismay.

"Yes. I've received word from FitzWilliam of a significant nature, relating to the government's support of the vaccinations, and I'd like to stop there for a night or two if you don't mind."

She pulled her hand from his. "I do mind. His wife is related to my mother's family. I would rather not." Her voice was low, and the three older women were doing their best to maintain a pleasant conversation a few feet away without turning in her direction.

"You can't run away your whole life."

Selina inhaled sharply at his unfamiliar contempt, and Diana turned her head quickly, no longer able to feign disinterest. "Is everything all right, Selina?"

"Yes, Aunt. It appears Lord Camburton has made other arrangements for his journey, so I will be taking the stagecoach."

All three women began speaking at once.

"That is preposterous—"

"Certainly not—"

"You will ride with us—"

"Ladies, please." Archie spoke carefully, looking briefly at her and then to the others. "I can easily write FitzWilliam and let him know I will visit him another time. I just thought since it was right along our route"—he stared pointedly at Selina—"it would not bother Miss Ashby one way or another if we stopped at Rockingham or at an inn in Northampton."

"Oh, it's Rockingham?" Vanessa was all enthusiasm. "It is a spectacular spot, Selina. You will simply adore it." Archie's mother always exuded an almost childlike joy. She clasped her hands as she described the castle from memory. "It would be the perfect setting for one of your novels—all medieval walls and hidden passages. You should see it, for research purposes if nothing else."

"I have visited the place, but thank you. I would hate to impose," Selina tried lamely.

Diana narrowed her eyes. "If it's Lady FitzWilliam you're worried about, she is no friend of your mother's."

There was a brutal silence as everyone in the room grasped the meaning of the words and the nature of Selina's resistance.

Steeling her voice, Selina fought the familiar and terrifying impression they were all joining forces to rally against her. "I would be imposing, Aunt." She had been in a room full of people rallying against her in the past, and it had not ended well.

Diana faced Archie. "Did you mention in your correspondence that you would be traveling with Miss Ashby?"

"Of course." Archie pursed his lips, apparently resenting that he would be questioned in this way. Selina almost smiled at how he clung to these rules of social order.

"And Lord and Lady FitzWilliam extended the invitation to both of you?" Diana pressed.

"Of course." He exhaled, and it was just shy of a huff.

"Selina," Diana encouraged, "please go. Take it as an opportunity to visit with one of your extended relations while Lord Camburton discusses his scientific matters with Lord FitzWilliam. I think it a fine plan."

Selina almost blurted that if Diana thought it such a fine plan, then she should accompany the marquess on his visit to Rockingham herself. They were all looking at her expectantly. "Oh, very well." She threw up her hands and everyone breathed a sigh of relief.

"Excellent," Nora said. "That's excellent. And then Vanessa and I will be back at Camburton in a fortnight or so, and all will be well. All of us tucked up in Derbyshire for the winter being productive as bees in summer, yes?"

"Yes, we shall." Selina tried to emulate some of Nora's enthusiasm.

Archie pressed the flat of his palm against the small of her back, and she felt it singe through her, the heat of that gentle touch making her grateful for the thick layers of chemise, corset, dress, and coat that kept her responsive breasts concealed.

His voice grew kind, nothing like the sharp tone he'd used with his running-away comment. "Are you ready, then?"

"Yes, thank you. I am ready." She hugged her aunt one last time, clasped hands with Vanessa, then Nora, and within a few moments she and Archie were settled inside the compartment of his luxurious traveling coach. She kept her gaze fixed on the passing homes and parks of Mayfair, then Kensington, then watched as the congestion of the city began to fade as they went farther into the countryside.

"Was it too cold for you to sit outside with the coachman this time?" she finally asked, regretting it immediately.

"Selina . . ." His voice was so tender, and she resented that too, the way it made her heat up and throb when he said her name, the way she imagined him saying it close to her ear, with the soft turn of his lips touching her sensitive skin.

She shut her eyes in frustration. He did not fancy her. In fact, she probably repulsed him. With eyes still closed, she replied, "Yes, Archie?"

"Please look at me."

Earlier this morning, she had hoped his repressive good manners would keep them both in check on the return journey. However annoying, at least his self-control had always been reliable. She turned her head and opened her eyes slowly. He was as beautiful as ever. His dark-blond hair combed perfectly, making her fingertips itch to ruin it, to ruin him; his amber eyes perceptive and kind, with an underlying hint of that avid curiosity that defined him; his lips . . .

She had to look away again. His lips always tormented her. She felt them on her body at night. They were firm when he spoke, but when they had kissed under that tree a few weeks ago, oh dear, they had been incredibly soft when seeking entrance to her welcoming mouth. Those lips, if no other part of his body or soul, wanted her.

"I can't." The countryside went by in a blur, and her eyes began to burn. "I can't look at you."

She heard and felt the shuffling movement of him crossing from the other side of the carriage to sit beside her. "Please." His voice was close and so gentle.

She turned to face him, and he was indeed close, far too close. He took her gloved hand in his and began undoing the small buttons at her wrist.

"What are you doing?" She was surprised her voice sounded normal while her heart pounded wildly.

"You despise gloves. I'm removing them for you." He was meticulous, neither rushing nor becoming frustrated with the small, annoying closures that always infuriated her. He slipped one, then two fingers into the opening and pressed against her wrist. "Are you well?"

She smiled despite herself. He behaved exactly like a country doctor, checking her pulse. "I seem to have a bit of a condition." She had never flirted with a man before Archie. She'd never had a season in London to perfect the snap of her fan or hone the edge of her repartee. But something about the marquess suddenly made her want to be that young woman, the wallflower who captures the attention of the most dashing man in the ballroom—neither the bookish writer spending the summer at Camburton Castle, nor the brash hoyden who revealed herself in a closed coach. Simply a young woman flirting with an eligible young man.

He began undoing the buttons on her other glove. "Tell me your symptoms."

"I feel extremely agitated on certain occasions."

He finished with the second glove and was inserting his two fingers in the same way. "Really? What brings it on?" The throbbing between her legs mimicked the pulse where he touched her, skin against skin.

"Whenever I am near certain people—"

"People?" He raised an eyebrow.

"Person." Her voice was no longer even. "A certain person."

"And this person makes you ill?"

She leaned back into the luxurious velvet squabs, tucked her feet up to the right of her thighs, and gave herself over to his playful tone. "Not ill, precisely. It's more of a passing fever."

"Is there nothing you can do to assuage it?" His fingers pressed more firmly against her skin, and her pulse skittered in response.

"I have tried."

"And did you find relief?"

She stared into his eyes. He was still nervous, she could tell, but he was eager just the same. "Yes and no. I've been told I'm very high-strung."

He began to pull at the fingers of the glove. "Perhaps you need something for your nerves."

"I do have certain . . . methods . . . for managing my condition."

The first glove was off. He began tugging gently on the other. "Excellent. I've always believed that once we learn how to manage our own health, we are so much better equipped to aid others."

Her breathing was shallow as he examined the back of her hand, touching his fingertip against her knuckles, tracing the creases and lines between her fingers, then turning over her hand as if seeing it for the first time. He bent down and kissed the center of her palm.

"What are you doing?" She gasped out the words.

"I am apologizing." His voice was so quiet, so sincere.

She reached up to touch his cheek with a trembling hand, loving the way he leaned into her palm.

"Archie . . ."

"You overwhelm me, Selina." His eyes closed, as if he were absorbing the power of her touch against his face.

"And you overwhelm me." She caressed his eyebrow with the pad of her thumb, then the edge of his temple where it met his hairline. "I never thought I would feel this way." More precisely, she never thought she would feel this physically attracted to a man, but she didn't see the point in saying so to him.

She tilted her head up and pulled his face to hers. He resisted ever so slightly, in a way that made her want him even more. The tension in his neck and shoulders seemed to say, *Show me you can take me, show me you will assuage my condition as well as yours.*

Chapter 5

When her lips touched his, Archie felt the air rush from his lungs. As the horses sped along at a brisk pace, his heart pounded right along with them. The kiss under the tree, and even her blatant, erotic display last week, were nothing compared to this possessive, greedy play of her lips over his. He let his hands move tentatively up to her hair, the gleaming blonde strands even silkier than he remembered. His grip intensified, and she pulled away slightly, speaking so her lips kissed him as she spoke.

"That's it, hold on to me."

Her encouragement roared through him. He tightened his hold on her, and she cried out. Worried he might've hurt her, he slackened his fingers.

"No, keep it like that, tighter," she panted. "I love the feel of your hands on me. I love the feel of you."

Something snapped inside him then—respect, lust, the future—everything fell away and there was only skin and heat and the molecular points where their bodies were joined, combining mouths, fingers, and skin to make this new element between them.

"Please let me see you." Her hand pressed suggestively against his hard length. "I've dreamt of you."

He thought he should protest. "We . . . I don't know . . . Perhaps . . ."

She rubbed him slowly and looked up into his eyes. Without glancing away, she molded and warmed the outline of his erection through the buckskin. Any hint of teasing was gone; the frivolity of last week was distinctly absent. "You don't have to *know*. Just let me look at you." Her eyes held his, offering so much.

He nodded, and her smile came; she appeared to be so pleased with him. She leaned in and kissed him again. "Thank you."

Why is she thanking me? His mind reeled as, starting with one of the top buttons, Selina began to undo his breeches with maddening patience. She worked the buttons free while petting him and rubbing her hand along his length, once or twice bending down to kiss him through the fabric or inhale the scent of his arousal. She started to speak without looking up. "I never thought . . ." But her voice faltered when his cock sprang free, her warm breath tantalizing along its length as she examined him.

It was bizarrely thrilling how much he wanted her to scrutinize him. She tasted him with small catlike licks, and then smelled him, sniffing and burrowing as if she were an animal familiarizing herself with his scent. His hands tightened uncontrollably in her hair, and she moaned her pleasure. "*Yessssssss,*" she exhaled, then took him full in her mouth.

Selina was crouched on her knees on the seat by then, trying different angles with her neck and mouth, swirling her tongue, attempting different levels of suction. Any time he responded—the slightest moan or sigh—she hummed her approval and did more of whatever that was. She was learning him.

He was lost in his own bliss, eyes nearly closed, when he realized she was moving her upturned hips and arse in time with her mouth. *Oh dear God.* He released one hand from the snarl he had created with her lovely hair, and reached for the turn of her bottom. As soon as he touched the fabric over her bum she cried out, a muffled burst against the head of his cock. He reacted by squeezing her arse and pushing his fingers greedily down between her legs. The fabric of her gray-blue velvet dress was warmer there from the obvious pleasure she was deriving from what she was doing to him.

The realization slammed through him of how much she *wanted* this, how natural and just it all was (in her mind, at least). Her pace quickened on his cock and with her hips. Unable to resist, he tugged at the heavy folds of her winter dress, bunching the fabric on her lower back, and finally found the warm, slick center of her through the slit in her drawers.

"Oh God . . ." He felt her—this other heart of hers—his fingers probing and inelegant at first, eagerly seeking her. Then he forgot every nicety as he discovered the smooth lips, the warm nest of pubic hair, the stiff nub of her arousal. Blindly, he penetrated her in time with her movements, first one finger, then two, dipping and searching for whatever would bring her the most pleasure. She was frantically sucking him now, sloppy and carefree, but he kept trying to please her, as best he could when he could barely remember who or where he was. He wanted to give and give and—

Her inner passage clamped around his thrusting fingers and her high-pitched scream reverberated around his cock like a primal cry. His body reacted immediately, filling her, shooting his hot seed into her mouth. Some shred of forgotten decency made him attempt to withdraw, but she was feral in her growling demand to keep him deep in her mouth until *she* was finished.

The haze of lust and forgetting receded as fast as it had come. Within seconds, he felt awkward and confused, his fingers stuck in a woman's vagina, his other hand tangled in her formerly beautiful coiffure.

He shifted self-consciously, trying to get out from under her, away from her, away from himself. Extracting his hand from between her legs, he wondered how best to get his handkerchief from his jacket pocket without making too much of a nuisance of himself. He pulled her skirts down and smoothed the fabric, just as he would smooth a tablecloth to remove stray crumbs after a meal. And tried to ignore the fact that his spent cock still remained in Miss Ashby's mouth.

Selina hummed happily and finally released him; escape was near, he thought fretfully. And then not. She turned slightly, but kept her cheek resting high on his buckskin-covered thigh. She looked up at him with an expression of angelic bliss. How could something so filthy make her appear downright beatific?

"You are delicious, Archibald Cambury." She licked her lips and sighed.

He blushed furiously and tried to shove his cock back into his pants.

"Oh, please don't." Her voice was listless and wanting all at once, as she rested her fingers lightly on his cock. "Let me revel in you for a few moments longer."

He was wretched sitting there, patiently waiting for her to recover her senses. And then the waves of awkwardness would crash over her as well, he assumed, and she would be brittle and angry and—

"Oh my, that was delightful!" She inhaled and came up to a sitting position and tossed her mussed hair over her right shoulder. Her eyes were gleaming, bright chips of emerald that shone with happiness. She stared into his eyes—which must have plainly shown his confusion and near terror—and then burst out laughing. "Oh, my darling Archie!" She reached up and placed the palms of her delicate hands on his cheeks, then leaned in to kiss him—

Kiss him with her mouth full of his semen!

"Selina!"

He held her away from him by her shoulders.

"Oh dear." Her face fell. "Are we to endure a period of regret and penance every time?"

"No." He shook his head. He could not process the combination of joy and trepidation the words *every time* evoked. She was tracing her thumbs over his cheekbones and it was exceedingly distracting.

"No? So . . . then . . . may I kiss you again?" She leaned in to do just that.

"Selina! Your mouth!"

"Ah. My filthy mouth that has been sucking your filthy cock, you mean?"

"Please. There's no need to be so . . . specific."

She released his face and kissed his cheek, a small smile playing on her lips. "Very well. I shan't go on and on about your beautiful cock . . ." She began fixing her hair while she looked at him. "Or about how wonderful it felt pressed against the back of my throat . . . especially when all that hot—"

"I am begging you," he interrupted desperately.

She raised a suggestive eyebrow, and then turned so she was facing out the window while she fussed with her dislodged hairpins. "Nor shall I talk about how it was the first cock I've ever tasted . . ." Her voice was low there at the end, and he was sure he had misheard. He was busily rebuttoning his buckskins, and the shuffling of fabric and the two of them putting themselves back to rights must have distorted her words. For the first time in his life he chose to ignore, rather than pursue, that which he did not understand.

He finished with his pants and then looked down to make sure his shirt was neatly tucked and his neck cloth still properly folded. "Do you require any assistance with your toilette or your dress? I'm sorry I've made such a mess of you—"

When she turned to face him, her eyes were even brighter, but this time it was the precarious sheen of emotion rather than raw lust. "Is that all you have to say to me?"

"What do you wish me to say? You confuse me beyond measure. I can barely think, much less speak, when I am around you."

"I have never been with a man before!"

The bounce and rumble of the well-sprung carriage, which had seemed nearly quiet during their lovemaking, was suddenly loud and clattering in the loaded silence. "I never would have known."

"Archie!" She huffed and clenched her hands into small fists. He wanted to kiss them and rub his cheek along her knuckles. "How can you be so brilliant and then be so *thick*?" She tugged on his earlobe as if he were an errant child, then released him.

"I only meant . . ." He was disturbed by how much he enjoyed her small punishment, wishing she would continue to chastise him. "I thought I was complimenting you."

She shook her head and widened her eyes as he sank deeper and deeper into this morass.

"I wished very much to compliment you. You were . . . You are . . . wonderful." He sighed like a schoolboy, letting the feeling of her wonderfulness wash over him. But she kept staring at him with that look of consummate disbelief. He furrowed his brow, suspecting that was perhaps not the right thing to say after all.

This was what he'd meant about being friends with Christopher! Christopher had never once, in their ten years of friendship and physical intimacy, looked at him in that beseeching way. Selina wanted some type of emotional recompense, and he had no idea how to provide it. He suspected he could offer her his hand in marriage long before he would ever be able to offer anything resembling sensitive understanding. And even *he* knew it was far too soon to tell her that he wanted to take the coach directly to Gretna Green.

On the other hand, when she *was* behaving like Christopher—laughing and enjoying the physical act for its own sake and nothing more—that didn't sit well with him at all. He wanted something far richer and deeper with Selina than simple physical release.

Unfortunately, he didn't know how to weave the myriad parts of her—or himself—together.

She kept reminding herself that Archie's confusion and conflicting desires were part of what she most adored about him. His honesty was raw and immediate; he couldn't help but show how he felt, poor thing. He was all torn up inside about how delectably raunchy the two of them had become in the heat of their shared passion.

He was a man—dear God, was he a glorious man—but he was not a typical one for his time or social standing. Archie's place in society had never mattered to him, insofar as he never courted the admiration or fawning appreciation of others. His respect for tradition and propriety were not mere social conventions to which he adhered to for public approbation. Archibald Cambury truly believed in the sanctity of his noble life and his aristocratic responsibilities, both in his public role and, apparently, in his private engagements as well.

Had she wanted some especial tenderness, some acknowledgment that it had been her first time with a man? Yes. Was that a sign of her own vanity or some coy neediness? Perhaps. Why should she rely on him to say things in a particular way? To flatter her? She almost laughed aloud because that was exactly what he had tried—in his very bumbling fashion—to do.

"Thank you, Archie." She meant it kindly. "I think you are wonderful too." She had finished repairing her appearance and waited with her hands clasped loosely in her lap while her temper righted itself. He turned to face her with a look of such profound relief that she realized he had been prepared for some bout of feminine weeping or flailing about.

"So, we are still friends?" He appeared nearly incredulous.

It was a wonderful, heart-pounding question coming from this man of so few intimate acquaintances. "Oh, yes, I—" Her voice snagged on an unanticipated emotion. "I am so grateful to be your friend. If my . . . eagerness has ever led you to believe that I have anything but the highest regard for you and the burgeoning friendship we now share, then I am desperately sorry. Perhaps in my foolishness, I had hoped my ardor would bolster, rather than hinder our feelings for one another."

He started to speak, but she held up her hand. "If I may continue?" He nodded for her to go on.

"If, on the other hand, it is not possible for *you* to be friends with someone to whom you are also, er, physically engaged, then I will respect that as well."

His face clouded, and she had a moment's pause. Was there someone else—someone for whom he felt both a physical *and* an emotional bond? She kept looking at him, trying not to convey too much curiosity . . . or envy. Surely there would've been whispers in London of his having a mistress or favorite merry widow. Her aunt was privy to all the latest on-dits. And most certainly there would be out-and-out talk of his having a favorite young virgin in the running to be the next marchioness. There was no such talk. He was so rarely in town, and when he did make the trip, it was invariably to attend a lecture or meet with his scientific colleagues.

"It seems to be difficult for me to reconcile." He looked at his lap. "I have never wanted someone the way I want you. I don't know how to go about it."

Her girlish heart soared, but she held her tone steady. "Then all is well. I shan't torture you—" he inhaled sharply and she forcibly ignored it "—with my constant advances. Please know that I am always thinking of you fondly, but perhaps it is best if we set aside our physical attraction." *For now*, she added silently.

"Yes, I believe that would be best."

"Friends?" She extended her hand.

He hesitated for a split second, probably dreading the jolt that always passed between them when they touched—the jolt she craved.

"Friends," he agreed, taking her hand.

She shook on it in one firm movement, as if they were a pair of old chums agreeing to an insignificant wager, then pulled quickly away. "Very well. It's all settled, then." She bent down to pick up a novel from her traveling bag and smiled at him easily before turning her attention to the pages.

She saw the words, but they hardly registered. Her mind wandered, imagining the upcoming days and weeks and months. Would his ardor fade without her prodding encouragement? Would Beatrix's return signal the end of whatever it was between Archie and Selina in any case? Would Archie ever be able to accept the arrangement of her dreams, that would give her the comfort and solidity of a happy home with him—children and a rich family life—as well as the recurrent intimacy with Beatrix that satisfied some integral part of her constitution?

The words of the novel flew past as these thoughts crowded her brain. Who was she to want such self-determination, to demand so much out of life? Who was she to want the world to revolve around her desires?

Who was she? This was her life, damn it! It was worth wanting and demanding and wringing out every possibility! In the past, she had fought hard for far less; she would fight even harder for this.

The stop at Rockingham proved to be a blessing in at least one regard. Her mother's cousin, the earl's wife, Lady Charlotte Ponsonby FitzWilliam, was charming and warm, welcoming her with what could only be interpreted as the greatest pleasure. Lady FitzWilliam assigned her to a splendid guest suite a few doors down and across the hall from where she had put the marquess.

Before dinner, Lady FitzWilliam came to see if she had everything she needed. "Not that it is any of my concern, but you and the marquess would be a wonderful match in so many ways. Such a boon for you, of course, and such a delight for your parents."

"I daresay my parents have no interest in my future, Lady FitzWilliam."

"Oh, but there you are quite mistaken. Your supposed failure in their eyes would be all but remedied, would it not? Were you to become the Marchioness of Camburton?" The elegant countess turned from the flowers she'd been adjusting and awaited a reply.

Selina knew she was being tested. Lord and Lady FitzWilliam had been close friends of Archie's father, and it didn't take a genius to figure out that the woman was trying to sort out whether she was merely seeking the protection of a title, or had deeper feelings for the unique marquess.

"You must know I have a modest income that affords me all the independence I require. Were I to become the Marchioness of Camburton—which is a possibility of such a remote nature that it hardly bears thinking about—such a decision would have nothing to do with anything except my feelings for the marquess."

"So you *do* have feelings for the marquess?" Lady FitzWilliam returned her attention to the delicate plant until it was exactly the angle she wished.

"Of course I do. I hold him in the highest regard. He has become a true friend during my stay at Camburton this summer, and I respect him immensely."

Lady FitzWilliam faced her with a kind smile. "The earl was also a true friend of mine before we decided to marry. Mutual respect is the best foundation for marriage, I believe. Shall we go down to supper?"

After following the countess down the immense staircase, Selina entered the drawing room and the two women were immediately greeted with collective enthusiasm. The earl was one of those rare aristocrats who was unabashedly in love with his wife. He excused himself from his conversation with Archie and crossed the large room to greet his countess.

"Don't you look lovely, Charlotte." The earl kissed his lady wife's hand, and they shared a brief, hot glance that made a flush creep up Selina's chest.

"Miss Ashby?" Archie was there a moment later to likewise greet her. It was far too easy to imagine him greeting her in just such a way if they were married, if they were . . . She shook her head to cast away the thoughts.

"Yes, my lord?" She gave him her prettiest curtsey and lowered her eyes.

Placing her hand on his forearm, he guided her into the room. "Please allow me to introduce you to my esteemed colleagues."

Archie proceeded to a group of four men and two women, who had their backs to her. As he told her the name of each man, she spoke politely and curtseyed. When he introduced the second woman, Selina's head shot up.

"Selina? Is it you?"

"Constance?"

They gripped their hands and smiled broadly at one another. "It has been three or four years, at least—"

"It was six years last month," Constance said quickly.

"Oh, you look wonderful! Are you studying?"

"Yes, well, as much as I am allowed, with women not being actual students. Professor Stroughton and I are recently engaged. We met in Edinburgh while I was helping Professor Jameson with his work there."

"I am so happy for you." Selina realized they were still holding hands and blushed despite herself. Miss Constance Forrester was several years older than she, and had been her neighbor throughout childhood. Selina had always harbored a secret (or perhaps not so secret) affection that went beyond neighborly.

"And I for you, my dear." Constance let go of her hands but stayed close. "You are looking *so* well." The other men resumed their discussion of Jenner's lecture, the details of which Archie had apparently been relaying before she and the countess made their entrance.

Selina lifted her chin toward the men. "Do you wish to join the discussion?"

"No, I attended the lecture." Connie led her slightly away from the other group. "I'm far more interested in hearing what has brought you to Rockingham, with the inscrutable Marquess of Camburton, no less."

She and Constance sat down together near the fire and caught up on one another's doings over the intervening years. Constance had always been the most agreeable, respectful child in the neighborhood, demure and soft-spoken, yet somehow she had always managed to pursue her rather unique ambitions. Botany. Anatomy. And finally, physiology. Selina had often wondered how different her own life would have been had her parents been as loving and encouraging as the Forresters. Or even half as loving. But they'd ceased to value her once it became clear she was neither demure nor soft-spoken, nor inclined to put her intelligence toward learning to manage a home.

"So, your parents . . . they are well?" Constance asked hesitantly.

"I wouldn't know." Selina didn't want to be curt, but the mere mention of her parents always made her churlish. Perhaps that too would fade in time.

"I understand. I shan't press." The dinner gong echoed in the hall. "Let us walk in the garden after supper. There is a meteor shower expected, and if I tell the countess we wish to observe it, I am sure she will excuse us from the ladies-in-the-drawing-room portion of the evening."

"Oh, I would love that." Selina blushed again, damn it, and looked away quickly so Constance wouldn't see the childish crush that lingered.

Constance reached for her hand. "I would love that too." Then Constance stood up and smiled at her fiancé, who was approaching to escort her into supper.

Chapter 6

*A*rchie felt the slight tremor in Selina's fingers as she rested them on his sleeve while he escorted her into the dining room. "Are you happy to see your childhood friend?"

"Yes, very happy."

"So, perhaps your childhood was not entirely awful?"

She looked up at him, and he wanted to get lost in her deep emerald eyes, to pull her into the alcove across the vast hall and smooth away every injustice that had ever befallen her. To soothe her with his kisses. He turned abruptly toward the dining room. It had been a glib, conversational thing to say, and he regretted it.

"Yes," she whispered. "Perhaps not *entirely*. Constance was always a mystery to me, how she managed to do what she pleased while still pleasing her parents."

"Not all parents are draconian, Selina." He couldn't seem to rid himself of that pedantic tone in his voice, especially when he said her name.

She scoffed. "I know that. One need only look at Vanessa."

It was his time to scoff. "Do not for one moment think Vanessa did not have her own ambitions for her children. She can be quite determined in her joyful way."

"But that's different. That all rises up from a place of love."

He laughed quietly. "It can feel just as constricting under certain circumstances."

She glanced up at him briefly then took her place where Lady FitzWilliam had seated her, down toward the far end of the table near the earl. Archie was given the place of honor next to the countess, of course.

Enjoying the meal immensely, he spoke at length with Lady FitzWilliam about her botanical garden and her extensive work in medicinal botany, and also conversed with several members of the Royal Academy who were in attendance. These men were in a position to ensure the smallpox vaccination was distributed throughout the kingdom in a concerted, thorough process, rather than the piecemeal allocation that had been happening for the past few years.

Occasionally, his attention was drawn to the other end of the table when Selina would laugh or smile at her companions. She had offered everything he supposedly wanted in the carriage. First her body—her beautiful mouth still made him feel faint every time he saw it—and then her calm acceptance that he was not the type of man who could partake of a fleeting sensuality. And after all of that, she had offered her friendship, her respect. Would he ever be able to offer the same in return?

He tried not to be distracted by her creamy skin, by the damnable strands of golden hair that refused to stay within the confines of her loosely styled coiffure, instead caressing the ivory of her neck. She was wearing another stylish gown, this one low cut and revealing, yet somehow innocent thanks to an inch or two of French lace trimming her bosom.

Professor Stroughton lifted his glass of claret in the direction of Constance and Selina. "Some things are even more compelling than Edward Jenner's thoughts on the subject, are they not?"

"What's that?" Archie asked, trying to pick up the thread of the conversation.

"My lovely wife-to-be and your lovely . . . friend . . . are very distracting together. A very charming pair." Stroughton swirled his wine, then took a sip. And Archie despised him instantly, with his suave assessment of the two women, as if they were chattel or horseflesh for him to weigh and measure for his potential acquisition. As if they were lovers.

He suffered through the rest of the meal, denying himself even the occasional pleasure of looking in Selina's direction lest he elicit additional smarmy remarks from Stroughton. The tedium abated somewhat when the ladies left the men to their port, but he was barely able to hide his relief when the earl finally finished his discussion of the recent happenings in Parliament and indicated it was time to join the ladies in the drawing room.

Crossing the wide hall, Archie scanned the drawing room quickly, only to be disappointed by Selina's absence.

Stroughton was right behind him. "The lovely Miss Ashby has gone to watch the meteor shower with Constance." His overfamiliarity and accompanying jab to the ribs indicated joviality—or perhaps to imply something salacious about the idea of Constance and Selina being alone together under the stars. Archie wanted to punch him square in the mouth.

"I believe I shall retire. Long trip from London today. I'm feeling the strain." He bowed slightly to the irritating Professor Stroughton, then spoke to Lady FitzWilliam and begged her forgiveness for retiring so soon.

"Please say you will remain a few extra days," the countess implored kindly.

"It is up to Miss Ashby. I welcome the opportunity to spend as much time at Rockingham as your hospitality will allow, but I don't wish to prevent her from resuming her work. She is very focused on her new book at the moment."

As soon as the words had left his mouth, the French doors to his right swung open with a brisk autumnal gust and two laughing women tumbled into the room. Constance and Selina were bright with joy— each with an arm slung loosely around the other's waist—both giddy from having seen the meteor shower.

"It was stupendous, William!" Constance cried. "Oh you should have seen it!" She reached for her fiancé and kissed him on the lips— in front of the entire drawing room—while her other arm remained around Selina's waist.

Archie looked away from their affianced theatrics, and his gaze happened to fall on Selina. He hadn't meant to appear so judgmental, but the combination of Stroughton's overly familiar behavior earlier at dinner, the other man's questionable implications then and now, and his own embarrassment at having depicted Selina as a hardworking novelist—only to have her blow into the room, as unthinking as a snowflake—well, all in all, he was ill pleased.

"Miss Ashby." He bowed formally in her direction, and then turned. "Lady FitzWilliam." He bowed to the countess far more deeply than he had bowed to Selina, nodded to the earl, and then strode from the room.

Was he really such a prig? He forced himself to take the stairs at a constant, respectable pace despite the urge to sprint to his chamber. Of course he was devoted to tradition, but he was not a prisoner of it. Who was he fooling? He was a prisoner to every convention, every thought. He couldn't even run up a set of stairs if he felt like it. Suddenly, he started taking the stairs two at a time, running as fast as he could.

When he reached the uppermost level of the castle, he kept running. He ran down a hall that must have been a nursery at some point. He ran past closed doors that smelled of cedar and storage. When he came to more steps, on he ran. Up a dark, circular set of stone stairs that must have dated back centuries, he sprinted, not caring that his jacket scuffed against the ancient walls. He reached a thick wooden door, and was surprised to find it unlocked. Panting and exhilarated, he turned the heavy, wrought iron knob, and pushed his way out.

He emerged onto one of the large circular keeps that were the defining architectural characteristics of Rockingham Castle. Looking up at the stars, he wondered at the stillness. His breath was coming in fast, satisfying pants from his exertions, but the celestial canopy appeared to be perfectly still. Of course it would be a riot of activity when Selina looked at it, and a staid gallery of immovable stars for him.

Leaning the palms of his hands down on his knees, he caught his breath at last and let his mind rest. Thoughts of Selina Ashby would never resolve themselves in a single night. Perhaps, like his work on the smallpox vaccination, Selina would take many years for him to fathom. For now, he would take her at her word and be her friend.

When he re-entered the castle and made his way down the stone stairs, he didn't recall which way he'd come. He started to run again, lightly this time, leaping to touch a high chandelier, twisting in the air for the hell of it. He found another set of stairs and then wended his way through what must have been the servants' quarters. He continued trotting down the back stairs until he careened, panting and probably red in the face, into a vast kitchen filled with about two dozen servants hard at work cleaning up the aftermath of the splendid meal.

Silverware clanged and then a pristine silence descended on the entire white-tiled space.

"My lord?" the head butler inquired carefully, while the remaining roomful of maids and footmen kept their heads bowed in quiet respect.

"Yes." Archie exhaled cheerfully. "I seem to have lost my way."

The butler looked at the nearest footman. "Please show the marquess to his chamber."

"Yes, sir. Right this way, my lord."

Following the deep burgundy of the footman's livery, Archie steadied his breath and his pace. He didn't bother paying close attention—as soon as they left the kitchen, he knew precisely where his room was. He'd been to Rockingham many times since he was a boy and hardly needed more than common sense to guide him around the main parts of the castle. But thoughts of Selina caused his common sense to evaporate.

The footman and Archie turned the corner from the far end of the house into the larger hall on the first floor where the guest suites were located. In the shadows at the other end of the corridor, he saw the silhouette of Professor Stroughton and his fiancée, Constance, bidding Selina good-night. Constance leaned in and kissed Selina on the lips, then patted her cheek with sisterly affection.

He tried not to stare, or make a sound. The footman was equally inconspicuous, one of his primary functions being discretion. Neither of them made a peep as they walked along the Axminster carpet that covered the center of the hall. After Stroughton and his fiancée had continued around the corner, ostensibly down the next passage to their own separate rooms, Selina turned and looked him right in the eyes. Even though the hall was only dimly lit by candlelight, even though she shouldn't have been able to see more than the shadowy outline of him as he walked behind the footman many yards away, he felt as though her gaze pierced his heart.

She wanted him. Why did that thought unnerve him so? Perhaps because, just like her cruel parents, he feared she simply *wanted*. In her moments of flirtatious levity, when she'd referred to her high-strung nature, he'd hated himself for worrying, but he had worried nonetheless. Was her behavior indeed unhealthy? More of a craving? A desire borne of an uncontrollable, insatiable animal lust, rather than the elevation of the human spirit through tender lovemaking and physical communion?

When she turned slowly and shut the door to her chamber, he felt as though a door was shutting on his heart. In his mind, he was left standing outside an imaginary home, the rest of his family and friends indoors, enjoying the comfort of the fire and one another's company. Always on the perimeter, he remained. This was the life he had chosen, one of detached observation; this was the life he thought he wanted. A life of scientific inquiry and purpose. Not a life made up of meaningless late-night assignations at the ancestral home of one of the most respected peers of the realm.

The footman opened the door to his guest room. "Do you have everything you need, my lord?"

"Yes. Thank you. Good night."

The footman bowed and left. And Archie stood there, alone in the middle of the room, and thought he might cry for the first time since his father had died, when he and his twin sister were seven years old.

He had never seen the bloated bodies of the Marquess of Camburton and his beloved brother after they'd been dragged from the ravages of the North Sea. He'd never seen his father nor his uncle in that morbid state, but he had envisioned them, imagined them inhaling water instead of air, struggling in the frigid water, sacrificing their own lives to save others.

Both of the Cambury brothers were famously strong swimmers, according to Vanessa and the engraved athletic boards at Eton and Cambridge. The Cambury brothers were famously strong at everything, or so it had seemed to Archie's young, impressionable mind. And then they had died and Vanessa had calmly informed him that *he* was now the marquess and *he* would need to be very strong and very wise like his father and his uncle had been. Vanessa explained how he would need to listen to his tutors, to observe the ways of different cultures, to empathize with the struggles of others, to investigate, to discover, *to cure*. In short, he needed to live a life that would honor his father's memory, a life that would make up for his father's tragic demise.

Over twenty years ago, a seven-year-old boy had accepted all those responsibilities—welcomed them and their weighty purpose—and lived up to them.

All of a sudden, he was unable to bear it. He didn't want to be a paragon for another minute. He didn't want to uphold some abstract ideal of British manhood. He wanted to taste Selina's mouth after she had devoured him. He wanted to taste Selina's hot center and then kiss her. He wanted to mingle every part of them, one to the other. And it was not filthy. It was glorious and perfect. In short, he wanted to marry Miss Selina Ashby, to marry himself to her in every sense of the word.

And he didn't want to wait another moment.

Selina stayed leaning against the door and traced the edge of her lip where Constance had kissed her. A few months ago—maybe even a few days ago—she would have welcomed Constance and William's overture; she would have seen their playful invitation to spend the night with both of them as a sweet interlude of physical satisfaction, nothing more. Constance's coltish childhood beauty had matured into a dark feminine allure. Her skin was as luminous as the finest Limoges, and under other circumstances, Selina would have longed to kiss her neck and shoulders, to taste the essence of her particular scent at her wrists and behind her knees. Between her legs.

And even though William Stroughton struck her as more than a bit too forward, Selina had always imagined a time she would enjoy both a man and a woman, all of them in bed at the same time, satisfying one another, taking and giving pleasure in so many new and joyful ways.

Closing her eyes in dismay, Selina realized she no longer wanted that with just *any* man and woman. She wanted to experience it with the impossibly remote Marquess of Camburton and her beloved Beatrix. She stomped her foot in frustration. Devil take him, the man had captured far more than her imagination. She wanted to protect him from the careless, public jibes of men like Professor Stroughton, but she also wanted to ravish him in private, to tear away all the layers that made him such a slave to convention. Not (merely) to torment him or tease him, but because deep down she knew he would shine like the sun if he were finally let loose in that way.

There was a quiet knock at the door, and it vibrated through her. "Who is it?" Selina whispered.

"Constance . . . I'm alone."

Turning to grab the knob, Selina didn't know whether she wanted to open the door a crack or fling it wide in welcome. If Constance was returning to speak as one old friend to another, Selina would certainly welcome her counsel. If she was back to renew some saucy sensual overture, Selina was simply not interested. Opting for a middle way, Selina opened the door enough to see Constance fully, but still blocked the entrance with her body.

"May I come in?" Constance asked softly. She had changed into her nightgown and white robe, and seemed as innocent as a fresh blanket of snow. For some reason, her appearance of innocence only exaggerated what Selina now clearly saw as the corrupt nature of her visit.

She felt the press of tears. How odd, she thought, rubbing her eyes as if she were tired, and barely grasping that the tears that threatened were those of disappointment that Archie had not been the person to knock at her door. "Yes. Of course. Come sit down and we can visit."

When they'd been out under the stars earlier in the evening, they'd lain on the cold grass and held hands like girls—excited by the mystery of night, thrilled by the expanse of the universe, and sharing in all that childlike natural wonder. Still, she had been acutely aware of the way their hands fit snugly together, because theirs were not children's hands: they were women's hands, their bodies were womanly bodies. As much as Constance laughed in that free, innocent way of hers, there was no denying the heave of her bosom as she did, or the images that floated into Selina's mind when she let herself remember all the nights she and Beatrix had lain under the summer sky at Camburton. Holding hands beneath the stars had always been a preamble to their most intimate lovemaking, with Beatrix tending to Selina's body as if it was the most precious gift ever created. As if she was precious.

She exhaled to rid herself of those tender memories. "Would you like a glass of sherry or port? Lady FitzWilliam has been kind enough to provide me with both." She remained by the small sideboard where the crystal decanters had been set on a silver tray.

"No, thank you." Constance smiled gently. "Come sit by me, my sweet friend."

Again, even though Constance used the words "sweet" and "friend," Selina couldn't help feeling like she was being invited into a den of iniquity.

"Constance . . ." Her voice was shaky, and she didn't attempt to hide it. Constance should know that this whole scenario was making her uncomfortable, but she sat down beside Constance on the small settee, despite her misgivings.

"Darling, you are trembling." Constance held one of Selina's hands in hers. "What is it?"

"I am confused. Surely I have not imagined the connection between us."

"Surely you have not." Constance smiled—a deeper, more provocative smile this time—then dipped her lips to Selina's palm.

"I have long admired you . . ." Her heart pounded with a confusing mix of unwelcome physical attraction and emotional distress. For once in her life, she was quite sure she did *not* want this type of physical intimacy. Never would she have imagined she would spurn the tender advances of such a lovely woman, of *this* woman.

Constance pursed her lips and looked adorably insulted. "Admired? You make me sound like a hat in a shop window."

Selina actually blushed, feeling the steady caress of Constance's fingers on her wrist, and gradually up along her forearm. "You know that's not how I meant it." She tried to temper her voice, but it was uneven. "I've always held you in the highest esteem."

Leaning down to kiss the sensitive flesh of Selina's forearm, Constance whispered, "That still sounds far too formal . . ." Constance placed a few more warm kisses up her exposed arm, then looked into her eyes. "I can see you want me. And I very much want you." She leaned in and kissed her lips, a soft, encouraging touch.

"I am not feeling at all myself." Selina's voice returned nearly to normal as she pulled back, but her treacherous body began to respond to Constance's advances nonetheless. Was this how she made Archie feel? This wretched combination of physical arousal and aversion? "I've been living with Beatrix Farnsworth these past two years—"

Constance smiled indulgently. "I know. I've met Beatrix, and I'm sure she would approve of a brief reunion between old friends."

Selina wasn't so sure. Before Beatrix had left for the Continent, the two of them had discussed at great length the nature of their commitment to one another. Beatrix and Selina had agreed that they were free to pursue other people in the time they were apart, but Beatrix had also cautioned her to be wise. Beatrix was seven years older, and she had given Selina so much more than a loving physical relationship. She had taught her how to respect her own passion, how to curtail her eagerness when the occasion demanded, how the rewards of postponement were often great . . . greater. Furthermore, wise caution was not to be confused with self-denial. The repression and cruelty she had endured as a child, Beatrix had explained, were not at all the same thing as choosing *not* to act on a desire that might prove to be less than glorious. Beatrix was all about glory.

Constance and her blithe fiancé suddenly struck Selina as quite *inglorious*.

Her feelings for Archie were glorious.

She extracted her hand from Constance's hold. "I know Beatrix will be happy to hear we met up after all these years, but she would also wish for me to follow my own inner voice. I am in a bit of a coil about the Marquess of Camburton—"

Constance laughed softly and, if Selina wasn't mistaken, with a bit of malice. "Darling, *really*. He's a puppy. And you are . . ." Constance let her gaze roam Selina's body with a look that was nothing short of ravenous. "Well, you are spectacular, my dear."

Constance reached for her bare shoulder, tentatively caressing her, then slowly trailing her fingertip lower, to the swell of her breast above the low-cut bodice. Selina inhaled sharply, wanting to cry again for how much she wished it were Beatrix or Archie touching her. Again, her body responded—her nipples hardening and her throat going dry.

"Spectacular . . ." Constance whispered, and leaned in to kiss Selina's breast. Before her brain could grasp what was happening, Constance had worked the delicate fabric away from her nipple and began to kiss and tease it with her wicked tongue. "You need a forceful lover." She pulled the nipple deeper into her mouth and sucked hard. Selina gasped and reached her hands into Constance's hair to push her away. Everything felt wrong.

And, of course, that was the moment Archibald Cambury, the Marquess of Camburton, opened the door to her chamber and whispered her name, peering around sweetly as if he were coming to pledge his troth. Then his eyes landed on her—or more accurately, his eyes landed on her bosom, where Miss Constance Forrester was suckling her flesh and moaning delightedly. Selina did begin crying then. She shoved Constance roughly away from her body as she watched Archie's tenderness and warmth drain away from his expression, and then he simply shut the door as quietly as he'd opened it. Gone like a ghost. The ghost—she belatedly realized—of everything she'd ever wanted and now would never have.

"Get out!" She tugged up her dress and stood quickly, then walked across the room and poured herself a drink. "I am serious, Constance." Breathing hard, she reached for the bell pull, wrapping her hand threateningly around the tassel. "I will call for a footman if you do not leave at once."

Licking her lips, Constance rose gracefully. "No hard feelings, I hope."

She tried not to roll her eyes. "No hard feelings. In fact, no feelings whatsoever. I wish you and Professor Stroughton every happiness in your married life together."

"Oh, not to worry, my dear. I know we will be very happy. Perhaps one day you will be mature enough to see *firsthand* just how happy we are together." With that parting volley, Constance left the room and, Selina hoped, left her life for good.

Chapter 7

*A*rchie woke up before the dawn. To be more accurate, he'd never actually slept, but he was out of bed before the dawn. He rang for a footman and asked for his horses and carriage to be readied as soon as possible. If Selina was going to spend her time in the arms of her *close childhood friend*, there was no point in his hanging about like some lovesick cub. He would return to Camburton Castle and send another coach back for Selina to return at her leisure.

Or perhaps he'd be lucky and Selina would decide to spend the winter at Rockingham instead of Camburton. Earl FitzWilliam had been quite taken with Miss Ashby and her literary aspirations, and over dinner last night the countess had even invited her to visit at length should she ever require solitude or inspiration for her writing. Perhaps Selina would eventually sleep with the earl and Lady FitzWilliam as well.

He scowled at the unfair bent of his thoughts as he packed his own bag and hoped that he could get out of the castle before encountering anyone. There was a light knock at the door and the footman informed him the carriage was ready and waiting just outside the keep. "We haven't brought it into the inner courtyard, so as not to wake his lordship and the other guests."

"Of course, thank you for being so considerate. I'm so sorry to have disrupted the household with my early departure."

"It's no disruption, sir."

"Thank you."

The footman carried his bag down the hall to the stairs, then led the way, step after silent step, until they crossed the palatial front hall and neared the front door.

"Lord Camburton?"

He thought he must have been hearing Selina's voice as some nightmarish punishment for his foolishness. The ghost of her sounded tentative and sweet. He kept walking.

"Archie?"

He turned abruptly. The footman also stopped. From the predawn shadows, Selina emerged from the alcove near the front door. "I thought you would want to leave quite early."

She was perfectly turned out in her rose velvet traveling dress and spencer. She was also wearing a warmer cloak—lined with some decadent fur, he noticed with irritation. Why did that bit of tantalizing fur against her milky skin have to drive him mad? Her hair was pulled back in a severe style, with a small jaunty hat atop her head. The small feather accent quivered slightly, although she appeared to be standing perfectly still.

He addressed the footman. "You may take my bag to the carriage. I will follow along momentarily." Once they were alone, he turned his attention back to Selina. "I will send a coach back for you tomorrow. The earl has invited you to stay, and it would be rude for you to leave in this manner."

"Is it not rude for *you* to leave in this manner?" Her voice held none of its familiar teasing or playfulness. She sounded fragile.

"Selina—"

She lunged for him, desperately clutching his upper arm. He stared down at her hold, and felt completely detached. She might as well have been holding on to a lamppost or an umbrella. He'd gone numb.

"It is not what you think. Constance was trying to seduce me—" She was crying dramatic tears, and he felt a twinge of sympathy, and then . . . nothing.

He peeled her gloved hand off his person. "You were flirting with Miss Forrester from the moment you walked into the drawing room last night. Not that it is any of my concern."

Her weeping was beginning to become hysterical. "I want it to be your concern! I thought she was my friend. I was happy to see her. She was my *childhood* friend. And she took advantage of me. You must believe me!" Her voice was low, but hoarse and emphatic.

"I must do no such thing." He took a deep breath and tried to think of the least troublesome solution to the immediate problem. She gulped back her tears, apparently awaiting his verdict. "And keep your voice down or you will wake the entire castle." He handed her a handkerchief out of habit.

She took it and patted her eyes, then held it close to her face, just as she'd done that first time they'd kissed. Had it only been a week? When it came to Miss Ashby, it seemed every minute was a year.

He sighed in frustration. "Come with me, then. There's no point in the two of us making a scene in the earl's foyer. I will ride up top with the driver."

He picked up her valise, but did not offer his arm. She followed him in silence, her shorter stride requiring two quick steps across the gravel to each of his longer ones. The sun was just beginning to hint at a magnificent autumnal morning, with the mist and the grass and the morning dew rising to meet the new day. A pair of songbirds began to trill, and both Archie and Selina stopped midstride and turned to listen to their spontaneous joy.

"So beautiful . . ." Selina's awed whisper unnerved him even further.

He started walking again and spoke without looking at her. "Get in the carriage and please refrain from falling in love with any more birds along the way. We have another long day of continuous travel."

She gasped, but said nothing. The driver held open the door, and she stepped in and immediately looked out the far window, avoiding eye contact with him or his servant.

"Please get my greatcoat from the trunk, Granger. I will be riding on the box with you."

The driver nodded, shut the door to the compartment, located Archie's coat, and they were off within a few minutes. The morning was clear and fresh, and they would be home at Camburton Castle in time for tea the next day. At least he would be home. Selina would be lurking about as usual.

The few times they paused to water the horses, Selina made her own way into the inns and saw to her own needs, and once again took her meal alone in her room when they stopped for the night. When they arrived at Camburton, she curtseyed politely and thanked him for his kind offer of transportation to and from London. One of the footmen carried her two heavier bags while she carried her valise, and they turned to walk toward her cottage on the other side of the formal gardens. Archie felt her departure like a thread being pulled from the fabric of his being, each step she took away from him unraveling his equanimity.

"Damn it." He turned to enter Camburton Castle, nodding as he passed the butler who held open the massive oak door. "I'll take my supper on a tray in my laboratory." He tossed his greatcoat on the bench in the front hall and headed straight to his workroom to stare into a microscope until he could banish every thought of Miss Ashby from his mind.

It almost worked.

He ran several experiments over and over, proving some of the hypotheses he and Christopher had been batting around after Jenner's lecture. He wrote his conclusions up in a lengthy report and sent it to London for Christopher's review. A single line came back in the return post: *Are you married yet?*

He crumpled it up and then, for good measure, lit it on fire in the incinerator he used to destroy some of his more dangerous specimens. "Yet? Ever."

Yes, he had started talking to himself. Full conversations about his research, about his obligations on the estate as they prepared for the long winter ahead. He spent two hours every morning with his steward and another hour on horseback overseeing any particular areas that required his attention. He was not nearly as good an equestrian as his sister, but he sat a horse—as he'd lived his life prior to meeting Miss Ashby—with quiet confidence.

At night, he was unable to rein in his wild imaginings. He began to dread nightfall, which, given the season, came earlier and earlier every day. He always took his meals in the lab, hoping to stay in solitude as long as possible. But eventually mental exhaustion would overtake him and the threat of making errors prevented him from working straight through until dawn.

After a fortnight of not seeing a trace of Selina, he was feeling far more temperate. He'd received word from his mother and Nora that they'd be returning to Camburton the following day. He dreaded the small family dinners that would be set for the four of them, Vanessa, Nora, Selina, and Archie. Perhaps it was a sign he should set up house in London.

Impossible. He had all of his work here. And why should he be driven from his own house because of some sex-crazed novelist? He'd done a fine job of ignoring her since they'd returned from London, at least during his waking hours.

He removed his leather apron and left the lab. Walking through the quiet castle had always brought him a deep sense of peace. Seeing his ancestors on the walls, a long line of honorable men and women painted throughout the centuries, had formerly filled him with a feeling of profound belonging. Now he felt he belonged nowhere.

Somewhere on his estate—he knew precisely where, often staring out his window at the small spiral of smoke that rose up from her cottage—Selina was probably warm and happy in her own skin. Or perhaps she was not happy—he experienced a pang of guilt for wishing she suffered even a fraction of what he did—given the strain of their last night at Rockingham, but at least she must have been engaged in her work and able to get on with her life.

He'd made sure she had a basket of food and fresh milk delivered to her each morning. She'd sent a note each day to his steward asking that he relay her gratitude to the marquess.

This was what he wanted, wasn't it? The protection of a formal relationship? The barricades of centuries of propriety? He entered his bedroom and looked around the perfectly appointed chamber. The fire glowed; the tester bed was turned down; the valet waited to assist him with his clothes.

He was patently miserable.

Apparently misery was a boon to productivity. Selina had never felt so lost or alone, yet the words—the good, subtle words—flew from the end of her quill. It was not the effervescent *pas de deux* she'd planned to write when she'd first proposed the plot to her publisher. Instead, she'd written to tell her editor that the story had taken on a darker cast. He'd written back immediately to tell her how pleased he was to hear it. *The darker the better, Miss Ashby.*

On and on she wrote, not giving a care to her appearance or her schedule. Sleeping some days until noon or writing some days straight through the night and then collapsing into bed at noon. Like a dog who misses its master, she'd found a scarf of Bea's and taken to keeping it nearby—on her desk while she wrote, or wrapped around her hand while she slept. She'd created a calendar, marking off the time until her lover returned. Only twenty-seven days remained. At the current speed of writing, she would be done with her manuscript by then and able to devote her full attention to Beatrix.

She'd been thinking perhaps in future it would be best if she followed Beatrix around the world, traveling with her from place to place while she performed. Obviously, the life of solitude and contemplation she'd thought she was so well suited to was not quite as charming as she'd hoped. Yes, she was productive, but at what cost?

She knew she must have the look of a wild witch in the forest, because the kind maid who delivered her basket of food each morning had lately taken to looking away, as if Miss Ashby couldn't possibly wish to be seen in her present condition.

"We've received word that Lady Camburton and Mrs. White are returning this afternoon, ma'am." Mary, probably in her twenties, was somehow respectful yet demanding as she kept her eyes downcast. "In case you wish to . . ."

Selina took the basket from her outstretched hands. "In case I wish to make myself presentable, Mary?"

Mary turned bright red. "I'm sorry, ma'am." She curtseyed again and turned to go.

"No, you're quite right. Please wait."

Mary paused and looked at her, then at the ground again.

"I've let myself go. Would you help me with my hair and getting dressed later today, in case the marchioness wishes to ask me for dinner?"

"Yes, ma'am. I would be very happy to. Shall I have a bath brought in?" She blushed again, obviously embarrassed that she'd implied Selina was in need of one.

Selina laughed, and it felt raw and unfamiliar. "Yes, Mary. I think I am long overdue for a proper bath. As Napoleon said to Josephine, I must take one after a fortnight whether I need it or not."

"Oh, I didn't mean to be sayin'—"

"No need to explain a thing. Shall we say five o'clock?"

"Yes, ma'am." With that, Mary turned and walked down the narrow path that led from the cottage. The late summer flowers had all been deadheaded by the gardeners and the beds had been turned for winter. As usual, Selina simply wanted to cry at the loss of vibrancy— the draining away of life—that seemed to be defining her existence at present. She shut the door, set the basket down on the small kitchen table, and went back to the desk where she worked. Her tea was still warm and her pen nibs were freshly trimmed.

When Mary next appeared at the door, Selina thought perhaps half an hour had passed. "Yes, Mary, did you forget something?" Her mind was presently in a dark dungeon, wet with moss and filled with the sounds of suspicious scuttling creatures and the drip of rank liquids. Her main character had been tossed into the secret prison after he was caught rummaging through the Italian count's private papers.

"It is five o'clock, ma'am. You said . . ."

Selina looked around confusedly, then saw the six footmen behind Mary carrying an enormous copper tub and large wooden buckets of hot water. "Oh! I didn't think you meant to carry out a full-sized bath." She stepped aside and let the footmen enter the cottage.

Mary, despite her youthful appearance, was a born dictator. "Yes. Put it there by the fire," she ordered two of the men impatiently. "Quit your gawking, Timpton. Pour the water and leave the lady in peace." The young man in question scowled at Mary, but did as he was told.

Once her minions had left, Mary shut the door behind them with a thud. "Men. Good for hauling things, I suppose, but I've yet to discover what else they're good for. Let's get you out of those . . ." She gestured vaguely at the motley items Selina had taken to wearing over the past two weeks. Around her shoulders, she had on a blanket-type shawl that usually hung over the back of the sofa. Then she wore a long men's shirt she'd picked up several years ago; it was cut wide in the shoulders and allowed her plenty of movement when she was working. She had on some loose trousers Nora had given her over the summer: Egyptian cotton with a drawstring waist. On her feet she sported a pair of mismatched socks in desperate need of darning.

She started laughing as she put one hand on her waist and the other on the top of her head, and then pirouetted. "Are you suggesting I am not properly attired for dinner with a marchioness?"

"It's nice to see you again, Miss Ashby."

"You too, Mary."

She removed her near-rags and slid gratefully into the copper tub. "Oh my, this feels delicious."

Mary brought a small stool to the edge of the tub behind Selina's head and began working through the mess of her long blonde hair. It was knotted and filthy, and she felt like a silly girl for having let herself go in this manner. "I apologize for my raggedy state."

"No need to apologize to me, ma'am. You are working hard, and there's nothing shameful about hard work." Mary spoke as she built up a thick lather against Selina's scalp. "I admire a woman like you, Miss Ashby, making her own life and living her own way. That's what I aim to do. Get a little cottage with a small garden and live out my days in peace. I save every farthing I make, and maybe in twenty years or so I will have enough for a modest place."

"That sounds like a lovely plan." Selina's voice was soft with gratitude. She relaxed more deeply into Mary's care, and hoped she would one day be in a position to help Mary realize her modest dream that much sooner.

After finishing with her hair, Mary scrubbed her back and rinsed it with a pitcher of warm water. Then she handed Selina a bar of soap and a flannel. "I'll go see to your clothes for tonight."

She scoured herself nearly raw, soaping and rubbing away the residue of the past two weeks that lingered on her body. When she stepped out of the tub, Mary wrapped her in a large towel and guided her to a seat near the fire. "Now, while your hair dries, I'll see to your hands."

She looked down and realized her fingertips were stained, her nails chipped, and her knuckles rough and dry. "Oh. Thank you." She extended her hands and let the maid rub them with oil and file the nails. She let herself be taken care of. It felt like the epitome of luxury, to be touched in this nonemotional way, to be tended to. "I am very grateful for you, Mary." Her eyes were moist with pending tears.

Mary patted the back of her hand where she was massaging in some oil. "Oh, it's nothing to be upset about. You've been very busy, and now you will look beautiful in no time. Lady Camburton and Mrs. White have returned and sent word that you are expected in the drawing room at eight o'clock. You won't have a hair out of place when you see everyone."

If Selina wasn't mistaken, Mary scowled.

"Will there be someone other than the ladies in the drawing room, Mary?"

Mary blushed in embarrassment, but still looked mildly angry. "I believe the marquess will be forced to leave his laboratory to greet his mother, yes. And the ladies have also returned with another gentleman from London."

Selina's heart—damnable heart that didn't care about heartless men who accused her of flirting with every songbird—began to beat faster at the mere mention of Archie. There was no point in worrying what Mary thought. They were going to be together for the next two hours at least—making Selina presentable—so she might as well wring some gossip out of the maid. "The marquess has been very busy with his research, is that it?"

Mary shook her head but kept her gaze focused on Selina's hands. "Research is one word for it. He's been hiding out if you ask me."

"Well, I *am* asking you. Isn't that his normal routine? To work long hours in his laboratory?"

Mary slipped a thick flannel glove onto one hand to help the oil soak in, and began work on the other hand. "Yes, he usually works in the laboratory."

"So, what's different?"

She sighed. "It's not for me to say, but he is behaving very strangely. He's taken to running around the castle late at night."

"Out on the grounds?" For some reason the idea of Archie running around Camburton Park like a wild werewolf made her smile despite herself.

"Yes, there too, but mostly down the long halls and up the stairs and all around. It's very odd."

Selina laughed. "Aristocrats are very odd, haven't you heard?"

"Of course, the marquess can run around naked and it's certainly not for me to say whether it's odd or not. I'm only remarking upon it because he was so much . . . happier this summer when you two would go on walks and that sort of thing."

"Mary!" Selina pretended to chastise her for her familiarity. "What *sort of thing* are you suggesting?"

Mary turned red as a beet. "I'm not suggesting . . . I was only . . ." She was practically blubbering.

"I'm only teasing. I know he and I were on much better terms this summer. And I must confess I'm rather pleased he's as rattled as I am after our . . . quarrel."

Exhaling with exaggerated relief, Mary continued, "I knew it. I haven't been gossiping with the other servants, but it's quite obvious he's *very* rattled. So maybe if you could, perhaps, be friends again? It's just awfully grim lately over in the castle."

"So if I were to . . . rekindle my friendship with him, it would be an act of mercy on behalf of his retainers?"

Mary smiled as she put on the other flannel glove. "Yes. It would be very charitable of you to be thinking of others. Very considerate. Now let me see to your hair."

Chapter 8

*A*rchie's valet was no longer hiding his displeasure. "If you do not finish the experiment now, my lord, you will be late to greet the marchioness and Mrs. White."

"They don't mind when I'm late."

"I do," the valet mumbled.

Archie stared into the microscope a moment longer. "Fine." He pulled away from his workbench and removed his apron, handing it to Reynolds. "Only because it will be such a trial for you. When hundreds of children die of the wrong variolation, that will be on your head."

"Lord Camburton—"

He smiled, and it felt like his face was cracking—he was that far out of practice. "I'm not serious. Let us go. I could do with a proper washing—I'm as ripe as old cheese."

Reynolds grunted in a way that was respectful but in no way disagreed with his less-than-pleasant assessment of his toilette.

As he bathed, he realized he was paying attention to his appearance for the first time in weeks. Reynolds sighed his appreciation and muttered a few disrespectful it's-about-times and well-that's-betters. After being Archie's father's valet, Reynolds had stayed on and had been dressing and tending to Archie for the past twenty years. The servant fussed with his neck cloth, ensuring the folds were immaculate. He pinned it with one of the finest emeralds.

"Is it a special occasion, Reynolds?" Archie kept his chin high so the man had room to work on the linen.

"There you are." Reynolds finished with the pin, stood back a pace, appeared to be pleased with his handiwork, then picked up the fabric brush and ran a few quick strokes down Archie's back to make sure the superfine nap was looking its best. "Seeing your mother after several weeks should be a special occasion, should it not?"

Perhaps Reynolds's voice should have given Archie a clue that something was amiss, but he was tired and hoping the evening would pass in the usual way. A relaxing supper in the small dining room, Vanessa, Nora, and Archie sharing details and observations of the past few weeks, a glass of port in the library, and a good night's sleep.

Alas.

When he entered the drawing room, it almost felt like a foreign place. He had not been in the main parts of the castle for many days—weeks even—except to sprint through its corridors like a madman, and he observed the splendid decoration with new appreciation.

"Archie!" Nora saw him first and crossed the room to hug him. "Oh, how I've missed you, my dear boy. Town is so loud and busy." She studied him and narrowed her eyes. "We will talk tomorrow. A long talk, yes?"

"Yes, Nora. I would like that very much."

She held his hands in hers for a few moments longer. "So would I."

He realized he was not merely being polite. He very much wanted to speak to Nora about what had transpired with Miss Ashby. Nora had always understood him in ways no one else did.

"Cambury!"

He turned and saw Christopher Joseph standing near the fireplace.

"Oh, yes!" Nora exclaimed. "Look who we found in London, and we simply forced him to come for a visit. You are so awful about going to town and seeing everyone, Archie. So we've brought town to you."

He smiled at his friend. They shook hands, and Christopher leaned in. "Are you married yet?"

Damn him and his blunt nature. "No. Highly unlikely outcome to that hypothesis, I'm afraid."

"Afraid?" Christopher raised a single eyebrow and took a sip of his whisky. "I can't imagine why."

Vanessa was speaking to someone and finished her thought before she leapt from the couch to greet her son. It was beginning to feel like a house party, and all he wanted to do was stare into a microscope.

"Archie!" Vanessa's high voice spread through the room, embracing him as much as her arms did when she hugged him close.

"Mother, how are you?"

She stepped back and looked at him from head to toe. "You are tired. I can see it in your eyes."

"I am. I've been working long hours as I get closer to understanding the final piece of this puzzle."

"There will always be one more piece, you know that."

"I know. But I've wanted to keep busy."

"You always do. At least you haven't been alone at Camburton."

He was about to reply that he had never been so alone in his entire life when a vision in emerald-green velvet rose from behind the tall back of the wing chair a few feet in front of where he was standing. Apparently Selina had been enjoying a few weeks of pampered leisure, from the look of her perfectly coiffed blonde hair and her immaculate ivory skin.

"Miss Ashby." He bowed formally.

"Lord Camburton." She curtseyed just as formally.

"What's all this?" Vanessa asked on a laugh. "We are all like family here, are we not? No titles, I beg of you."

There was a slight pause that Vanessa likely missed. He was fairly certain Nora picked up on the subtle tension, but she smoothed things over in her usual way.

"Of course we are," she said gently. "Archie, I would love a glass of sherry, and I believe Selina would like one as well."

Selina looked at Nora, not at him. "Yes, please."

"Allow me." He walked over to the table that had been stocked with a small selection of spirits and poured drinks for the ladies.

Nora followed and took both of the small, etched-crystal glasses from him. "I will bring Selina her glass, shall I?"

"Yes, thank you." Once again, he felt like a guest in his own house. In his own castle, damn it. He poured himself a stiff whisky for his troubles and walked over to stand near the fireplace, as far away from Selina as he could get without being obvious about it. Christopher came and stood to his left and began speaking about an experiment he was working on with an element related to osmium. Within seconds, Archie was barely paying attention.

"And then I let it dry in the phial overnight to see if it would crystallize a second time and thought it would be worth bringing it back up to a boil, just to see if it happened again. I lit the burner with a strand of Selina's beautiful blonde hair—"

He nearly choked on his whisky.

"Are you all right, dear?" Nora asked him from across the room.

"Yes. Thank you for inquiring. I've had a bit of a sore throat this past week. I'm better now."

Nora nodded and resumed speaking with Vanessa and Selina.

Did she have to look so damned delectable? Of course no one would ever suspect Selina Ashby was a scheming voluptuary, the way she sat up so straight, taking only the most ladylike sips of her sherry, while she listened attentively to Vanessa's description of the latest finds in the rare book room at Hookhams.

"You'd best put your panting tongue back in your mouth or she will have to scrape it off the floor with a shovel." Christopher spoke mostly into his glass so no one but Archie could hear him, but he realized Christopher was right: his lips were slightly parted. He slammed his mouth shut into a firm line.

"When was the last time you saw Miss Ashby?" Christopher asked casually.

"Two weeks ago."

Christopher burst out laughing. Again the three ladies smiled kindly in the men's direction. He waved them off. "Archie has the driest wit."

"He does!" Vanessa agreed. "When he was younger I thought he was being serious all the time, and then I would think over what he had said and burst out laughing ten minutes after he had left the room. He has his father's dark sense of humor."

Selina looked into her glass, and Archie wanted to smack it from her hands and be very dark indeed. Her beautiful, delicate hands. She obviously hadn't been writing or doing anything productive, if her lovely hands were any indication. Perhaps she'd gone back to Rockingham to have some debauched ménage with the affianced Stroughtons these past two weeks while he'd been hunched over his bench or running his legs off in the middle of the night worrying about her and how to reconcile their friendship. He nearly growled into his glass.

"Bad whisky?" Christopher asked.

"No. The liquor is fine."

"You might start by talking to her. She's sitting right there." Christopher took a meditative sip. "And she's quite spectacular. Why didn't you tell me she was such a beauty?"

"Is she?"

"Are you blind?"

"I think I may be when it comes to her. Let's change the subject."

"Oh, you are such a one for changing subjects, Lord Camburton. Very well. If you are not going to pursue her, may I?"

He had never felt a fury of such immediacy. He turned slowly, and Christopher did not laugh. He didn't even smile.

"Ah." Christopher shook the ice in his glass. "It's like that, is it? Dog in the manger? If you shan't have her, nobody shall?"

"Stop it this instant."

Narrowing his eyes, Christopher set his drink down on the mantle. "I'm glad I've come after all." He lowered his voice and spoke with near malice. "I'm going to fuck some sense into you tonight, you brilliant, stupid man."

Archie's stomach fell a few inches. "How dare you speak to me like that in my own drawing room?"

Christopher tilted his head to one side and gave him a collegial slap on the arm. "Someone has to. Apparently the job has fallen to me. The dinner bell's about to ring—"

"Now see here—" He was interrupted by the gong sounding in the hall.

"Dinner is served." Christopher winked at him, then approached Selina. Archie suddenly despised his best friend and *former* bedmate, as he watched him bow slightly with easy grace and offer to take Miss Ashby into the dining room.

Nora and Vanessa had also stood up at the sound of the gong, and Archie walked over to them and set out each of his arms. "Ladies?"

Vanessa kissed him lightly on the cheek. "Aren't you the kindest gentleman in all of England?"

He began to lead them to the large formal dining room, but Vanessa tugged in another direction. "Oh, since it's only the five of us, I asked for the meal to be set in the family dining room."

"Of course." He turned down the hall, and dread crept up his spine. The small round room was for intimate suppers among immediate family. He had hoped the twenty-foot table in the formal dining room would grant him a much-needed physical distance from Selina. As usual, his hopes were dashed.

Vanessa released his forearm when they entered the cozy room. The fire crackled and the round table was set for five. He did feel a moment's pyrrhic victory when he thought he heard Selina inhale with equal displeasure at the intimacy of the room.

"How snug," she remarked pleasantly.

"Yes," Vanessa agreed. "I love this family room after all the crowded suppers of summer, don't you, Archie?"

"Yes, Mother." *Especially when it's reserved for actual family*, he wanted to add sarcastically.

"Please sit here, Selina." Vanessa pointed to the chair next to the one that Archie usually occupied. "And of course, Archie, you always sit here. Then Nora, Christopher, and I am on your other side, Selina. I am simply *dying* to hear what you've been working on. Do you think you can bear having Camburys to the left of you and Camburys to the right?"

Archie supposed she was answering truthfully when she said, "I'm certain I can bear it if I must."

Vanessa laughed at her supposed joke. "That's the spirit."

If only there were one of Aunt Diana's trapdoors beneath this lovely *family* table, perhaps Selina could expire in peace. As it was, she had to pretend to be jolly when she felt like weeping, had to pretend to enjoy the food when she could barely taste it, and worst of all, she had to pretend *not* to feel the heat of Archie's body mere inches away from her own.

She made it through the soup course. And she was almost through with her probably delicious main course. She would beg off dessert and flee soon enough. When Vanessa asked her how she was progressing on her latest novel, she swallowed her bite of tasteless food and replied, "I've nearly finished."

"You have?" Archie and Vanessa replied in unison. She smiled at Vanessa and ignored Archie. It was all she could do. The few times she had looked at him, she had wanted to ravish him, and she knew how little that appealed to him. She vowed to herself that she would get through this meal and kindly decline any future invitations from the marchioness. Which would be easy because she planned to vacate her charming cottage the next day.

"Yes. The quiet and solitude of Camburton at this time of year have provided me with the greatest inspiration. I'm writing close to twenty pages each day . . . or night . . . as the case may be."

"Camburton is so beautiful at this time of year. Lots of long walks and contemplation in nature; that gets the muse going, doesn't it?" Vanessa was a glutton for the creative spirit, always celebrating those around her and spurring on their achievements.

Selina laughed, and it came out sounding more bitter than she had intended. "I'm sure it is quite beautiful, but I haven't left the confines of my cottage in two weeks."

The table fell silent, and she realized it sounded quite odd to admit that she had been holed up in a tiny shack when all the comfort and pleasure of Camburton Castle was a stone's throw away.

"Surely you mean that figuratively," Vanessa suggested. "Didn't you dine at Camburton? Didn't you invite her to dine at Camburton, Archie?" His mother was the picture of bohemian liberty about most things, but apparently this lack of hospitality was a breach of some importance.

"Miss Ashby chose to stay in her cottage, and I did not wish to disrespect her privacy."

Vanessa set down her knife and fork. If Selina wasn't mistaken, Vanessa might've preferred to slam them down if she hadn't been in company. "Would someone please tell me why you keep referring to Selina as Miss Ashby? As we all know, that is her family name and she dislikes it."

Apparently, Archie *didn't* know that. He looked at Selina for a brief but meaningful moment. "I beg your pardon, Selina. I didn't know. If you'll all excuse me. I have a terrible headache." With that, he stood up in the middle of the main course, and left the room.

Vanessa appeared to be on the verge of exerting her maternal rank and telling her son he had not been excused, when the door closed and she exhaled. "What in the world?" She turned to Nora for guidance and found none, then to Selina. "Have you quarreled? I thought you two were such good friends? Surely you can get to the bottom of it?"

Selina stared at Vanessa, then Nora, then turned to this stranger named Christopher Joseph who seemed to have such an easy intimacy with Archie. She was jealous of the friendship and camaraderie she had spied across the drawing room—the low comments and answering smiles the two men had shared. She and Archie had almost had that.

She paused, inhaling through her nose to temper her reply. "Yes. I'm afraid we quarreled. It seems we have some differences of opinion about which . . ." She hesitated. "About which we cannot agree to disagree. I thought of leaving and sending you a letter of gratitude—"

"Gratitude! This is preposterous! What could you and Archie possibly disagree about? He worships you—"

"Perhaps that's the problem," she interrupted softly. "I don't believe I measure up to his idea of me."

"Oh." Vanessa finally showed the beginnings of understanding.

"Well, this is all very dramatic," Christopher said in his easy manner. "May I be excused, Lady Camburton? I believe Archie needs some sense beaten into him."

Nora smiled. Vanessa nodded. Selina was jealous. She would very much like to beat some sense into Archibald Cambury's hard male body.

"Mrs. White. Lady Camburton . . . Selina?" Christopher stood and bowed slightly to each of them.

"Yes, please call me Selina. And please tell Archie I'm sorry if I've upset him . . ."

"Yes. I will tell him." Christopher pushed his chair back under the table and departed.

She couldn't bear it another moment. She pulled her napkin up to her face and began to weep.

"Oh my sweet dear!" Vanessa gripped her hands together in frustration. "I am such a dunce. Nora, you should have told me something was amiss. You are so prescient about these sorts of things and I am so dim-witted."

"It's not for you to worry, Vanessa." Selina tried to speak between jagged sobs. "He is your son after all . . . your wonderful son . . ." She started crying harder.

"Oh! Oh! This is terrible!" Vanessa threw her napkin on the table and stood. "You must go talk to him, Selina. That's all there is to it!" But she looked almost laughably uncertain. "Isn't that what she must do, Nora?"

"I think we all need a stiff drink." Nora stood up and helped Selina do the same. "Come. Let's get all this out." She guided Selina down the hall and into her painting studio, which also doubled as Vanessa's study. The two women were nearly inseparable after twenty or so years of living together, and the spacious room reflected all of their shared interests.

Nora's easel and paints had been put away for their recent stay in London, but the smell of linseed oil and canvas still lingered after her absence. Vanessa's desk took up much of the other side of the room. It was a large partners desk with a tooled leather inlay top and a beautiful brass lamp at the corner. The desk was neat and free of papers, but there were a few stones and feathers, as well as a small self-portrait of Nora.

"What a beautiful room." Selina sniffed. "I don't want to impose."

Nora soothed her and set her down in the soft corner of a red silk chaise. "Don't be silly. We have both longed to get to know you better and we all know the summer months tend to be a riot of activity and fun, but rarely afford us the opportunity to talk at length. Will you have a whisky?"

Selina sighed and settled into the downy back cushion. "I think that sounds heavenly."

Vanessa sat in the chair opposite the chaise and clasped her hands together. "Now start at the beginning. From what I could see, Archie's been mooning over you since he first saw you in June. And then I thought you might have passed the mooning phase and, well, become friends. He's very hard to know, and so private and reserved, and you are—" Vanessa held out her hands in a gesture of all-encompassing admiration. "You are splendid! And just the person to bring him out of his shell. And since he admires you so, and you are in love with Beatrix, I assumed you would pose no threat to his . . ."

Selina began weeping again. She had held on to the thick linen serviette from dinner, finding it much more efficient than her ladylike handkerchief, which would have been soaked through by now. "I do love Beatrix, but I fear I have fallen in love with Archie. Is that so wrong? I don't even think there is a name for it. I want us all to be together. I am beginning to fear my parents are right and I am a damaged, selfish girl who dreams up fantastical stories that make no sense to anyone but my deranged self."

"Drink this, Selina." Nora handed her the whisky and sat down next to her on the chaise. "You are not deranged. You are human. You have a grand capacity for love and that is not something you should be ashamed of or fearful about. But . . ." She looked into her own glass of whisky, then lifted her chin and smiled across the small distance to Vanessa. "But sometimes society sounds loud and powerful in our ears. Especially in the ears of a man like Archie—"

Vanessa leapt up and began pacing the room. "I resent that."

Nora pursed her lips.

"Oh, I don't resent you saying it, darling." Vanessa circled behind the chaise and trailed her hand on Nora's shoulder for a moment, then she scowled and kept pacing. "I raised him to be open-minded and loving, to be a good man who didn't let society dictate his actions. Why is he behaving in this deplorable manner?"

"I think I've shocked him," Selina said quietly.

"Well, I should certainly hope so! He needs to be shocked." Vanessa stopped at the far end of the room, behind her desk, and picked up a glass paperweight from the curio shelf. "He reminds me so much of his father sometimes, all that restraint. But, oh my dear, when he would let himself be free of that, when he would let his guard down . . ." Vanessa was lost in the memory, moving the heavy glass from one hand to another. When the silence of her reminiscence had filled the room, she set down the paperweight and turned to face Nora and Selina.

"His uncle was just the same," Nora recalled fondly. "That is how Vanessa and I first met, you know. She'd come to Spain to find the woman her brother-in-law had intended to marry, to deliver the harrowing news that both brothers had died at sea. I was not in very good shape when she found me."

Vanessa picked up the thread of conversation. "All of that is to say that Nora and I are perfectly familiar with the species *Camburton Male*."

It was delightfully typical of Vanessa to refer to her husband and the other Camburton men as if they were part of some Linnaean system.

Nora continued in her gentle way. "They need to be cracked open like one of those French bonbons with the almond inside. You need to break through that hard shell to reveal all the sweetness in the center. And that is just what you must do with Archie. You must break him, perhaps physically, but mostly in his mind—of the shackles of convention with which he has imprisoned himself."

"He has seen things . . ." Selina pictured Constance at her breast and the look on Archie's face when he saw them together. "Unforgivable things."

"Nothing is unforgivable, dear." Nora patted her arm. "Is it something you can share?"

Wiping her runny nose with the thick napkin, she looked from Nora to Vanessa. "I don't know. It happened at Rockingham, and I think Archie believes it proves my guilt or some such thing, but . . . This all feels far too forward."

Vanessa kicked off her shoes and sat back down in the comfortable armchair, tucking her stockinged feet under her legs. "Oh good! I love *forward*! Let me guess . . . did he walk in on you making love to another woman?"

"Vanessa!" Nora gasped.

Selina's eyes widened, but she remained silent.

Vanessa started laughing. "Oh my dear! He did, didn't he? You are quite certainly the best thing that could have ever happened to my son."

Still, Selina could not let the impression rest. "In a way, that is what he thinks he saw."

"Oh. I can tell it was not what you wished, is that it?" Again, Nora provided the gentle counterpoint to Vanessa's bold nature.

Taking a deep breath, Selina thought about how best to describe what had happened with Constance. She ended up blurting the whole episode out in one breathless recounting, from the moment she had walked into the drawing room and seen her childhood friend, until the moment she'd threatened to tug on the bell pull and have Constance forcibly removed from the chamber.

Vanessa leapt up again, unable to quell her anger. "Haven't I told you how infuriating this is, Nora?"

"Yes, darling, you have."

"What exactly?" Selina asked.

Vanessa turned with her hands fisted on her hips. "This absurd notion that only men can be rapacious, that only men can use intimidation and raw sexuality to bend someone to their will. This so-called friend of yours is as much of a predator as any man who takes advantage of any young innocent woman. Of course I am disgusted with her behavior. But oh, Archie!"

She started pacing again. "For him to see you in such circumstances and refuse to understand your side. If you had been weeping and struggling beneath a man he would have called him out and shot him dead a few hours later. But because it was your supposed friend, all he could see was the... well... never mind. It's been on my mind recently, regarding a few people, and Nora has had to hear my soliloquies on the subject. I suppose I should see it as the pinnacle of equality when a woman can behave as abominably as a man, but let's just say I had hoped for better."

Vanessa unclenched her fists and then refilled her glass.

Selina took another deep breath and set aside her barely touched drink. "I think at this point it's best if I go, don't you?"

"Yes, you must go to see Archie at once." Nora nodded her encouragement. "With your eloquence and persistence, I know you can make him see sense."

"Oh, no. I meant I think it's best if I leave Camburton."

"Absolutely not!" Vanessa was vehement.

"You really believe he cares for me?"

"Oh, Selina." Nora spoke kindly and patted her shoulder. "He is only behaving in this bizarre fashion because he is so overwhelmed by his feelings for you. You should speak with him tonight. Please don't give up on him just yet."

Feeling restored after the kindness and honesty from Nora and Vanessa, Selina stood up and collected her courage. "I think you're right. I will speak with him now." She glanced down at her favorite green velvet dress, then touched her fingertips to her puffy cheeks and eyes. "I thought I'd turned up rather pretty when I first arrived, but now I must look a fright."

Vanessa opened the door to the hall. "You look perfectly gorgeous. Now go to him in that blasted laboratory of his and tell him he must know the truth of your feelings and own up to the truth of his."

Hugging each of them before she left, Selina gave her heartfelt thanks and turned down the dimly lit hall toward the back of the castle and Archie's laboratory.

When she reached the closed door to his workroom, she thought she heard Christopher and Archie speaking through the thick wood. She knocked and waited until she heard Archie say "Yes." And then another slightly louder, "Yes."

Taking this to mean he wished her to enter without waiting for him to let her in, she turned the knob and pushed open the heavy door.

Chapter 9

*H*e'd only just begun to recover from his embarrassing departure from the dinner table and already he was being interrupted.

"Get out." Without looking up from his microscope, he could tell it was Christopher. The man wore some kind of bay rum scent that was subtle enough not to offend, yet potent enough to keep Archie in a confused state of partial arousal whenever he smelled it.

The door closed. "I think I'll stay."

Still not caring to look, he heard Christopher removing his jacket and his footsteps as he approached. "What are you working on?" Christopher's strong, knowing hand cupped the back of Archie's neck. He began to massage the strained muscles at the base, near his shoulder.

"Stop that." He knew his voice was ragged and it was a weak protest.

"I think not." Christopher let his other hand massage down the length of Archie's spine, then down the cleft of his arse. "Have you missed me, darling?"

Archie laughed bitterly at the saccharine endearment. "Not you too, I hope. I can't stand one sentimental lover, much less two."

Christopher reached between Archie's legs and grabbed his balls with possessive force. "So she is your lover, then?"

"No—" His voice was choked with lust. God, he needed to be fucked in the most terrible way. To have all of these rampant, useless feelings pounded out of him.

"So she's just sentimental?" Wrenching Archie's head away from the microscope with a forceful tug on his hair, Christopher bit the side of his neck. He gasped in primal pleasure. "Answer me."

"No, she's not just sentimental. She's a whore."

Christopher pulled his neck back even harder. "A whore like me? Did I tell you I fucked the Duke of Wexham just this morning? He was still in my bed at the inn when I left to meet your mother and Nora's coach for us to carry on with our journey."

Archie nearly wept with frustration. "Selina is a woman, you bastard."

"And this past weekend I let that pretty little Earl of Sunningdale suck me off in the shower at Gentleman Jackson's after I'd beat the daylights out of him in the ring. Did I mention that? Is she a whore like that?"

"No, damn you! Stop this!"

"Stop this?" Christopher bit his neck again and reached one hand around to Archie's steel-hard rod. He rubbed Archie's length through his silk trousers. "Stop making you feel everything your body was born to feel? Stop saying everything you need to hear?"

"Yes." But his body betrayed his words, as his hips began to thrust and retreat in time with Christopher's clever hand.

"That's it, you nasty boy. Let your body tell me what is right and what is wrong. You picture that splendid creature taking you like this, don't you? All that long blonde hair uncoiled and draped around your face and chest as she rides you . . . because that's what she will do, won't she?"

"Yes, damn you . . ." Archie was now sprawled facedown over his workbench, gripping the far edge with desperate firmness. Christopher unbuttoned the fall of his own trousers and somehow pulled Archie's down to his thighs as well, kicking Archie's ankles as wide as they would go.

"Tell me how she takes you in hand in your fantasies, Archie."

"I can't . . . I can't speak of her like that . . . when you are . . ." He said the words into his forearm, hating himself and wanting what Christopher was about to give him all the same. Wanting Selina beneath him, to slide his cock deep into her silken warmth while Christopher—

He gasped, hot tears springing to his eyes, when Christopher slammed into him. He. Wanted. Everything.

"Yes . . . yes . . . yes . . ." he panted in rhythm to Christopher's thrusts, imagining the simultaneous counterpoint of Selina's softness, a counterpoint he would never have the opportunity to actually experience—either due to respect or shame, he wasn't sure.

He didn't hear the knock at the door, if there had even been one, but his endless string of yeses would have made any sane person think he was inviting them to enter. It was only when Christopher stopped abruptly, inside him to the hilt, that he realized something was amiss. "Don't stop now, you bastard," he growled in frustration.

Christopher grabbed the back of his sweaty hair and forcefully turned his head so he was facing the door to the laboratory.

Where Miss Selina Ashby stood with her hands folded politely in front of the pleated waist of that spectacular green velvet gown.

"Selina." Christopher's voice was rutty and charming all at once. "Do come in."

Archie stared in horror as she shut the door behind her and then turned to look into his eyes. "This explains so much, my dear Archie. Why didn't you simply tell me you preferred the company of men?"

She approached the two of them slowly, never taking her eyes from his face. *Perhaps she won't notice Christopher's cock is in my arse*, he thought madly, as if she could somehow fail to observe that salient fact.

He must be hallucinating. That was the only explanation. No histrionics. No tears. No censure. No (very warranted) accusations of hypocrisy. Just the most profound tenderness in those green eyes of hers, as if he were some elusive woodland creature she had always longed to see, and had finally happened upon in a secluded glade.

"May I?" She reached for his cheek but paused before touching him, apparently asking Christopher for permission.

The bastard pulled out slightly and then pushed back into him, the momentum jerking his face against the lab table.

"Be my guest," Christopher answered. "He was just talking about you."

She touched his cheek, petting him like she petted all skittish, powerful creatures, with admiration and animal curiosity. "So beautiful," she whispered.

He shuddered, and his eyes slid shut, no longer able to process what was happening. He wanted to disappear. He wanted to reappear. He wanted to melt into her touch.

"He is a work of art, is he not?" Christopher pulled out and thrust in again while Selina's delicate fingertips traced the angles of his face, then trailed down his neck. He shivered, and Christopher groaned in answering pleasure. Selina hummed her agreement, and Archie opened his eyes slowly to see her.

"A masterpiece," she agreed. "May I watch you finish?" Her fingers raked through the hair at the base of his neck, a tender touch compared to Christopher's firm grip a few inches away.

"You only want to watch?" Christopher asked.

"I'd hate to impose." Selina began toying with Archie's ear while she spoke. "He gets very . . . remorseful . . . when I attempt to please him."

He growled into his forearm at the sound of their drawing room niceties while they played with his quivering body.

Christopher nearly laughed. "Well, it's not his decision just now, is it?"

Selina stepped back as Christopher pulled him clear off the table, hauling him up to a standing position and turning him to face Selina. He couldn't hold her gaze, and let his eyes drift shut again. "He'll do as I say when I have him like this." Christopher began a slow rhythm, using his controlling hands to manipulate Archie's body—one hand still firm in his hair and the other flat across his lower abdomen to keep him close. "He becomes very agreeable . . . and he can always ask us to stop. Isn't that right, Archie?"

Archie could not open his eyes, paralyzed by mortification and lust, but the word came just the same. "Yes."

"See?" Christopher said. "Quite agreeable."

Then Selina's hands were on him, and he wasn't sure he could breathe. Christopher kept up that slow, methodical pace in his arse while Selina's satiny fingertips began to explore every inch of him. She undid his neck cloth, slowly and with great care. He was in a dark sea of sensation, the heavy anchor of Christopher behind him, the light wind of Selina before him. And then her lips were on his skin, licking and exploring his neck, humming her approval. The tantalizing velvet of her dress billowed against the thin linen of his shirt, which was already wet from his seeping cock. He pulled back to avoid soiling her extravagant fabric. The movement only served to shove him harder against Christopher on his next thrust, and the two men groaned in unison.

She pushed her hips more firmly to him, cradling his leaking cock against layers and layers of her feminine warmth. "Are you worried you will sully my gown, Lord Camburton?"

He nodded and nearly whimpered.

"Perhaps I need to clean up your messy cock?" she taunted.

Christopher laughed devilishly in his ear, and Archie's eyes flew open. Selina's beautiful face was mere inches from his, the light citrusy scent of her spiraling around him.

"But I think I'll kiss you first, before my mouth is full of your delicious, filthy seed. And then I'll kiss you again, after." She leaned in and traced his quivering lips with the tip of her tongue.

"Kiss her properly, Archie. I want to see how you do it. Does she know you've never let me kiss you on the lips?"

He could no longer repress his desire. His arms flew around Selina, grabbing her close and nearly knocking the wind out of her. Her mouth was heaven, warm and welcoming; her small grunts and moans made his blood roar while their tongues tangled and played.

"Is this really you?" She was speaking between hot kisses. "Is this what you need?" She held his face in her hands. All he could think was how spectacularly beautiful she was in this moment—raspberry lips wet and swollen, jade eyes smoky with lust, golden hair coming loose.

"I need you," he admitted hoarsely, closing his eyes and resting his forehead against hers. "I need you both."

"And so you shall have me. Us," she added after another kiss. Then she withdrew slightly and he missed her horribly.

"Selina—"

She pulled his shirt up and over his head, and tossed it carelessly on the floor. Kissing her way down his chest, licking and sucking on each of his nipples in turn, she slowly dropped to her knees, a vision of billowing green fabric settling around her as if she were a woodland sylph alighting on a lush, delicate fern. And then she took his length into her mouth and his body left this earth. His mind scrambled and then miraculously calmed. Christopher, bless his virile endurance, had never ceased his relentless rhythm, and Selina began to match him thrust for thrust with her eager, welcoming mouth. Everything about his body—his being—was finally locked into perfect alignment, and he began to vibrate with joy.

Of course Selina had been shocked when she first saw Archie bent over the table and being fucked from behind like a common serving wench. But dear God, how fantastically erotic! Of course she should have told him what a terrible hypocrite he was for making her feel like such a hussy when he'd happened upon her with Constance, but none of that mattered anymore. The man was an angel. She could feel the tension coiling in every muscle of his body while her mouth hummed with pleasure around his cock. The scent of the two men together made her breasts swell with longing, her pussy throb in time with Archie's thrusts. Or were they Christopher's thrusts?

Bless Mr. Christopher Joseph. Her fingertips trailed around Archie's exquisitely firm hip and touched the other man's thigh when he slammed into Archie. Christopher wove his fingers together with hers and pressed their joined hands against Archie.

"We've got you." Christopher voice was low and clear against Archie's ear, but loud enough for her to hear. She sucked harder and pulled deeper, not caring that her breath was short and her head light. She wanted Archie to feel the power of what the three of them had, the beauty of it, free of any of his misconceptions about propriety or what was *supposed* to constitute right or wrong. Archie's hands were tight in her hair and she began to weep from a combination of joy and pain, the coiled heat of everything—emotional and physical—that was about to be released.

Christopher's movements finally became jerky and erratic and his hand pressed hers even harder into Archie's flesh. There would be bruises on him; the idea pleased her. She whimpered, or cried, or moaned around Archie's cock and then dragged her fingernails roughly down his hair-dusted abdomen.

When he thrust into her with a final victorious groan, she felt the hot jet at the back of her throat and her own body responded instantly. She hadn't touched herself in the past two weeks and—with the combination of Archie's joy and the presence of the domineering Christopher and her stockinged heel rubbing against her clit—her orgasm exploded in a quick sharp flare of ecstasy.

She kept licking and tasting Archie as his cock softened, afraid to part from him in this heightened state; she dreaded the reappearance of another postcoital, penitent Archibald Cambury. Finally, licking him clean to her satisfaction, including the underside of his heavy cock and the sensitive balls beneath, she kissed him one last time and then, filled with trepidation, looked up to see which Archie awaited her.

"See, Archie?" Christopher still held his friend in place. "She likes you anyway . . . even though you're such a dirty boy."

She smiled at Christopher, then, more tenderly, at Archie. She stayed there resting on her heels, liking the way it made her feel, as if she were Archie's loyal pet; she realized she liked worshipping him. In fact, she loved it. She loved him.

Her heart pounded anew when the depth of her feelings crashed through her. He was still in a daze of physical satisfaction, his eyes glassy and stunning.

"Archie?"

"Yes?" he croaked.

"Will you kiss me?"

Christopher helped Archie lower himself to the floor, then ruffled his hair affectionately. He buttoned up his own trousers as he walked toward the door. "Always a pleasure, Lord Camburton." Once he was fully dressed and had his jacket back on—his person not even slightly disheveled from their recent doings—Christopher bowed and added, "Miss Ashby." Then he left the room.

She pulled Archie to her, not wanting even a few inches between them. A part of her had wanted Christopher to stay—so much had happened in such a short span of time that they needed to discuss— but for now she was deeply grateful to have Archie to herself.

"You stupid, beautiful man. You should have told me." She stroked his hair tenderly. He somehow coiled his large, muscled body into the swath of green velvet, nestling into her. Leaning down, she kissed him tentatively on the forehead. "Is it all right for me to kiss you now, on the lips, with my filthy mouth?" She smiled and caressed him, letting her fingers luxuriate in the silk of his hair and the slight stubble of his cheek, while she waited for him to reply. They looked in one another's eyes, and her body cried out for his. She wanted to tie him to his bed and take so much more than kisses on the lips, but asking for his permission this once felt profound.

The silence lengthened, and then Archie licked his dry lips. "It is all right for you to do anything to me that you wish." He looked away briefly, earnest and bashful all at once. "I want you so much it has twisted my mind, Selina." He turned back and wound a strand of her hair around his finger, then tugged slightly to bring her closer.

Cradling his face, she pulled his mouth to hers and pressed her breasts to his chest. Within seconds they were nearly mauling each other on the hard floor.

He tried to stop her. "Bed—"

"No—"

"What—?"

"No bed. I want you again now."

He laughed into the next kiss, and it was the most wonderful sound she had ever heard. Archibald Cambury laughing in the midst of lovemaking was the best of all things imaginable: tenderness and power and love all rolled into one delicious, muscular package.

"Come with me." He stood up, bare-chested and glorious with his buckskins around his thighs and his hard cock jutting away from his incredibly firm body. He glanced down at his exposed self and then smiled at her. "I am officially beyond the pale."

"As long as it's official." She accepted his offered hand, and he pulled her up easily.

"This way." He led her toward the back of the laboratory. She thought perhaps there was a chaise or daybed of some sort that they could use, but he pressed a panel and the wood opened to reveal a hidden staircase. "Long hours and crazy ancestors. You know how it is."

Preceding her through the door, he drew up his pants and buttoned them enough to keep them low around his hips. The turn of his arse was charming, but the view was quickly swallowed into the darkness when he shut the door behind them.

"You're not afraid of the dark, are you?" He squeezed her hand.

"No." Her voice echoed into the void and then he was guiding her up a circular set of stone steps.

When they reached the top, he opened the door and led her into what must be the marquess's suite.

"How divine!" She squeezed his hand tighter as she looked around the lavishly appointed room. The ceilings were high and intricately carved, but they were not gilded or showy. The bed was raised and covered in the finest pale gray silk.

"I'm glad you like it. I want you here—"

"You have me." She turned into his arms and kissed him again. All of his hesitance and worry of the previous weeks seemed to have slipped away. He was eager and joyful in her arms, touching her waist and reaching for her bosom through the velvet. She pressed her hand over his when he finally cupped her breast. "Yes, just like that." She guided his hand and sighed her pleasure when he began kneading and shaping her flesh.

"May I take your clothes off?" His voice was utterly polite and his fine manners were incredibly stimulating under the circumstances.

"Yes, my lord. You may." She turned and presented him with the hooks at her back. His fingers were quick and steady as he undid her overdress, then the laces of her bodice.

"Where did you learn how to undress a lady with such dispatch, Lord Camburton?" She glanced seductively over her shoulder as she held her hair off her neck to give him room to work.

His cheeks reddened. "I'm very good with knots and that sort of thing from many years of sailing."

"What a wonderful skill to have," she nearly purred. For some reason, being with him made her want to purr.

He hesitated when she was undressed down to her shift, with nothing but her stockings on beneath. The lamps around the room and the glow of the fire cast them both in a warm light, and she was sure Archie could easily see the dips and shadows of her body through the sheer linen that covered her. Her nipples hardened as he watched.

"Archie?"

He seemed to be lost in his own thoughts, reaching out to touch her body . . . but not quite managing to do so. "I knew you would be beautiful, but I had no idea." His fingertip traced the arch of one breast, so hesitantly she almost didn't feel it, but the sensation was exquisite, light and hot.

She pulled her shift up over her head and put it on the back of the armchair where Archie had carefully placed the rest of her clothes. After removing the few remaining pins from her hair and setting them on the small table next to the chair, she shook out her long blonde tresses and enjoyed the clean scent of citrus and verbena that wafted around her. "Look your fill, my dear man." She stepped closer to the fire to stay warm, then bent to remove her stockings and garters. "Take the rest of your clothes off, beautiful. I want to see you too."

The sound of his stilted breathing, of his nearness, made her body heat from the inside out. She closed her eyes in anticipation, then stood up straight and looked at him.

She felt the press of tears . . . again. What would that be? The tenth time this week? "You should not be permitted to wear clothes. It is a crime. Stand still while I look at you." As she closed the distance between them, he shivered and stared at the carpet. "Don't get nervous now, silly. This is the best part. I finally get to touch you . . . everywhere."

He was, quite simply, an Adonis.

Leaning in close, she inhaled the essence of him. She licked his neck and adored his answering moan and quiver. Tracing the hard edges of his arms, the turn of his ribs, the columns of muscle along his spine—she marveled at his physical perfection. "I can see why you've been saving yourself for the right woman. You are quite something, my dear." His hard cock jolted at the sound of her voice, at her compliments.

"And are you the right woman?" His voice was strained as he tried to remain still for her examination.

She kissed one of his nipples, then pulled away slightly and smiled up at him with mischief. "That depends upon whom you ask. I'm sure some people will tell you I am very, *very* wrong." She teased the hair leading from his navel to the base of his straining shaft. "But I think I may be the right woman for you. What do you think?"

"Yes, I think—I think you are." The way he said it, with that stuttering reluctance, gave her a peculiar thrill. She loved him eager and open, as he'd been in the laboratory, but she also loved him like this, when he was fighting himself just a little. Because she was the *wrong woman* in so many ways. She was complicated and willful and damaged.

She loved Beatrix.

She loved Archie.

"Have you ever been with a woman?" She touched him while she spoke, circling his nipple with one hand and grazing the hair on his stomach with the other.

"No." It came out like a gasp.

"Ah." Selina's heart slammed again, making her ribs feel too tight and her lungs feel too full. "We shall be each other's firsts. A jumble of awkward grabs and thrusts, yes?"

He moaned and shut his eyes.

"Yes. Even though you thought me a whore, no man has ever touched me."

He moaned again and shook his head in what might have been self-reproach.

"Do you enjoy the idea of deflowering me?" she pressed.

He nodded and hummed, and his body said yes, but he didn't actually say the words.

She leaned in closer. "Does the marquess want to do unspeakable things to my innocent body?"

His chest heaved, and he exhaled through his nose in seeming disgust, yet he nodded.

"Open your eyes."

He obeyed her immediately, and a thrilling joy ran through her. She brought both her hands to his cock and stroked him lightly while she looked into his eyes. "Take me to your bed, Archie. Now."

Chapter 10

$\mathcal{H}$e swept her up in his arms, and nothing had ever felt so perfectly right in his life. No experiment. No familial duty. Only this. Only Selina Ashby, naked in his arms, as he carried her to his bed. Her skin was soft and warm, feminine silk against his masculine roughness. He dipped his face into the crook of her neck and inhaled the scent of her, then pressed his lips to her neck with wet, hot kisses.

The bed had been turned down, and he settled her delicately on the clean linen. Her blonde hair spread across the pillow, and he was torn between wanting to preserve her in this perfect state of innocent purity and wanting to imprint his possession on every inch of her creamy skin, to leave his mark and his scent all over her. She arched her back and stretched out her legs, moaning delightedly. "This bed is quite wonderful. I can see why the floor of your laboratory seemed quite inferior. Will you join me?"

He dove at her like a beast. And she fought him admirably, clawing at his back, nipping at his neck. They wrestled at first, like a pair of drunken louts, and he relished all of it. Her slick body wound around his, scratching or soothing, sucking or biting, until he was blind with lust. His body needed hers like his lungs needed air. Just as Christopher had said, she rode him. Straddling his hips, Selina rose up with her neck extended and her long hair falling in decadent waves around her breasts and shoulders, and then she descended onto him and they were locked together. All the frantic groping ceased, and she looked down to where they were joined, then up into his eyes.

"You are perfect." Then her eyes slid shut, and he'd never felt such a profound sense of joy.

"Selina . . ." He wished he could have been more eloquent, but his mind was stripped of words, awash in pleasure.

"I know." Then she began to move, and he reached for her waist to follow her rhythm, to feel her feeling him. When she threw her head back and he knew she was taking her pleasure, he lifted his hips to join her.

"That's it. Right there."

God, how she worked him, rotating her hips and grinding against him and then withdrawing slightly before taking him again, deeper. Every cell in his body felt as if it were preparing to leave his body, to gather and reside inside her.

"Selina . . ." His voice was more urgent.

"Hold on . . . hold on . . ." And he did. For her. And then he felt the crashing pulse of her orgasm around his cock, and she cried out his name and fell against his chest, clawing at him and calling his name again and again. "Now," she whispered against his ear, and he joined her then, pulling her close, closer, until they both quaked and finished.

He didn't feel any of the shock or shame he'd felt in the coach several weeks ago, nor any of the chaotic lust he'd felt in the laboratory earlier that evening. He only felt . . . whole. He stroked down the length of her silken back and breathed in her delectable scent.

"Did I hurt you?" he asked quietly.

She kept her cheek against his chest, and he felt the jolts of her laughter. "Hurt? If that's hurt, I beg you, please hurt me. Often."

He smiled and kissed the top of her head. "Do you want to get married straight away or take the time to plan something quite grand?"

She stiffened in his arms, like a blanket that had been dipped in water and left outdoors in the middle of winter. Lifting her head, she looked him in the eye. "Don't be silly. You don't want to marry me. I'm a filthy whore, remember."

He was instantly furious. "Don't you dare say that! How could you throw my own foolish misconceptions in my face at a time like this? How could you?"

She wriggled to get free but he held her firm.

"Are you the one who is feeling penitent now?" he tried to tease.

Her face stayed serious. "No. I'm neither penitent nor deluded. We don't need to make this into something more than it really is."

"There is nothing more, as far as I'm concerned." His heart pounded as the ground of certainty shifted beneath him. "I love you and I want to marry you and I hope my seed is embedding itself in your body right this moment and that you will be with me until my dying hour."

He could feel her heart beating frantically against his chest. She pressed her small hands between them and forced him to release her.

"Please, Archie." She slid off the bed and reached for her shift, pulling it over her body. She was just as alluring out of bed covered in a bit of linen as she had been resting naked against him.

Shaking her hair behind her, she attempted to collect herself and appear formidable. He sat up a bit, punching the pillow and then clasping his hands behind his head. "Yes?" he prompted.

"Don't sit there in that manner."

"In what manner?"

"As if you are the lord of all you survey."

He smiled arrogantly. "But my dear, I *am* the lord of all I survey. And many hectares beyond those I can survey with the naked eye."

She stomped her foot, and he crossed his ankles at the far end of the bed, liking the way she glanced at his naked body and then reluctantly forced herself to look away.

In her typical fashion, she began pacing around the large chamber. *Pace away*, he thought happily, enjoying the turn of her ankle and the flex of her thigh through the fabric as she did.

"You can't possibly want to marry me now when you couldn't stand the sight of me only an hour ago." She swiveled around to face him. "You couldn't even bear to be in the same room with me! You couldn't eat at the same table!" Her voice was fierce and her cheeks flushed.

He lifted his chin and licked his lips. "I think I'm over that. I'm quite pleased to be in the same room with you. Very well pleased. And I'm perfectly happy to order a tray of fruit and cheese, if you like, to be sure I can also eat in the same room with you." He reached for the embroidered silk pull that hung near his bed in order to summon a servant.

"Don't you dare!" She ran back to the side of his bed.

He placed his hand behind his head again. "Fine. As long as you concede I was in a state of unrequited . . . longing . . . and that's the only reason I was ill at ease during dinner. Now that I am . . . requited . . . we shan't have any such disputes in the future."

"Disputes?" she scoffed. "You couldn't even ride in the same carriage with me! You accused me of falling in love with a songbird!"

He smiled at how ludicrous that sounded, and shrugged easily. "Obviously, I have a very jealous nature."

She stared at him in disbelief. "A jealous nature? You were a *beast*. Constance was taking advantage of me and all you could surmise was that I had somehow seduced her, like I seduce every man, woman, and *bird* in my path, apparently."

"Please accept my sincerest apology." He sat up and then stood naked in front of her. "I was falling in love with you and, well, I did not recognize the evidence."

"Evidence? Are you mad? I am not a science experiment. I'm a woman."

He smiled as he placed his hands firmly—possessively—around her hips. "I know what you are. And I love you."

She inhaled sharply, and he had the first hint of a realization that she might not share his feelings. He loosened his hold on her, and she shook her head slightly. He didn't know whether that meant she wanted him to hold on tighter or release her entirely.

"Archie . . ." Her voice was soft and soothing, but it was also placating, and the alarm bells began to ring in his mind. His arms fell away from her, and he felt suddenly exposed. He'd been relaxed and natural without his clothes on a few minutes ago; now he was embarrassed and at a disadvantage. He reached for a sheet and wrapped it around his waist.

"You can't mean to say you thought I would do that—" He gestured toward the tangled sheets on his raised bed. "That we would . . ."

"We *fucked*. You can't even say it outright. What is the *matter* with you?"

Her words hit him like a punch in the gut. "Matter? *Matter*!" He took a breath so he didn't continue shouting. He did not shout. He had never shouted at another human being until he met this woman. He exhaled slowly. "Of course I can say the word 'fuck.' There. I just said it."

She smirked.

He sighed and continued, "But that is *not* what we just did. That is not what *I just did*, in any case. Perhaps I mistook your interest for something more than a meaningless romp." He lifted his chin, baiting her.

She stomped her foot again, and his heart sped up. There was nothing meaningless about her physicality; he wanted to be there for every stomped foot, every clenched fist, every kiss. He reached for her without thinking, reached his hand out to her cheek.

"Selina . . ." He whispered her name like a breath. "Please . . ."

She softened against the palm of his hand, and her eyes slid shut. "It was not meaningless, Archie. But it wasn't . . . It doesn't need to be . . ." He began caressing her neck and then the smooth turn of her shoulder.

She leaned into him and rested her cheek against his bare chest. "You scare me."

"Don't say that. Please don't. Tell me what you want, and we will make it work."

"Talk of children scares me."

He swallowed. "Are you saying you never wish to have children?"

"No, that's not what I'm saying. Just . . . not right this minute, if you take my meaning."

"Oh!" He held her closer against him, one hand at her lower back, the other still gripping the sheet at his waist. "I will have a large delivery of French letters sent up from London immediately."

He felt the rumble of her laughter against his fast-beating heart. "You plan on using a large quantity of French letters?" She looked up at him, and he was so grateful to see the spark of mischief had returned to her deep-green eyes.

"A very large quantity." He kissed her forehead and released the sheet. "Because you may not wish to have children for many years, which is fine. As long as you do wish it . . . eventually?"

"I do wish it," she answered breathlessly. "In my dreams I have pictured my children . . . your children . . . our children."

His heart pounded at her words, from the sheer blessed relief of realizing he had not been imagining a shared future in some solitary, demented dream of his own. "That is more than enough for me." He still sensed her residual tension, something held back. "What else? Tell me." He hugged her close in his arms, and they stood together like that for a long time, breathing into each other.

She gathered her courage and, after a few long minutes, finally said, "It's about Beatrix."

He exhaled and kissed her neck, then pulled back slightly to look in her eyes. "You mean that you love Beatrix?"

His eyes were so caring, so earnest, so true. She didn't want to lose him, but she would never give up Beatrix; yet some part of her was certain he would never abide an ongoing relationship outside of their marriage. "Yes. I can't give her up, Archie."

"Of course you can't. Giving her up would be like giving up your family. You would never ask me to give up my family."

She stared at him in stunned disbelief. "You mean it?" When he caressed her cheek and traced the outline of her lips, she melted into him.

"I mean it. Your happiness is the root of my happiness, darling. I want you with me—always, I suspect—" he laughed and pulled her tighter against him "—but I know you will also want to be with Beatrix when she returns. She is always welcome here. We can build her a house if you like, for her own particular use."

The blood roared in her ears. She had spent so many hours and days consumed with visions of what she'd imagined would be one of the most difficult conversations of her life, and here was Archie showering her with generosity and love beyond anything she could have conjured. "Truly . . . are you certain?"

"Of course, I am," he answered without hesitation. "I love everything about you. I love your creativity and your boldness. I love your loyalty to your dear friend. You scare me too, with your spirit and your . . ." He traced the line of her neck, and she shivered beneath his touch. He was somehow gentle and provoking all at once, tugging at the edge of her shift and exposing her breast to the cool air. "Your exquisite beauty," he whispered reverently before dipping his mouth to the tip of one breast.

She leaned down and kissed his forehead while he made love to her tender skin, and she felt the circuit of adoration and desire whip between them, coiling them tighter together. "I love you, Archie. I will marry you."

He dropped to his knees and kissed his way down her stomach, mumbling endearments and love-filled fragments. "You will not regret it . . . I will make you the happiest woman in England . . . in the world . . ." When his mouth dipped between her legs, and she held fast to his hair lest her knees buckle, she believed him with every cell in her body.

The next few weeks were a blissful mix of productivity and passion. Rather than the autumnal changes reminding Selina of loss of life or decay, she saw every bright-orange leaf and frantically busy squirrel as a dramatic last gasp of celebration. Vanessa and Nora were thrilled with their marriage news and seemed especially happy to hear that Beatrix would be returning to Camburton when she was not traveling for her performance schedule. Their eyes shone when Selina explained the details of their future arrangements.

"So you are the next Marchioness of Camburton." Vanessa beamed. Then she laughed and turned to Nora. "I shall be a dowager marchioness. Shall we move into the dower house, my dear?"

"No!" Selina cried.

Nora laughed across the breakfast table. "Why ever not? Don't you want to be mistress of your own home?"

Archie smiled at Selina and took another sip of his coffee. When she remained quiet, he said, "Selina fears she will disappoint you if she confesses the truth, but I told her I suspect quite the opposite. Tell them, Selina."

She and Archie had spoken at length about her role as the new marchioness. In short, she wanted nothing to do with it. Other than being married to Archie, that is.

"Vanessa," she began respectfully, "I think you run the castle perfectly. Archie has his work in the lab and I have my writing, and I think I would be a terrible housemistress. Details often escape me. I go for days where I forget to do anything but trim the nibs of my pen!" They all laughed and she continued, "Would you think very ill of me if I asked you to stay living in the castle and running it as you always have? Would I be shirking?"

Nora smiled at Archie, then looked down at her lap.

"Surely you must have opinions about redecorating the yellow drawing room . . ." Vanessa tried.

Selina shook her head slowly. "No. I confess I do not."

"Or the rotation of the winter menus . . ." Vanessa suggested.

She smiled and shook her head again. "I can try to develop an opinion, if you wish?"

"You've no opinion on the type of slate we should use to repair the roof on the south wing?" Vanessa was beginning to smile as well.

"I have complete faith in the slate you choose." Selina smiled through her words.

Archie took another sip of coffee and looked from Nora to Selina, then to his mother. "She is the ideal daughter-in-law, is she not, Mother? She has no interfering relatives and she will defer to you in everything." He turned to Selina, and his eyes darkened. "And she loves me."

She blushed from the tingling roots of her scalp to the tips of her toes. "Archie," she whispered hotly.

"Well, if for no other reason than that," Vanessa declared, "yes, I do believe Selina is quite certainly the perfect daughter-in-law for me and the perfect wife for you, my dear."

Later that day, Selina wrote to Beatrix with her wonderful news. She received a letter back a few weeks later of congratulations and shared joy. Bea praised her for saying what she wanted, for grasping after her own pleasure and for securing Bea's happiness as well. She signed her letter with a promise that she would return by the beginning of December and she would show Selina then all the ways she had missed her, all the ways she loved her.

Christopher had remained for a few days, but he had never participated again in their lovemaking. She decided not to press Archie on the subject, nor did she feel the need to discuss her relationship with Beatrix with him at any greater length. He was—miraculously—fine with her ongoing intimacy with Beatrix, and she didn't see the need to dwell on it. In fact, there was little time to dwell on anything but Archie: he was spectacular—an attentive, eager lover; a charming companion; a blessing in her life. In short, Archie had blossomed.

They posted banns nearby, in the small town of Beeley, and had a quiet wedding ceremony in the family chapel three weeks later. Apparently Vanessa had satisfied all of her societal and maternal urges for an enormous tonish wedding when Georgiana had married Trevor in London.

Selina and Archie fell into an easy, intimate routine. He rode around the estate every morning, then they met up and worked on each of their projects for about six hours in the middle of the day. She occasionally still used her cottage as an office of sorts, but more often she enjoyed being in his laboratory, at a large table Archie had cleared for her particular use. He'd arranged it so it faced out a window toward the formal gardens and the deer park beyond, and he placed a small vase of fresh flowers on it every morning.

They didn't speak very often during those industrious hours each day, but the nearness of Archie, the quiet comfort of his presence or a passing smile, managed to work him deep into her soul. In the afternoons they would tromp out into the woods or go riding. At night, they ate dinner in the small family dining room with Nora and Vanessa.

And later at night, dear lord, the man was insatiable. He rarely touched her during the day; by the time they reached the marquess's suite after supper, they were ravenous for each other. He'd been adorably tentative at first, asking permission to touch her in certain ways, afraid of behaving in some ungentlemanlike manner of his imagining. After many days of delectable assurances, she'd finally convinced him that she was quite capable of saying no if she wished, as was he. Since then, they'd simply devoured each other.

Some nights he was patient and methodical, touching her slowly, watching her swollen cunny with rapt attention as he licked or stroked it. Other times he was impatient and rough and clumsy and beautiful in his desperation. They never fell into a routine or any specific roles of leader or follower when they were in bed. Selina had spanked him once, in jest, and quickly realized how much it pleased her to do so. Archie tied her up one time, with all of his spectacular nautical knots, and they both discovered the joy of that as well. And in the pursuit of understanding their own unique proclivities, they nearly always forged an even deeper trust in each other.

She adored being tied up: the stiff confines of the rope made her breasts and pussy feel all the more tender and sensitive, desperate for his inquisitive touches and admiration. God, the look in his eyes at those moments, as if he had discovered the cure to every disease, righted every wrong, just by loving her and giving her pleasure.

He also adored being taken in hand: when she spanked him that first time, a playful swat really, she'd seen the flare of dark lust in his dilated eyes.

"You like that, do you?"

"No . . ." He always said the word "no" in that hesitating, insecure way—as if looking for her guidance and approval to lead him away from the *no* of it—and then his head would nod in silent encouragement, begging her to continue with whatever filthy delight she was set upon. That tiny uncertain no had become a powerful trigger for her own lust. She spanked him hard after that initial no, and kept on spanking him that time until he was weeping and gasping with pleasure and she was so wet from the joy of it that when she finally turned him on his back and straddled his steely cock, she exploded around him before she had finished one full thrust.

Chapter 11

By the beginning of December, Archie was convinced his life was nigh on perfect. Selina was finished with the first draft of her novel, and Nora and Vanessa and Archie begged her to read it aloud in the evenings after supper. The four of them would retire to his study and sit together in front of the fire. At first Selina had been shy, both of reading her words in front of people, and from the way he sat on the floor at her feet. He adored her. Shamelessly.

When she'd pointed it out on their walk earlier that day, he had laughed so hard he'd almost choked. "I'm too adoring of my own lady wife?" he'd asked with joyful disbelief. They'd been walking briskly through the forest and both of them had flushed cheeks and pounding hearts from the exercise.

"You are wonderful. You know I think you're wonderful. But you're so, oh, I don't know!" Selina had thrown up her hands but kept up her rapid pace. "You're so *attentive*. It makes me feel examined or something."

"Examined? Of course I'm examining you. Everything about you fascinates me. I'm a scientist. You know that. You are quite possibly the most exciting experiment I've ever conducted."

She'd pulled a branch out of the way, held it aside for him, and then they'd both carried on walking. "That's exactly what I'm talking about. You're so avid!"

They'd both been laughing by that point, and he hadn't been able to resist reaching for her waist and pulling her back to him, his large body enveloping hers.

"Archie!" He'd nearly knocked the wind out of her, then she'd swiveled in his arms and faced him as he squeezed her close.

"I love you, Lady Camburton." He adored calling her by her new name—his name. He'd kissed her then, a peck really, and then he'd seen how even that small contact enflamed her and he'd kissed her more deeply. She'd responded like a struck match—like she always responded to him now—with immediacy and fire.

That was why they rarely touched each other during the day; there were always immediate consequences. Seconds later he'd had her up against a tree and she was crying out her orgasm after a few rough strokes of his hand through the fabric of her dress.

"You're spectacular," he'd panted into her mouth between kisses.

"I'm a selfish cow, is what I am." Selina was breathless. "You are spoiling me terribly."

"Good. I like spoiling you."

He certainly did. Lately, he'd taken to giving her expensive jewelry and baubles, and at first she'd tried to decline them all, telling him that everything felt overwhelming. But he had been so crestfallen, and she must've sensed it. She'd finally relented and accepted his gifts, but also told him that if he wanted to give her presents, she would look favorably on his gentlemanly offer of a half-dozen orgasms a day. He'd blushed fiercely and then bowed his agreement.

That night, Selina was in his cozy study reading aloud from the final chapter of her manuscript. He was sitting casually on the floor, leaning against her leg, while Nora and Vanessa reclined on the large sofa. As she read from the climactic scene in which the heroine rescued the hero from the dreadful rat-infested dungeon, the door from the hall flew open and Beatrix Farnsworth came in like a gust of autumn wind.

"Hello!"

Without hesitation, Selina let fly from her lap all the pages of her manuscript and ran across the room to greet her beloved friend. She flew into Beatrix's arms, crying her relief at her return. "Oh, how I've missed you."

Archie watched with something akin to pride as his wife embraced her dearest companion. Selina's loyalty and fervor were the things he'd come to admire most about her.

Holding Selina close at her side, Beatrix looked up. "I'm so sorry to have interrupted—"

"Come in! Come in!" He beamed, treading carefully over the sprawl of papers and reaching out to shake Beatrix's hand. "Welcome home."

He could see how those simple words pleased Selina: the two people she loved most in the world were together in the same room—and loved her—and the world had not stopped spinning. She had shared her concerns with him, that he would be jealous of their friendship, that he would not wish her to continue their correspondence. Nonsense. Beatrix and Selina were the best of friends, and it was ludicrous to think he would (or could) prevent the continuation of their affection.

Beatrix curtseyed formally. "Thank you, Lord Camburton."

"Please, you must call me Archie."

"Thank you, Archie."

Selina's smile widened.

"Vanessa, Nora." Beatrix turned to the other two and kept hold of Selina's hand. He gave Selina a small smile and then turned and began picking up and organizing the spilled pages of her manuscript.

"How wonderful to have you back, Bea!" Vanessa cried with her usual enthusiasm. "You must tell us every last detail of your time on the Continent. You're so brave and fearless to go abroad in the midst of all this Napoleonic rubbish."

"Yes, it was quite chaotic at certain points, but even men at war want to hear beautiful music—perhaps even more than men who are not at war. But don't let me interrupt you. Were you reading, my dear?" She turned to Selina and squeezed her hand slightly.

"I was. I finished the novel and I was reading the last chapter."

"Oh, I want to hear it! Will you continue?"

"Yes." Selina cleared her throat, and he noticed her flush of excitement. "You don't mind hearing the ending before you hear the rest?"

"You know I love your words no matter the order in which I hear them."

Archie now knew that Beatrix had been more than a supportive friend when it came to Selina's writing; she had been the true instigator of her entire career. It had never dawned on Selina that she could actually get paid to do what she'd always done for her own pleasure—and sanity. For as long as Selina could remember, she'd told Archie, she had written things down. But only with Beatrix's encouragement had she dared to submit her writing to publishers.

Beatrix and Selina sat together on the small settee. Archie handed Selina the collated pages, smiled again, and then sat where he'd been before, on a pillow on the floor, loving the tenderness and camaraderie that filled the room.

"We're very happy to have you back," he repeated, looking at Beatrix and then at Selina.

"And I'm very happy to be back," Beatrix replied warmly.

Selina started the final chapter anew and read the words with an intensity and joy that he had never heard before. They all cheered when she finished. He ordered a celebratory bottle of champagne, and they all toasted what they were sure would be Selina's best novel yet.

Vanessa begged off near midnight. "You all have much to catch up on, and we are both exhausted."

Nora yawned her agreement. "And Bea, you must come practice in my studio as you often did last summer. The piano has been tuned, and I would love to paint while you play."

"Thank you for the invitation. That sounds wonderful. I will find you in the morning."

"Oh how fabulous!" Vanessa sighed and Archie thought she looked as if she might cry. "One big happy family." She hugged Beatrix briefly, congratulated Selina again on her accomplishment with the book, and then hugged Archie as well. She whispered something about *how very good* he was and then she and Nora departed.

He knew that Selina would be eager to spend time with Beatrix, filling her in on all the details of her new life here, and the surprises they'd arranged for Beatrix's future life there as well. "I know you two wish to enjoy one another's company after so many months apart, and I shan't intrude." He leaned in and kissed Selina lightly on the lips, then turned and kissed Beatrix on each cheek. Something continental, he'd decided. A handshake or bow would have been too formal, and a kiss on the lips would have been too intimate.

Selina grabbed his arm. "You don't need to leave, darling."

He smiled and caressed her cheek lightly. "I am tired, and I have an early meeting with my steward. Spend time with your friend."

She blushed and kissed him again on the cheek. "Very well. I'll be up shortly."

"Take your time, my dear." He nodded again, saw the happiness in both Selina's and Beatrix's eyes, and left the room.

As he walked slowly up the grand staircase—the late-night sprints were now long past—he heard a bubble of joyful laughter and then the soft chatter of the two women he'd left behind. Being able to provide Selina with the life she'd always craved but never thought she deserved was turning out to be the greatest gift of his own life.

He arrived in his dressing room to find his valet waiting for him. As Reynolds helped him remove his close-fitting jacket, he thought about all the turmoil and upset he'd experienced earlier in the fall. The trip to London; the trip to Rockingham. He wanted to re-experience everything with Selina and Beatrix happily settled.

An idea popped into his head and it pleased him. "Perhaps we should go to London for Christmas, Reynolds. What do you say?"

"It sounds very unpleasant." Reynolds had always hated going into town and never hid the fact.

"Then it's decided. Please begin packing my things, and I will speak with the marchioness and Miss Farnsworth later about when they would like to go."

"Yes, my lord." Reynolds made no attempt to hide his displeasure.

"Your enthusiasm is downright infectious."

Selina stared at the door as it closed after Archie and then simply breathed in the scent of Beatrix as the other woman's arms slid around her waist from behind. Laughing at the sheer joy of being in her lover's arms, in her husband's house, she leaned back into Bea's strength.

"God, how he adores you. It's so beautiful to see." Beatrix rubbed the flat of her hand across Selina's smooth belly. "Are you carrying yet?"

Her heart began to race and her pussy throbbed. "No, I told him I wanted to wait." She gasped when Bea's hand moved higher to cup the underside of her right breast.

"And what did he say?" Bea's words were warm breaths close to her ear.

"He said he was happy to wait as long as I wanted. And then he put in an order for a hundred French letters to be sent up from London at once."

Beatrix laughed this time, pressing her forehead against Selina's shoulder and trembling with happiness. "You've done it Selina. You have conquered the world with your goodness." Bea's other hand went lower, then pressed hard and possessively over her mound. "Have you missed me?"

"You have no idea." She turned in Bea's arms and kissed her with all the desire and ferocity she'd had to keep at bay while Archie and Vanessa and Nora were in the room. Not that any of them were in the dark about the nature of her relationship with Bea, but it would have been inappropriate under any circumstances for her to kiss Bea in that way in front of others. She might have been an exhibitionist when it came to closed-carriage rides with Archie, but even Vanessa and Nora, who had been together for twenty years, rarely did more than hold hands in front of anyone.

And even though she had enjoyed when Christopher and Archie and she had all made love together, it did not seem like something Archie was interested in pursuing. Even tonight, when she'd invited him to stay, he'd chosen to go. At some point in the future, she would be more direct; she would seduce him while Beatrix was there in the room, and see where it led. He seemed to be more comfortable with two discrete relationships for now, rather than one that melded all three of them together. Given the extent of his generosity and understanding, she wasn't about to push him beyond that at present.

"I want to rub up against you." Selina proceeded to do so while undoing the fastenings of Bea's dress.

"Right here, darling?" Bea's voice lowered slightly.

"Where else? You can't possibly expect me to wait another moment to have you." She pressed Bea down onto the couch and shoved her petticoat and dress up impatiently. "God, how I've missed you." Tugging roughly at her drawers, she heard a slight tear. "I'm sorry, love." She looked up quickly to see Bea's eyes glowing with lust and happiness, her breasts heaving in anticipation.

"No need to apologize for your ardor, sweet Selina."

Then Selina dragged her tongue across Bea's neatly trimmed pussy, and Bea's head fell back against the arm of the couch. "Oh dear God, your mouth—"

Selina pulled the drawers the rest of the way off and pressed Bea's legs wide apart. She blew a light stream of air on Bea's slick pussy. "I love you, Beatrix." Then she leaned in and circled Bea's clit with her tongue. As Bea's hips rose, Selina pressed her mouth more firmly, sucked harder, then softened and licked the entrance to her cunny. She could already feel the beginnings of Bea's orgasm, as the tender flesh began to throb and quiver against her lips. Humming her approval, she slid three fingers into Bea's slick opening.

Bea cried out at the welcome invasion, then began rocking her hips and keening with desperate need.

"I love you, Bea," Selina repeated between erotic kisses, as her fingers matched Bea's rhythm, and then she leaned in and closed her lips around Bea's clit and drew out her orgasm, sucking and licking until Bea's body finally stopped quaking and her breathless cries for Selina to *never stop* were reduced to nothing more than vague whispers of gratitude and love.

By the time Bea began to recover her senses, Selina had undone Bea's bodice enough to reveal her splendid bosom, and had lowered her own dress so their breasts could rest against one another. The sensation was intensely erotic for Selina, and Bea was often able to bring her to a climax without ever touching anywhere but her breasts.

Bea tilted up slightly and brought one of Selina's breasts to her mouth. It was Selina's turn to cry out. She buried her face in Bea's neck, licking and sucking and kissing the long-missed familiar scent and taste of her. "God, I have missed you. It's so good to have you back." Her hips were tilted provocatively, and Bea's hands worked to pull up her skirts. When Bea's long, knowing fingers found her wet and exposed, Bea drew her mouth away and laughed. "You no longer wear any undergarments? I thought you enjoyed wearing vaguely scandalous drawers as much as I did."

Selina blushed, which she knew was rather preposterous under the circumstances. "Archie and I . . . We . . . It's easier that way . . ." She kept her face buried in Bea's neck.

"Look at me, darling." Even as Bea's familiar hands caressed the turn of her bottom and then down her inner thigh and back again, Selina was suddenly shy. "Your happiness is my happiness. And I can tell he makes you happy. I don't need to know the specifics of your lovemaking. Perhaps one day all of us could be together in one bed—"

Selina inhaled and felt her breasts tighten in obvious excitement.

"Would you like that, my naughty, lovely girl?" Bea pinched her nipple.

"Yes," she gasped.

Bea pinched harder. "Tell me everything you would like. Do you want him to fuck you while I devour your gorgeous breasts—" Lowering her mouth again, Bea pulled the taut bud of Selina's nipple into her mouth.

"Yes!" Rocking her hips, she pressed her pussy against Bea's fingers. "God, yes!"

When Bea bit down on her nipple and pinched her clit at the same moment, her body exploded in a fury of all-consuming ecstasy, and she collapsed against Bea.

"Oh God . . . I am so glad I've already been to hell."

Selina's trip to hell on earth had finally become a joke between them, after she had frequently collapsed into tears after their lovemaking early on in their relationship. Bea had ultimately convinced her that neither of them were going to hell, especially not Selina. She pointed out that Selina had already been to hell— when she'd been confined in the asylum in Yorkshire. Therefore, Bea rationalized: Selina had served her time.

Bea dragged her fingertips lightly along Selina's exposed hips and legs. "You like the idea very much, of all three of us together. Is that it?"

She sighed and reveled in the simple joy of feeling her body flush up against Bea's. "I do . . . but only if you wish it. Or if Archie does. I can't tell how he feels. He's so respectful all the time." She turned to rest her cheek against Bea's shoulder and pulled a strand of her beautiful chestnut hair between her fingers. She began to twirl it as she spoke. "I want to know that he will not be hurt if I suggest it. The male ego is a surprisingly fragile thing."

Bea laughed and kissed her forehead. "So I've heard."

She looked at Bea more seriously. "Do you have any desire . . . any curiosity? For men, I mean?"

Bea quirked up her lip, as she might while listening to a new piece of music for which she had yet to determine an opinion. "For men in general, I would've said no. But Archibald Cambury in particular intrigues me. Very much."

Tugging on Bea's hair to get her attention, Selina pretended to be affronted. "I say! Do you have designs on my husband?"

Positioning herself so they were even more closely pressed together, Bea whispered, "I certainly have designs on his wife."

"Thank heaven for that." She kissed Bea's neck and then the two of them lay like that for many minutes, finding the familiar pattern of their shared breathing, their breasts somehow soft and firm all at once, their bodies aligned.

Startling awake when a log split and sparked, she sat up quickly and realized the two of them had dozed off. "Wake up, love. I have a surprise for you."

"Mmm, I'll be there in a minute," Bea mumbled.

Selina stood and adjusted her dress. If one of the servants happened to pass by, at least her breasts were no longer cascading out of her bodice.

"Now, sleepyhead. You will be pleased."

"Yes, yes, I'm coming." Bea was notoriously difficult to rouse. Selina leaned down and began to kiss her awake, something they both adored. After the kiss went from light lips against lips to hot, hungry tongue against tongue, she pulled away.

"Wake up, you beautiful creature."

In a perfectly awake voice, with her eyes still closed, Bea replied, "But I'm still very, *very* sleepy. More kisses, please."

"Up!" Selina laughed. She tugged on Bea's hand until they were both standing. Bea stood still and smiled while Selina fixed her dress for her. "There. Now we are somewhat presentable. Come with me."

Holding hands, the two women walked the length of the main hall until they were approaching the orangery.

"Are we going to make love in the greenhouse?" Bea asked.

"No! I mean—" She stopped abruptly and kissed Bea hard and quickly on the lips. "Yes, but not right now."

They continued through the orangery and along another glassed-in corridor that led to a smaller building.

"Where are we going?"

"To your house."

"What?" Bea stopped in her tracks. "Our cottage is in the opposite direction.

"I didn't say cottage. I said house." She smiled and waited for Bea to grasp what was happening.

"I don't have a house."

"You do now. You have your own beautiful house right here on the Camburton estate, with the most beautiful piano and furniture and bedrooms and antiques and lovely paintings—"

She tugged on Bea's hand and pulled her along until they were nearly running. Pushing open a heavy door, she was breathless from both effort and excitement when they came to a halt. They had entered through a side door, but they were standing in the small entryway of a beautiful home.

"But this is the dower house." Bea's voice was awed.

"It is your house. For as long as you want it."

"It's too much. It isn't right."

"You are my tender love, my only real family until Archie. Of course it is not too much. Archie and I have spoken about it at great length. He knows that your travel schedule will keep you away and you may not use it for any great length of time, but we both agreed you should have your own space, as you've always wished. And in the future, when perhaps you decide to settle . . ."

Bea was weeping slow tears. "I don't deserve you, sweet Selina."

"You saved me. You saved my life." She brushed away Bea's tears with her thumbs as she spoke. "You made me believe I had a life worth saving. You deserve every wonderful thing."

They kissed tenderly in the hall and then she showed Bea upstairs to the large bedroom that overlooked the informal gardens at the back of the estate, and the rolling hills that were all limned in icy moonlight. She pulled back the covers, and then they undressed each other slowly. After another hour of slow, attentive lovemaking, she finally kissed Beatrix good-night and returned to Archie.

As she walked back through the orangery, her steps echoing through the night, she realized she was willing to pay any price to be living this life of openness and freedom.

Chapter 12

hen Selina returned to their marital bed a few hours later, Archie, half-asleep, reached for her warm naked body like a flower reaches for the sun, with instinct and gratitude.

She snaked her hands around his waist and twined her bare legs with his. "Did you miss me?" Her body rubbing against his warmth made him hard within seconds.

"Mmm. Absence definitely made me grow—"

"Archie!" She laughed and then softened into him, kissing his lips and his shoulder, then licking one of his nipples playfully.

"Your scent is different." He burrowed his face into her neck, then pulled up her arm to smell her wrist and the crease at her inner elbow "You smell like Beatrix." He kissed the spots and then kissed her on the lips.

She inhaled sharply. "You don't mind?"

He paused, not understanding the hint of worry in her voice. They'd decided together that Beatrix would live in the dower house, that she would be a part of their family. In his mind, Beatrix would be a maiden aunt to their children, a loving fixture in all of their lives, for the rest of their lives. "Mind? It's what we decided. And now she's here and you are so obviously delighted. Why would I ever mind?"

Her arms flew around his neck and her legs flew around his hips. "You have kept your promise . . ." He was on his back, and she was straddling his hips.

"Which promise is that?" He grabbed her hair and pulled her down to kiss her nape as he spoke.

"You've made me the happiest woman in England."

He looked up into her shining eyes, then down the length of both their bodies where they were about to be joined. As she began to lower herself onto him, he released her hair and held her hips, stopping her. "Wait, I'll put on a sheath—"

"I don't want to wait any longer. I'm ready. Are you?"

They stayed poised in that moment, both realizing they were on the cliff edge of their shared future. "I think I've been ready since the first day I came upon you in the maze and heard your voice through the hedgerow."

"Oh, Archie." Her voice was so full of trembling love he was unable to say anything more. He loosened his grip on her hips, and she touched her slick pussy against the very tip of his straining shaft. "I love you."

Then she lowered herself completely onto him, and they both inhaled through the power of the connection. Her fingers dug into the muscles on his chest, the sharp turn of her fingernails adding a hint of something fierce to the emotion that was passing between them. After a few long seconds, he tilted his hips and began a slow rhythm. He watched as gooseflesh spread across her belly and breasts, and she tipped her head back.

When she arched forward and pressed harder onto him, he was lost. They were lost in each other for hours—light touches and rough scratches, soothing words of love and crashing cries of passion. They fell asleep at last, her back against his front, his hand resting over hers low on her belly, as he thought of the new life they were creating together.

When he woke the next morning, the room was still dim in the winter dawn. Selina was awake and looking at him, her face a few inches from his on the large pillow they shared. "Good morning, beautiful." His hand reached for her belly. "How do you feel?"

She smiled dreamily. "I feel like you are inside me . . . even when you're not."

He kissed her and then remembered his London plan. "I was thinking we could go to London for Christmas. You could meet with your publisher and we could celebrate at Camburton House in Mayfair." He rubbed her stomach lightly as he spoke. "I want to experience London with you, properly this time. And I think Georgie and Trevor and James will be returning soon and, well, I just thought . . ."

She smiled wider. "You are a magician."

"How so?"

"Bea was telling me last night that she's been invited to meet with a renowned teacher named William Dance. She was going to postpone until after the New Year, to spend the holidays with us, but this is divine." Selina rolled onto her back and stared at the canopy over their bed, then sighed happily. "When would you like to leave?"

"I have a few things I need to do here." He moved over her and pulled the covers over both of them to keep the cool air from touching her sleep-warm body.

"Really?" she asked provocatively, lifting her hips to his. "What sorts of things?"

He leaned down and kissed her, and they didn't emerge from the bedroom for two more hours.

At breakfast that morning, he announced that they planned to go to London for Christmas. Nora and Vanessa looked disappointed, but since they'd been there for two months in the fall, they did not want to return again.

"You promise you won't stay overlong?" Vanessa asked.

Selina replied quickly, "Oh I promise! After I turn in my manuscript and speak to my publisher about my next idea, I will want to sprint home and begin writing the next series of books."

"Very well." Vanessa toyed with her coffee cup. "I always traveled when I was your age and I'm happy to see Archie wanting to leave the nest for once, but— Oh, I'm just spoiled, I suppose."

Archie had to suppress a laugh. "Spoiled? You, Mother? Never!"

"Mind your tongue, Archibald Cambury." She tried to chide him but she was smiling nonetheless.

Nora put her napkin on the dining table and stood to go. "I'm going to paint the rest of the morning. Bea, would you care to practice in the studio?"

Beatrix was sitting across the table with her hand resting lightly on Selina's shoulder. Archie and Selina had told her about the London plan before they'd all gone in to breakfast, and she'd been thrilled.

"Yes, I'll come with you now." Beatrix turned to Selina when she stood up. "Would you like to hear me play, love?"

Selina blushed, and Archie had an answering roll of desire as he watched her. He thought of that moment on the carriage in London—with her face turned to the sky as if she were receiving the universe into every cell of her body. Whether it was her best friend or his touch or the way she wrote her stories, Selina exuded a brilliant light of joy.

She caught him staring at her and smiled in return. "Would you like to join us to hear Bea?"

He pulled out his pocket watch and declined. "I have a timed experiment that I have to check on. Leave the door open, will you? And then I will be able to hear it wafting through the castle."

Selina nodded and that small connection throbbed between them. "Excellent." She stood and joined Beatrix and Nora and the three of them left the intimate dining room.

Vanessa took another sip of her coffee and pretended to read the paper.

"What is it, Mother?" he asked as soon as he knew the others were out of hearing distance.

"Hmm?" She kept her eyes downcast and acted like she didn't know what he meant.

"Catching up on the latest changes to the French Penal Code?"

She looked up, then looked back at the words in front of her, then smiled and refolded the newspaper. "I'm proud of you, Archie. That's all. You have married for all the right reasons. I'm not sure how to go about saying it without sounding—oh, I don't know, patronizing or something."

He knew his mother was an emotional being, and it didn't surprise him that she would be more proud—if that was even the word for it—of his having found the one perfect person to love, than if he had developed a stable vaccination for smallpox for all mankind. "I'm glad you are happy, Mother. I am ecstatic."

She stood up and walked to his side of the round table. "I can see that." She kissed his temple. "Selina has opened your heart."

Leaving the breakfast room together, they parted ways at the end of the hall. He entered his study and Vanessa went to join the ladies in

Nora's studio, where she would work at her large desk. He could hear the powerful chords of a Mozart sonata trailing into his workspace, as though Beatrix's notes were somehow weaving them all together.

They spent the rest of the week at Camburton Castle and then he, Selina, and Bea took the coach and four down to London. The inside of a closed carriage brought back all sorts of salacious memories, but Selina behaved herself during the day, only occasionally holding Bea's hand while she rested her cheek on his shoulder. She was now sated in a profound way, he thought with masculine pride.

The house in Mayfair had been prepared for their arrival. The front portico was festooned with greenery and all the lights inside the mansion were ablaze. The last day of the journey had been rather treacherous—contending with heavy snow and rough road conditions on the outskirts of the city—so all three of them were grateful to finally settle in.

A pile of invitations awaited them and, rather than pitch them in the bin, Archie decided to set them aside until the next day. For the first time in his life, he actually wanted to attend balls and routs, wanted to stand in a stuffy crowded ballroom with his wife at his side, wanted to get a box for concerts and plays, where Beatrix and Selina would sit nearby in rapt attention.

The servants bustled past them with all the parcels and luggage, as Selina, Archie, and Beatrix removed their cloaks and stomped off the snow that had clung to their shoes in the brief walk from the curb to the front hall. Archie told the butler to take the stack of invitations and set it on his desk for him to review tomorrow.

"Oh, Archie, may we go through them now?" Selina asked. "Perhaps we might sit in front of the fire, just the three of us, and plan all of our adventures?"

He looked at Selina then, so bright with hope and love, and realized he would give her anything—large or small—that she ever wished for. "Of course, my love." He turned back to the butler and asked him to set the pile in the blue drawing room and to send in a tray of meats and fruit, as well as a large pot of hot tea.

Selina rested her cheek on Archie's strong thigh and gazed into the fire. She had been sitting on the pale green silk sofa next to him, and had begun to feel the weariness from the journey stealing over her, when she decided to lean down. Bea was reading a letter from Mr. Dance and smiling gently as she scanned his words.

Breathing contentedly, Selina looked up to see Archie staring at her. "What is it?"

"Was the journey too much for you?"

"No, I'm just sleepy. It's late."

He turned his attention back to the invitation he was holding, one of the last in the original stack. "Devonshire is having another one of his masquerades. What do you think?"

The three of them had gone through dozens of invitations and decided on the concerts and balls they wanted to attend. Without looking away from the card he was holding, Archie toyed with a strand of her unruly hair, tucking it behind her ear, then grazing the edge of her jaw. She shivered, and he hummed his approval.

Bea glanced up from her letter and caught her eye. As Beatrix watched, Archie traced the turn of Selina's shoulder and then let his hand rest on the fabric of her dress over the swell of her hip. Looking at Bea while Archie touched her, even in that absentminded way of his, turned her insides to pudding. She wanted to kiss Bea while Archie held her in his lap; she wanted to kiss Archie while Bea massaged her tender breasts.

Her body was changing; she could feel it already in the swell of her bosom, the tingling sensitivity of her nipples. She suspected she had become pregnant the first night they had been together, so all the French letters had been for naught.

She gasped when Bea smiled and slowly licked her lips, trailing her clever tongue back and forth across the edge of her lower lip, just as she had trailed her tongue along the edge of Selina's pussy that morning in the room at the inn while Archie had been collecting the horses.

Selina was a woman in love—with Archie and Beatrix of course, but it was more than that. She felt as though she were actually living in a world of love, a deep, embracing pool of affection and comfort and desire. She shifted her upper arms to press her breasts closer together and watched Bea's eyes darken with desire. Archie kneaded her flesh absently as he spoke. "I think a masked ball would be quite entertaining, don't you, darling?"

She bit her lip as the combination of Archie's big hand and Bea's fiery gaze stoked her pleasure. "I do," she croaked.

"Then that settles it." He patted her hip and tossed the final invitation on the side table, then lifted her off his lap so they were both standing. He took a deep breath, stretching his arms toward the ceiling. "Off to bed we go. Come, come." He reached out his hand, and she took it.

"Where are we all sleeping?" She hoped one day soon Archie would take the bait and choose for all of them to sleep together.

"I thought Beatrix would enjoy the large guestroom closest to our suite. I imagine you two will want to get up to whatever it is you get up to when I'm at the Royal Society tomorrow and Thursday."

She reached for Bea's hand and laced their fingers together as they walked up the wide stairs. "That sounds perfect, darling."

"But tonight we all need a good night of rest after that taxing journey, don't you agree?" He led them down the hall and opened the door to a beautiful room that had been decorated in soothing yellows and creams. A few hothouse flowers had been placed around the room as well, and there was a small fortepiano in the corner.

"This is heavenly!" Bea exclaimed when she entered.

"Vanessa thought to have the piano moved into this room. I hope it's not too crowded or bothersome." Archie looked concerned for Beatrix, and Selina had never loved him more.

"As long as you don't mind hearing me play at all hours of the day and night, I won't find it bothersome in the slightest." Bea trailed her slender fingers along the brightly polished wood, and Selina shivered in Archie's arms.

"Come to bed, Selina. I don't want you to catch cold."

Bea turned and smiled at both of them. "He's right, love. You need your rest. Come visit me in the morning after Archie leaves for his lecture, and I will play the new sonata for you."

"You are both far too concerned for my welfare," she huffed, but she blew Bea a kiss and left obediently with Archie.

His suite of rooms was nothing short of spectacular, with a riot of golden angels above the bed, the frescoed ceiling depicting men and women, angels and putti, all frolicking in the clouds overhead.

"You are a sybarite at heart," she crowed. "I knew it!"

"It was my grandfather's doing." He looked at the ceiling as he turned her around and began to undo her dress. "I've always thought it was rather a bit too much."

"Well, I adore it—I especially adore how everyone is touching everyone, without a care for propriety. And how happy everyone looks." She was stretching her neck to take in the full array of characters and activities when he let her dress drop to the floor, and she was standing with her back to him, in nothing but the sheerest shift. He had spoiled her the previous week with a trunk full of undergarments sent up from London, and he'd told her he wanted her fitted for many more lacy things while they were in town.

He leaned down and kissed her neck. "You are going to be the belle of every ballroom in London, my dear. The Marchioness of Camburton has arrived." As he untied the shift, his nimble fingers touched the sensitive skin along her spine, and she moaned at the pleasure. When she was fully naked—and he still fully clothed—he lifted her in his arms and set her onto the enormous feather bed. "Now go to sleep, my little vixen, and rest up for the days and weeks to come."

"But I'm not tired."

He smiled down at her as he began to untie the folds of his cravat, and that was the last thing she remembered before she fell into blessed sleep.

The sweet smell of rich dark chocolate roused her the next morning. A gold ormolu clock on the marble mantle rang nine times, with a lovely clear tone. Further in the distance she heard Bea on her piano. A maid was straightening up the room, and she realized it was her own Mary.

"Well, hello to you," Mary boomed cheerfully. "Don't you look all bonny and fresh."

"I feel bonny," she agreed. "Will you pass me my robe, please?"

"Of course, my lady."

Mary came to the side of the bed holding yards of heavy Japanese silk. The pale ivory had been embroidered with a blue heron and soothing gray swirls of mist along the water scene at the hem. Her slippers were at the edge of the bed, and she put one foot and then the other into them. "I will have my chocolate with Beatrix this morning."

Selina began to pick up the breakfast tray, and Mary intervened abruptly. "You shouldn't be lifting that, my lady."

"Whyever not? Just because I married a marquess doesn't mean I can't carry my own cup of hot chocolate."

The maid blushed slightly and then looked stern. "You'll be carrying a babe soon and I don't want any worries on my head that you tripped or anything of that nature. So you just leave the carrying to me, my lady."

Ever since that first night when Mary had transformed her from a ragged hermit to a lady fit to sit at the marquess's table, the two of them had been fast friends. She had asked Archie if Mary could be her lady's maid. "Not that I need one, mind you," she'd quickly added.

He'd laughed and told her she could have twenty maids if she had a mind to. And that had been the end of it.

She huffed. "Very well. You can bring the silly tray into Bea's room if it makes you feel better." She walked out of the room with her chin held high, in a mock approximation of a Japanese princess. "Remember you are to remain five paces behind me at all times."

"That man has created a monster," Mary grumbled good-naturedly.

Selina laughed. "I heard that."

"Good!"

They reached the door to Bea's room, and Selina waited a few moments until Bea paused in her practice, then knocked on the door.

"Come in!"

She and Mary entered the yellow guestroom, now bright with morning sunshine.

"Thank you, Mary. That will be all for now." She used her haughtiest tone and the maid rolled her eyes and then smiled at Bea. After she had left the room and the door had shut behind her, Selina turned around and flipped the lock.

"Well, well, well. What are we going to do that requires locked doors?" Bea asked, standing up from the piano bench and walking toward her.

The heavy silk robe dragged along her skin, stimulating her breasts, smoothing down her thighs. "I have many things in mind." She untied the knot at her waist, and the robe slipped open a few inches, not enough to reveal her breasts, but enough to show the triangle of hair at the apex of her thighs. "I woke up wanting you, Bea." She let go of the belt and reached one hand out for Bea and pressed her other hand against her mound. "When Archie was touching me last night and you were looking at me . . ." Her voice caught. "I was nearly overcome."

Bea drew her into her arms. "I know, darling. I know." Bea kissed her hard, nipping at her lower lips and then kissing her way around to Selina's sensitive earlobe and biting her there too. "But I don't think Archie knows," she whispered.

"What?" Selina pulled back roughly. "Of course Archie knows. You are living with us. I am with you as often as I am with him."

Stroking her fingers along Selina's exposed belly, Bea slowly removed the robe to reveal her shoulders. "He sees what he wants to see, Selina. He sees two close friends—intimate friends, even—but he sees two *girls*."

She tried to get away. "That's ludicrous. He is a grown man. He has had sexual relations with Christopher, for goodness' sake. He must know what two people do . . . What we do . . . when we . . ."

"When we 'get up to whatever it is we get up to'?" Bea echoed Archie's words of the night before.

"Exactly!" She smiled. "That's quite precisely how he would describe any sexual act. You know how prudish he is with language."

Bea shook her head slightly. "I don't know, darling. I think you might be seeing what you want to see as well. Has he ever actually seen us kiss?" Bea pressed her lips against Selina's and kissed her senseless, devouring her mouth in an endless barrage of thrusts and parries.

Breathless, Bea tore herself away and continued, "Has he ever seen me ravish your breasts?" Leaning down, she took the tip of one nipple into her slick, warm mouth and began to torture and tease the hard skin. She sucked and scraped her teeth across one and then the other breast until Selina was begging her to stop. "Has he ever seen me make love to you? *Really* make love to you?" Bea pushed her against the wall, then knelt, pressing her mouth against Selina's pussy. Bea's moaning pleasure when she kissed her there ricocheted through Selina's body.

Bea was relentless, licking softly and then tugging on Selina's clit with her teeth while her slippery fingers found their way into her. And then Bea twisted her fingers in exactly the way Selina wanted—needed—and teased her clit with light flicks of her tongue until she was begging for release, begging for the culmination rather than the tease. When Bea finally gave it to her, sucking with her mouth, fucking with her hand, she pitched over into a realm of blind, splintering pleasure.

Before she had fully recovered her senses, she was cradled in Bea's arms and heard her whisper, "No, my darling Selina. Archie has never seen that, not even in his mind's eye."

Chapter 13

*A*rchie and Christopher decided to have lunch at White's after attending a morning lecture. Christopher had been out of town for nearly a fortnight and Archie was looking forward to seeing him.

"How is married life treating you now that you have two wives instead of one?" Christopher asked with a slow smile.

"Married life is divine. And I only have one wife, thank you very much. More than enough to keep me busy." Archie cut into his beef and took a satisfying bite.

"Really?" Christopher picked up his wineglass and swirled the claret. "You've never... you and Selina with Miss Farnsworth, I mean?"

He set down his fork and knife with a slight clang. "No, Christopher."

It was unusual for a silence of more than a few seconds to pass between them, especially when they hadn't seen each other in many weeks. Christopher pressed on. "It's not as if you and Selina and I didn't—"

He felt a hot rush up his neck and cheeks. "We are at White's, for Christ's sake. Have you no shame?"

"Thankfully, no." Christopher brought the glass of wine to his lips and swallowed as he stared at Archie.

Shaking his head and taking a deep breath, he picked up his fork and knife and resumed eating.

"So the ladies just fuck in the other room, then?" Christopher asked, raising his eyebrows as if he were inquiring about nothing more scandalous than the Duke of Bedford's new carriage.

Another clanging drop of fork and knife. This time, he made enough noise to turn a few heads. He composed himself, then breathed hard through his nostrils. "Are you willfully trying to upset me?"

"Egad, man, I hadn't thought to upset you at all—willfully or otherwise. When your letters arrived describing your—" Christopher gestured around to encompass a small circle "—*arrangements* with Beatrix Farnsworth becoming a member of your household—a member of your *family* even—it had seemed obvious enough."

"Well, it's not."

"Not obvious to you, you mean? Now *that* is obvious."

Archie smiled. "You are merely trying to irritate me. Stop it at once."

Christopher leaned in. "I'm not sure if you are trying to be upstanding for me, old friend, but given our past together, it seems a bit absurd. Perhaps marriage makes you feel particularly protective of your lady wife's honor. I shan't say a word."

"Damn it. There is no word to say. Selina and Beatrix are the closest of friends. They hold hands. They go on long walks. They are very dear to one another. They don't . . ." He lowered his voice and looked around the room guiltily. ". . . *fuck*."

Christopher started laughing into his napkin, the pale blue fabric a small concession to repressing his uproarious amusement. "Oh, you really are a peach." He took a sip of water between gasps of laughter. When Christopher finally settled, Archie sat with his arms folded across his chest, his appetite lost, and the rest of his roast beef sitting untouched on the plate in front of him.

"Are you quite done?" he asked coolly.

"Oh, my good friend. I'm afraid you are the one who is done for." Christopher's face turned serious in an instant. "I suggest you go home to your lady wife and her *very dear* companion. And open your damn eyes."

Archie stood up from the table and tossed his napkin back onto his chair. "I'll thank you to mind your own damn eyes and let me mind mine."

Christopher was clearly nonplussed. "Very well. I'll see you next week at the masquerade. I'm going as Dionysus; why don't you go as Ampelos?"

Leaving the room with as much quiet dignity as he could muster, Archie seethed inside. Why did Christopher have to turn everything into a sordid game? He walked off his anger, trudging through the snow-dusted sidewalks along St. James's, then along Piccadilly, and through the bare trees of Berkeley Square, until he reached his front door. The footman had the door open before Archie reached the top step.

He removed his hat and handed it to the servant, along with his greatcoat. "Is the marchioness at home?"

"Yes, my lord. She and Miss Farnsworth are in the library."

"Thank you." He tried to set aside Christopher's prurient suggestions, but he couldn't help imagining Selina and Beatrix in some preposterously compromising position when he entered the room. He knocked lightly, and Selina's sweet voice beckoned him to come in.

She was standing next to Beatrix, and glanced at him over her bare shoulder. Both women were dressed as Grecian goddesses. Selina lifted the diaphanous white fabric so as not to trip, and ran to greet him. "Are they not spectacular? We've been adjusting the clasp at the shoulder and pinning the hems to get it just right. For Devonshire's party next week, remember?" She kissed him on the cheek and then lifted a gold-feathered mask to cover her face. Her blonde hair was piled high on her head, with a delectable tangle of unruly curls trickling down her neck.

"You are splendid as always, my love." He leaned in and kissed her bare shoulder.

"Darling. It's the middle of the day."

"I want you now," he whispered, and an answering tremor of desire rocked through her body where he held her hip.

"This instant?" she teased, keeping the gold mask in place.

"Upstairs. At once." He looked over Selina's shoulder and smiled at Beatrix. "I'm so sorry to intrude. We shan't be a moment."

Beatrix smiled and lifted a similar gold mask to her face. She was dark to Selina's light: her chestnut hair a sharp contrast to her creamy skin, her deep chocolate eyes rich compared to Selina's of pale green jade. "Farewell, sweet Sappho."

"Farewell, wise Athena!" Selina replied, laughing as she tripped out of the room and followed him up the stairs.

They were both breathless when they reached the master suite. He pushed the door shut behind him and tore at the fall of his trousers. Selina stepped slowly away from him, keeping the mask in place as she lifted the gauzy fabric of her costume with her free hand. As she revealed more and more leg, he felt more and more like a rutting Pan come to defile her.

"This isn't going to be pretty," he growled.

"Good," she purred. "I hate pretty."

Before she could get out of reach, he grabbed her wrist and pulled her to him. His cock pressed into her soft belly through the fabric; she gasped and pushed harder against him.

He shoved the fabric out of the way and held Selina so she was firmly against to the wall. He reached his fingers to her slit and felt how ready she was for him. She looked up at him, eyes ablaze with lust and invitation.

Her voice was seductive and irresistible. "Ready and waiting as always, my love."

He thrust into her with one powerful stroke, and her head tipped back against the wall with a thud.

"It's only you, only you who can do this to me."

He knew it! Damn Christopher Joseph and his lascivious imaginings! Only he did this to her!

"And you, Selina—" He slammed into her again and again, both of them wanting this powerful, unequivocal declaration. "Only you." He thrust again and knew he was stroking her inside and out, exactly where she wanted—needed—him the most, and then she cried out her pleasure, grasping desperately at his lapel with one hand and squeezing her breast with the other.

He held still, thrust deep inside her, while she quaked around him. Her eyes were glassy, but open enough to lock onto his. As wave after wave took her, she never looked away. She was his damn it. *His*.

She ground out the last of her pleasure, coiling one leg around the back of his hip, and then she bit down on her lip and used her inner muscles to push him over. "Mine," she whispered. He came and came, his legs barely able to keep them upright through the storm of ecstasy that overtook him.

Her head fell forward against his shoulder, and she sighed. "I am in love with the Marquess of Camburton." She said it with a hint of wonder, as if the fact still perplexed her.

"I am in love with the Marchioness of Camburton. Madly in love."

She looked up at him and caressed his cheek. "Not mad, darling. Just the opposite of mad." She kissed him as his cock slid out of her body. "Are you finished with me for now?"

He kissed her palm. "Yes. For now." When he reached for his handkerchief, about to clean himself off, Selina smiled wickedly and slid to her knees.

"You and your silly handkerchiefs." She licked him clean and buttoned his trousers, leaving him immaculately attired and partially aroused, before returning downstairs to continue her preparations with Beatrix for the costume ball.

He had set up a small laboratory in town several years ago, and he spent the rest of the afternoon testing the new version of the vaccination that he'd been working on. It was by far the most stable he'd achieved, and he was looking forward to sharing his work with Jenner the following week. If they could get the vaccination to stabilize in the mercury distillation, then widespread distribution—and the complete eradication of the disease—would not be far behind.

The following week, he, Selina, and Beatrix had an animated supper before getting ready for Devonshire's ball. The invitation was for ten o'clock, and they'd decided not to attend either of the other parties beforehand to which they'd been invited.

Feeling well pleased with his work—and his wife—he returned to his dressing room after supper. Selina had ordered a costume for him as well, a patrician toga with an elaborate cape and preposterous crown of golden laurels that matched the hand-held masks worn by Selina and Beatrix. His mask was made of exotic amber feathers— "to match your eyes," she'd told him—and it tied in the back.

When they met in the hall at half past nine, the three of them were a trio of Greek gods.

"Oh, this is going to be so much fun!" Selina cried. "All my favorite people in one place." Beatrix slid her hand into Selina's arm and Selina slid hers into Archie's. "You will finally get to meet the dashing Christopher Joseph," Selina told Bea.

He nearly tripped at the mention of his friend's name.

"Careful, Archie! You're not accustomed to walking in a dress!" Selina laughed.

"It's not a dress," he said with haughty good humor. "It's a toga."

"I forget you're such a *man*, darling. Very well. You are not accustomed to walking in a *toga*. Have a care."

He helped each of the ladies up into the carriage, and they rode the short distance to Piccadilly. Even though Devonshire House was only a few blocks away, the narrow winter streets were congested with snow and traffic, and it took them nearly an hour to get there. They spoke of Selina's excitement about her next book, about her upcoming meeting with her publisher, and Beatrix's future concert schedule. She would be performing primarily in England and Scotland for the next year, which made Selina sigh with pleasure.

By the time they arrived, the party was in full froth and all three of them buzzed with anticipation and excitement.

The past few weeks in London had put many of Selina's demons to rest, at last. Her parents held no sway here. Her cousin, the Marquess of Hartington and future duke of Devonshire, William Cavendish, was a popular man about town who insisted on including Selina in all of his numerous social gatherings. She had visited her aunt in Tavistock Street several times, as well as having her for supper. Aunt Diana was enamored with Archie and his gentlemanly ways, and thrilled that Selina had been able to keep her close ties with Beatrix even after she and Archie were married.

All of their costumes were from Aunt Diana and the prop room at the theater where her latest show was now running. Tonight felt like a celebration of all the strands of Selina's life finally weaving together in a harmonious whole. The crush at the front of Devonshire House was a pretty kettle. The press of aristocrats in costumes and cumbersome headgear, capes, and coats, created a sea of hot, teeming flesh. In the commotion, she lost her grip on Archie's hand and looked at him desperately as the throng pushed him farther away from her. He gestured toward the ballroom and pantomimed that he would meet her there.

She held tighter to Beatrix. "Can you breathe?"

"Yes." Bea smiled. "I love this kind of crazy mash vat."

Selina took a deep breath and tried to assume some of Beatrix's festive enthusiasm. Ever since her time in Yorkshire, she had never done well in tight, crowded spaces. Her breathing tended to become shallow, and a sheen of cold sweat formed on her upper lip and brow.

"You're fine," Beatrix whispered, soft and close to her ear. Bea squeezed her hand, and she settled somewhat. "I'm not letting go." Bea gripped her fingers tighter to let her know without words that she was not going to be abandoned in this conflagration.

Trying to steady her breathing, she finally caught a glimpse of a long hall that led off from the front entry. The footmen were frantically trying to collect all the coats and shawls without stemming the incoming tide of people. At last, she and Beatrix were through the worst of it, but when she turned to face the ballroom, she saw it was nearly as crowded as the front hall had been. She'd very much been looking forward to a night of gaiety and had known it would be crowded, but she was starting to feel ill and asked Beatrix to join her in a quiet room for a few moments.

"Of course. Do you know your way round the mansion?"

"Vaguely..." She looked up and saw Christopher Joseph emerging from a room at the far end of the hall. "Christopher!"

He smiled when he saw her approaching, and something flipped in her stomach. He looked as though he'd just rolled out of bed, and it reminded her hotly of their time with Archie in the laboratory at Camburton Castle.

"Lady Camburton, what a pleasure to see you again. And this must be Miss Farnsworth."

Beatrix curtseyed and kept her gold mask over her face. "Athena, at your service."

Selina still felt as if the crowd were pressing in on her, even though the three of them were now relatively alone in the hall. "I need to sit down. Is there someplace quiet nearby?"

"Right this way." Christopher put his hand around her waist before her legs gave out, and led them into a small library. There was a man standing behind a desk, and he looked up with a playful smile. "Christopher? Back so soon?" When he saw that Christopher was now accompanied by the two ladies, he continued more seriously. "Pardon me. How may I be of assistance?"

She realized it was Geoffrey Standiford, one of Cavendish's cousins from his father's side, and he was dressed as a twig-and-vine-covered satyr. "Hello Geoffrey," she tried lamely, then collapsed onto the silk sofa. "I'm having a bit of a swoon, I'm afraid."

"Allow me to fetch Camburton."

"Yes, would you? That would be lovely. I believe he's in the ballroom. Don't upset him, if you please. Just tell him I'd like to see him privately, or some such."

"Very well. He's become a protective husband already, is that it?" Geoffrey was a few years younger than she, and he carried himself with the jovial gait of a carefree man about town. He had chosen his costume well.

After the door closed behind him, she saw Christopher staring after him for a few extra seconds, then he turned back to look at her with a residual smile.

"A new friend, Christopher?"

He laughed and waved her off. "These young men are all so *curious*. Who am I to tamp down his enthusiasm for new experiences?"

"Come sit and talk to me until Archie arrives. I don't want to spoil the evening for everyone. I'm feeling better already."

Beatrix returned from the sideboard with a glass of water. "Drink this, darling."

Christopher watched them as Selina drank and Bea fussed with the pillows behind her, then caressed her cheek in that familiar way, with her knuckles. It had always soothed her, from as far back as she could remember. When she was finished drinking, Bea took the glass from her hand without asking, and returned it to the tray with the decanters.

Christopher definitely had something on his mind, and Selina wasn't able to ignore his curious expression. "What? Why are you looking at me like that?"

Sitting on the edge of a wingback chair, Christopher slung one of his legs over the other and rested his forearms on his thighs. "Like what?"

Bea came back to the sofa and sat at the far end, lifting Selina's feet and putting them on her lap.

"Are you two lovers?" Christopher asked plainly.

Selina and Beatrix both laughed.

"What do you think?" Bea asked provocatively, letting her palm run up Selina's leg, beneath the white layers of her silk costume.

Christopher only smiled. He nodded once, then stood up and walked toward the sideboard. "I need something stronger than water, I'm afraid. Anyone else fancy a bit of Dutch courage before poor Archie arrives?"

"What do you mean by *poor* Archie?" Selina sat up straighter so she could see Christopher over the back of the sofa, and pushed Bea's hand away from her leg.

"Yes. Whatever could Mr. Joseph mean, Selina?" Bea asked peevishly, her arms crossed in front of her beautiful chest. "That perhaps Archie is not as *fully* aware of our circumstances as you would like to believe? That you have been lying to yourself *and him* in the hopes that everything between us would just—" she snapped her fingers loudly above her head like a flamenco dancer "—miraculously become clear to him."

Christopher poured a healthy serving of amber liquid into the glass and downed it in one gulp. Then he poured a more appropriate amount, walked back to the seating area, and took up his spot on the edge of the chair again, as if he didn't want to take a seat and participate entirely.

"He doesn't know." Christopher sipped his drink and stared at Selina, then Bea.

All feelings of claustrophobia and paranoia evaporated. She felt a wave of something far worse. She stood up and began pacing behind the sofa. "It's simply not possible. He smells you on my body. He is with us all the time. I hold your hand. I—"

The door swung open. "Selina! Are you all right? I've been looking all over and— Oh, hello, Christopher." Archie dropped his gaze to his rabble-rousing friend with a look of contrived disinterest. "Fancy meeting you here."

"Yes. Fancy that." Christopher took another sip of whisky. "I'd be happy to leave—"

"No!" She cried, then realized her voice was shrill. "I mean . . ." Composing herself, she continued, "Would you please stay while we get to the bottom of this potential misunderstanding?"

Christopher smiled that lazy, provocative smile of his and slid all the way into the armchair, settling in for the duration, it seemed. "You know how much I love to get to the bottom of things, Lady Camburton."

Archie stared at Christopher and breathed through his nose; she had never seen him more like an angry bull. She almost laughed, but when he turned to her, his eyes were so full of anger and hurt, she gasped. "Archie?"

"Are you all very amused?"

A chill crept over her skin. One of her shoulders was bare due to the costume, but she suddenly felt cold and naked all over. "No. Darling, no!" She reached for him, but he pulled away.

"Do you love her?" He pointed to Beatrix without looking at her, as if she were some piece of trash on the floor.

Selina took a sharp breath and stood up ramrod straight. "Of course I love Beatrix. I have never said otherwise."

"I am not talking about platonic love, Selina," he boomed.

"Neither am I," she whispered. She spoke without fear of the truth, although she feared her marriage might well be floating away just as the words floated into the barren silence.

"How could you?" Archie's eyes revealed so much pain and confusion, and then raw accusation so palpable she took a step away from him. He straightened and all the emotion drained from his face, just as it had that morning at Rockingham. The loving, joyful Archie was gone; the cool, distant Marquess of Camburton had returned once more. And just as she had that morning, she dove at him. So much more was at stake now. They were married. She was likely carrying his child.

"Don't do this. Nothing has changed!"

He stared down at her hands where she gripped the white fabric of his costume. "Unhand me."

The silence in the room crackled and none of them said a word. He never looked at Christopher or Beatrix, only at her. When she didn't remove her hand, he tugged his arm away.

"I need you." She wept shamelessly.

He stopped at the door with his back to her. "I'm sure your *lover* will console you in your time of need." He left the room without a glance.

Chapter 14

*A*rchie left Devonshire House in a fog of his own disbelief and rage. A few people called to him and he may have replied, but he never stopped walking, except to demand his greatcoat from the footmen who were still trying to retrieve all the coats from the crush of newly arriving guests.

Some doyenne asked after his mother, and his look must have frightened her. The woman recoiled when he nearly growled, "She is not in town."

For the first time in his life, he hated Vanessa, for her free-spirited nature that he did not inherit; and then for her controlling, demanding nature that he did.

"Archie?" Christopher was pulling at his arm.

He turned slightly to face him. "Yes?"

The other man shook his head sadly, but Archie merely grimaced. "There's no need for any histrionics, old friend." He secured the fastenings on his coat. "Selina's made her choice, and I see I must learn how to live with it."

"Archie, no!" Christopher's face was etched with rage, the gas streetlamps casting him in a demonic light. "You also have a choice in this matter. Don't do this. Don't discard her because she is—"

"Discard her?" He nearly spit the words. "Me? Discard her? How could you possibly say such a thing? She just told me she is in love *with someone else.*" He broke after that. Came apart completely. His stomach was as tight as a fist; his spine felt as if it were disintegrating into a crumbling stack of vertebrae. He turned quickly to take hold of a nearby wrought iron fence that separated Devonshire House from the riffraff of Piccadilly, lest he slip to the ground like some actress with a touch of the vapors. Now he despised himself just as much as he despised all these hideous liars and cheats who'd called themselves friends.

"I'm leaving," he announced formally. "If you'll excuse me." He bowed coolly to Christopher, as if they'd only just met at Almack's, then strode toward Camburton House. He could walk there far faster than any carriage could take him. He would change out of this preposterous costume and simply disappear.

"Archie, don't!" Christopher yelled, chasing after him. He realized he had never heard his friend raise his voice, not once in twenty years. Such a charming effect his wife had on everyone's equilibrium.

He scraped his palms over his face, but did not turn to look back. "God damn it, Christopher, I won't share her. Not like that."

Christopher wheeled him around by the shoulders, forcing him to face Christopher. Without actually hurting him, he gave Christopher a rough shove, and strode away without a word. He reached Camburton House in less than a quarter of an hour. The two footmen in the hall would have plenty of gossip to share with the rest of the servants over breakfast tomorrow. The thought spurred him on even more. He ran up the stairs to his suite and began tearing off the infernal Greek toga.

"May I assist you, my lord?" Reynolds was there. Of course he was.

"No, you may not." He no longer cared that he sounded rude.

"My lord—"

He turned on his valet and nearly struck him. "I am going to dress myself alone. And then I am going out into the city alone. If you care to have a position when I return, I suggest you leave this room at once."

Without a word, Reynolds bowed and turned to leave.

"And don't you ever bow to me again."

The door closed quietly. He knew he was destroying everything in his path, but he didn't flinch. In fact, he welcomed the sensation. Destruction was so much swifter than creation, he realized. Let the viruses attack the innocents. Let the fields choke with weeds and lack of attention. Let Camburton Castle rot. He would make his way into the stews of the city, to the darkest corners with the most wretched wastrels, and he would remember why he was put on this earth. To help the poor. To heal the sick. Not to play bedroom games with an oversexed young woman who laughed at him while she pranced into the beds of others. He decided to forgo his watch and family ring, bringing only a pile of coin and paper money.

He stormed out into the night and headed east. As he passed St. George's Hanover Square, he was reminded of his dear sister Georgie. The last time he'd been here was to celebrate her marriage. Georgie had written from Cairo just last week to say that she and Trevor and James would be home by the New Year. He'd envisioned all sorts of harmonious scenarios, with shared parties at Camburton Castle, or Mayfield House, where Georgie would be living with Trevor Mayson and James Rushford. And he had envisioned his beautiful bride on his arm, and perhaps her beautiful friend as well.

Alas.

Archie was dead tired of *alas*. He wanted to kick *alas* in the throat.

He began to walk farther east through the dark, snowy streets. Maybe if he walked long enough and far enough, he wouldn't be a marquess anymore.

He headed along Oxford Street, meandering through smaller streets where drunkards and louts emerged, laughing and raucous, from bawdy houses or gambling hells. Wending his way slowly through the fashionable parts of Russell Square, he saw housemaids and cooks about their predawn chores; he continued east for many miles. He ended up in Spa Fields and rested in the park as the winter dawn crept through the branches of the desiccated, bare boughs. One sad bird began to trill weakly and Archie let his chin fall to his chest. She could fall in love with a songbird, he thought miserably.

He recalled that dismal morning at Rockingham, how the dawn had been so glorious. Even through his fury and hurt pride, he'd known that his reaction to seeing Selina with Constance Forrester was merely further proof of his passion. He'd known when he'd seen Selina's eyes that night, with that corrupt villainess making love to her bosom, that Selina had been distraught. Still, it had seemed so much easier to default to convention and run. If she hadn't been waiting for him in the foyer the next morning, he might have even been able to convince himself it was all for the best.

But Selina *had* been waiting in the corridor. And she had come into his lab while Christopher was . . . God, she was right. He could barely say the word "fuck," even to himself in his very unquiet mind.

"Fuck," he snapped.

There were a few tramps and vagrants in the grim park around him. One of them looked at him askance upon hearing the word. Archie realized that even in his most unassuming clothes, he was a glimmering specimen in the midst of all this squalor and depredation. He took a coin out of his pocket and gave it to the desperate man, toothless and filthy, curled into his rags to stave off the cold wind as best he could.

Disgusted with himself and his comparatively insignificant problems, he walked out of the park and headed south to the river. His mind continued down the self-flagellating path. At least at Rockingham, he'd been wrong. The thought made him laugh bitterly. Better to be wrong? What pathetic reasoning was this?

This time he was dead right. And it certainly didn't make him feel any better.

As he walked, he decided that if he was going to traipse around the city like some wandering fool, he might as well collect a bit of research. Jenner had mentioned clusters of infection in certain parts of the city, and Archie wanted to see for himself how the disease was spreading. While many members of Parliament and the upper class felt that diseases spreading in the poor areas of the city were merely the result of moral corruption—a form of social justice, even—Archie knew better than to think the smallpox virus had any care for morality or justice. It was blind and direct, perfectly clear in its mission to infect and kill.

He walked for hours, entering the most hideous streets and alleys. He was accosted several times, and usually a tossed coin and an autocratic word of warning sufficed.

Unfortunately, there were one or two more aggressive types, and he was forced to retaliate, finally resorting to punching one man in the jaw. It was unfortunate, mainly because doing so gave him such a visceral pleasure. He *wanted* to fight. He wanted to feel his fist slam against human flesh and bone. What a hypocrite! Down to his bones he was a liar. Help the poor and heal the sick, indeed. He wanted to destroy . . . everything.

He wandered into the next night and all through the following day. He purchased questionable food from mangy street vendors; occasionally he slept under a tree for a few hours, pulling his coat around him. He wasn't sure about the day of the week after a few such dozes. It was quite possible he'd slept for minutes or hours, and it didn't seem to matter in any case.

When he had given away his last bit of money, he started walking west along the Thames. Apparently he looked grimy (or crazy) enough to be of no further interest to thieves, because no one came near him after that. By the time he realized where he was, he was standing in front of Christopher's lodgings at the Albany. The wizened man who guarded the entrance took a cursory look at the marquess and immediately welcomed him as if he'd arrived atop his shining curricle, perfectly turned out in his finest silk neck cloth.

"Lord Camburton."

"I'm here to see Mr. Joseph. Is he receiving?"

"Allow me to check. It won't be a moment." The unflappable man sent a young lad running. A few moments later, the breathless messenger reported formally that Mr. Joseph was "at home."

Archie showed himself through the front courtyard and into the main part of the former royal residence. He got to the top of the stairs and saw Christopher standing casually in the doorway to his flat holding a glass of something brownish and likely alcoholic.

"Have you taken to drinking in the morning?" Archie tried to appear relaxed as he walked down the corridor toward his friend. Finding himself indoors felt strange and confining, and he had to measure his steps to walk in a straight line.

"It's six o'clock in the evening—Wednesday evening—Lord Camburton."

"Is it? I must've lost track of the time."

Christopher pulled the door wider to allow him entrance. "I think you may have lost far more than that, my friend. Christmas was yesterday—"

The room began to swim, and he reached out to steady himself. The last he remembered hearing was Christopher's desperate plea, "Not the Etruscan vase—" before collapsing to the floor.

Despite her confusion and sadness—or because of it—Selina found peace in Beatrix's arms that first night of Archie's disappearance. But when the gray light of day crept into the guestroom overlooking the bare trees of Grosvenor Square, her feelings of loss and misery about Archie crept right in along with it. She cocooned her body closer against Bea's and tried to keep the desolation at bay.

"Are you all right, love?" Bea whispered.

"No." She had never been able to lie, or even equivocate, with Bea, nor Bea to her. It was one of the things they most loved about each other.

"Tell me what you love about him, why he is worth fighting for." Bea gently stroked her shoulder.

She lifted her chin and looked into Bea's sleepy eyes. Bea's dark-chestnut hair framed her strong face, and Selina was filled with a profound gratitude. "How can you be so wise?"

Bea kissed her forehead. "I'm not wise. At least, I don't think I am. I see you. I love you. I see you love this man. I want to know everything you feel. And why. He is struggling. You are struggling. For some reason, I don't feel like I need to struggle when I am with you."

Selina hugged her close, loving the feel of their naked skin against skin—stomach against stomach, thighs against thighs, breasts against breasts. It wasn't an erotic feeling, exactly, it was more of a grounding, anchoring feeling of humanity, of being part of all humanity, connected.

"Oh, Bea. He is so good." Selina rested her cheek against Bea's shoulder. "He's sincere and eager and brilliant and . . . in many ways he's trapped in all sorts of conventional prisons. But he is his own gaoler."

"So you must free him." Bea started to kiss Selina along her neck and then her shoulder.

"Like you freed me?"

"If you like . . ." Bea whispered near her ear, then bit her lobe playfully. "You were so full of rights and wrongs when I met you. So agitated. All fear and righteousness and adamancy." She kissed along Selina's neck. "Pushing every which way."

Selina pushed her hips against Bea's. "I thought you liked that about me."

"Mmm," Bea hummed as she nudged her onto her back and slowly pulled the sheet lower to reveal her breasts. Her nipples puckered immediately from the cool air in the bedroom and the nearness of Bea's warm lips. Beatrix cupped one of her breasts and took the tip into her mouth, sucking gently and humming.

Her back arched and her hips pressed up against Bea's stomach. "And it is not all Archie's fault either. You were right—I must have been equivocating in some way, afraid to tell him the true nature of what is between us." She gasped. "You are distracting me . . ."

Bea's mouth came away, and she blew on Selina's breast teasingly. "You are distracting me, darling. I can't get enough of you. Archie will come back. And if you want to go speak with him alone, you should. Or if you want me to go with you, I will do that too. If you want me to make love to you while he watches, I will do that."

The thought sent a thrilling desire up her spine. "You would do that?" She was awash in a terrible combination of guilt and desire.

"Mmm, I would love to show him how much I love you."

She arched into Bea's touch and raked her hand through Bea's long, dark hair. "Would you come to bed with both of us?"

Beatrix exhaled gently, and her warm breath tickled Selina's skin. "Oh, my love. When he was touching you the other night, the fire in your eyes was so beautiful. I want to touch you—kiss you here—" Bea pressed her hand against Selina's mound "—while he touches you in that possessive way of his. You will simply combust, I know it. I want that for you."

"I love you." Lifting her head from the pillow, Selina looked Bea in the eye as she touched her cheek and smiled. Her head fell back to the pillow. "And it seems I also love Archie."

"Tsk-tsk. Poor Selina has too much love in her heart," Bea teased as she kissed the skin over Selina's beating heart for emphasis. Then she returned her gaze, no longer teasing. "I revel in your happiness. Do you hear me? I want your happiness."

"Yes," Selina replied, her throat tight. "I hear you and I love you and I want your happiness too."

Bea rested her cheek on Selina's breast and sighed. "This is my happiness. You. And the freedom you give me to play my music and to come home to you when I can, with that glow of love in your eyes and no censure and the warmth and tenderness—"

"Stop, you're going to make me cry again."

"Cry all you want. I love your tears as much as your laughter. Do you know what I loved about being away? I loved being in Berlin or Milan and thinking, 'Selina is here in my heart.'" She patted her own chest. "'Selina loves me and I love her. I know Selina will be there when I get home.' While I was gone, I realized that you had become a fact of my life. I see all these people running around, frantically searching for trust, for comfort. And I have it. I have it with you."

She wept quietly as Bea spoke, and replied haltingly. "That's exactly how I feel." She wiped her eyes. "I know now that I didn't make that clear to Archie, that I was immature and selfish in my desire to just float through the wonders of our lovemaking without confessing the truth of my feelings for you. I knew deep down he would not approve, and I dreaded that. I think he must have assumed—probably logically on his part—that I would cast you aside or something like that, because he and I had fallen in love. But when he accepted you, I just assumed. Was there the seed of wary questioning in the back of my mind? Yes, I think all men dismiss the notion of passion among women because—" she choked out a bitter laugh "—where would that leave them?"

Bea smiled up at her. "Well, it's all out in the open now. He will come around. He must." She leaned down and kissed the slight swell over Selina's womb. "He must," she repeated reverently, "for you and the babe."

"I know. But— Oh, but the look on his face last night!" She turned away from Bea and put her face into the pillow.

"It's all right, love. It's all going to be all right." Bea pulled the sheets and blankets over them as she settled in behind Selina and wrapped her body protectively around hers. "Shh, just try to sleep for now. He'll be back today or tomorrow— I'm certain he'll return before Christmas. We will make him see that I am not a threat to his happiness."

Somehow she was able to get a few more hours of sleep and then, when the butler informed them the marquess was still not at home, the two of them spent the rest of the morning walking through the park. She continued to chastise herself for her lack of clarity with him, for not telling Archie directly that Beatrix was her lover in every sense of the word. But she knew now she had to make him see that this made their life much richer, rather than the other way round.

That night after supper, when Archie had still not returned home, she began to worry about far more than their tangled love affairs. She wrote to Vanessa and Christopher, asking if they'd received word from him, and directed the messenger to wait for a reply. She wouldn't hear back from Vanessa for several days, but perhaps Christopher would know where Archie had gone.

"Is the marquess always so rash?" Bea asked the next morning.

Selina laughed bitterly. "Never. Except when it comes to me, apparently. Then always."

She proceeded to tell Bea what had happened at Rockingham, everything about Constance, and Archie's hasty, furtive departure the next morning.

"I remember meeting Constance in Edinburgh a few years ago, before you and I had met. She was a bit overconfident for my taste. Sounds as if you handled her perfectly."

Selina shrugged. "I don't know if I *handled* her at all. But it was satisfying to stand by the servant's bellpull and know I was quite prepared to actually pull it."

Bea held her close in a one-armed hug. "Yes. That's what I meant. You are your own mistress now."

Something fluttered in her chest when Bea said it in just that way, reminding her how Archie frequently called her his *loving mistress* when he was being tender. "I'm different when I'm with Archie. In bed, I mean."

Bea gave her a knowing look. "I should hope so."

"Do you want to know?"

"Perhaps in time I will see for myself." She smiled. "But yesterday morning, when I asked what you loved about him, I hadn't meant to inquire after your lovemaking. I only meant . . ." Bea looked at the sparkling, snow-edged trees, and farther afield at the pale winter sunshine across Grosvenor Square. "I wanted to know your heart, if that makes sense. What you do in bed with Archie is private . . . between you and Archie. I don't need to pry apart what you two have. I know what we have; I know what you like with me," she added with a little bump of her hip against Selina's as they walked.

Selina blushed and took a deep breath. "And you with me."

"So tell me what you would have if you could have anything," Bea prompted. "Everything."

"In my dreams?"

"Yes, in your beautiful dreams."

"In my beautiful dreams, it's like this, how we are right now, walking together in a splendid morning, except Archie is right there at home, or here with us on my other arm, and you are here—when you can be, when your work doesn't take you away. And I am here for you *both*, always."

"That sounds lovely."

"But maybe Archie is right." Selina looked down at her boots as they peeked out from under the hem of her winter walking dress with every stride. "And I am wrong. Maybe it simply isn't allowed."

Bea laughed, deep and sure, and Selina was reminded of all the reasons she adored this woman. "Allowed by whom? We can live our lives the way we wish, all of us. You especially. You have no financial constraints on your behavior, as long as you live modestly, which is your natural tendency. You have no social restrictions—or at least none that you need to countenance—your parents' cruel censure, for example. You believed you were telling Archie the truth about us before you got married. Perhaps you could have been more forthcoming about the details, but on some level he must have known what you were really asking."

"I feel greedy," Selina whispered guiltily. "Emotionally greedy."

"You feel greedy for wanting your own happiness? Greedy for wanting to love a man who obviously loves you in return? Greedy for thinking you deserve my love as well as his? Well, if that's greed, then you *should* be greedy, because you *do* deserve it. You are a light, my dear. You shine in a way that warms those around you. Archie must know that. Perhaps it is *he* who is greedy—wanting all of you to himself—and fearful, I imagine." Bea sighed with something like understanding. "I shouldn't be too hard on him if I were you. He is probably convinced that you do not have enough to give, that love is finite, or that your love for me will somehow diminish your love for him. He does not yet understand your capacity for love, that's all."

"You make everything sound so reasonable." She rested her head on Bea's shoulder and slid her hand through her arm. She felt slightly mollified, but she would never feel whole again unless Archie was there. Her voice cracked. "I wish he would come home."

Chapter 15

hristopher took a slow sip of his Turkish coffee and stared at Archie. "Well, well. Look who decided to rejoin the human race."

When Archie attempted to lift his head off the pillow, the weight of his skull prevented him from doing so. "Have I been drugged?"

Shrugging, Christopher set down his demitasse and folded his arms in front of his chest. "I suppose it's quite possible. Where have you been? You're a complete disaster."

He rubbed his temples and tried to compose himself. His thoughts were thick and murky. "I've been here in London."

"Really? Where in London?"

"I don't know precisely. I meandered." He was able to get himself up to a partially sitting position. He looked around slowly and realized he was in Christopher's bedroom, in Christopher's bed, in a clean nightshirt. "I'm very sorry to have inconvenienced you in this manner. I shan't bother you any longer." He tried to sit up all the way, but the pain in his head wouldn't let him.

"Have you seen yourself?" Christopher stood and began to pace the floor at the foot of the bed. "You have a black eye that is healing nicely." He tossed his hand in Archie's direction. "Abrasions on your scalp. Contusions on your ribs. I don't even know whose shoes you were wearing when you stumbled in here last night." Christopher quit pacing and looked out the window impatiently. "The shoes have been discarded, in case you were wondering."

"Oh dear." Letting his hand cover his eyes, then wincing when he realized his right eye was indeed still sore, Archie had nothing more to say.

"Yes. 'Oh dear.'" Christopher turned and stared at him with complete exasperation. "Setting aside, for now, all the worried correspondence I've received from your family this week—and missing your first Christmas with your wife—what the hell got into you?"

"Week? How long have I been out?" He struggled to sit up again.

"Just stop trying to do anything but lie there, would you?" Christopher resumed pacing. "You bolted Saturday evening after that ridiculous scene at Devonshire House and it's now Thursday morning. Five days later."

"*Five days!*"

"Yes. Five days."

"Jesus."

Pausing, Christopher took hold of one of the turned wood posts at the end of his bed. "When I visited Camburton Castle a few months ago, you and Selina were in each other's pockets. Then when I got news of your marriage, and having seen you in town these past weeks— Well, she's an angel. And she obviously loves you, for some bizarre reason that I cannot possibly fathom."

"Why do you act as if she is blameless in the failure of our doomed marriage, and that I am somehow guilty?"

"How is *she* to blame?"

He gestured vaguely. "She obviously wants nothing to do with me."

"Selina wants nothing to do with you?" Christopher coughed out, as if that were the most ridiculous thing he'd ever heard.

"She doesn't want me. Are you deaf?"

"What gave you that idea, my brilliant friend?"

He groaned and turned his head away. "Now you're merely trying to hurt me. She has made her choice."

"You're such a fool!" Christopher cried. "She has made her *choice*, you say?"

"Yes. That's what I say." A surge of resentment reignited inside him.

"She is desperately trying to see you."

"She is?" He flipped his head quickly—too quickly—and immediately regretted it. His skull was pounding.

Christopher narrowed his eyes and held on even tighter to the bedpost, likely to prevent himself from punching Archie like everyone in most of London seemed to have done in the past week. "She loves *you*, you idiot."

"She loves Beatrix Farnsworth, you ass!"

"So what?"

He spun his head back and didn't even mind the crushing pain. If Christopher wanted to fight, he was happy to oblige him. "'So what?' You bastard." He forced himself out of bed, stumbling and reaching for Christopher's shirt, to grab him for support or punch him in the face, he wasn't sure which.

Christopher moved out of reach easily. "You, my friend, are pathetic."

The room tilted awkwardly as he tried to keep his balance, then he collapsed to the floor, vaguely hoping he didn't hit his head this time on one of the many antiquities that crowded his friend's chamber.

It was dark outside the tall window across the bedroom when next he woke. He was safely resettled in bed, and there were voices in the living room. He kept his eyes closed and hoped everyone, everywhere, *ever* would simply go away. He groaned pathetically into the pillow and a few seconds later the door flew open.

"If you weren't so hurt, I would hurt you so!" Selina cried as she crossed the room, then she must've caught a glimpse of him in his *pathetic* state; she gasped and covered her mouth with one pretty dove-gray gloved hand.

"Why are you wearing gloves?"

She burst into tears and looked like she wanted to leave the room, but she stood where she was. Christopher peeked in through the door across the room. "Everything all right in here?"

"Yes," Selina answered hotly, wiping away her tears. "Now shut the door and leave us."

"Yes, ma'am." He dropped a silly curtsey and closed the door.

Archie groaned again. Could this entire situation be any more embarrassing? Women weren't even allowed into the Albany. "Wait a minute. How did you get in here, anyway?"

"As you can see." She struck a mannequin's pose.

He looked away from her beautiful jade eyes and then down at her attire. She was a very attractively dressed . . . man. Her blonde hair was pulled back from her face and tucked up into a jaunty top hat. Her coat was immaculately tailored. Neck cloth folded artfully. Snowy-white shirt. Brocade vest of the finest maroon silk. Black satin breeches. Shiny boots.

His eyes skidded back to the tight-fitting breeches. "Your legs are obscene."

She finished wiping away her tears, and she smiled at him. "Damn you. What do you care about my legs? You don't care about me in the least. You missed our first Christmas as husband and wife. I just had to see for myself that you weren't dead. And you appear to be recovering just fine. So I shall leave you. Good day, sir." She bowed just like a man, and he smiled despite himself.

Just before she turned to leave, he whispered her name, then, "Please don't go."

"What's that?" The male clothes made her seem cooler somehow, less excitable. She lifted her chin. "Did you ask me something?" She had her hands behind her back and one leg slightly in front of the other, in that arrogant pose so typical of all the young bucks who swarmed around the prince lately.

"Yes." He hesitated. "I asked you to stay with me."

"I'm standing right here."

His voice faltered as he spoke. "You know what I mean. I need you, Selina. You are my wife. This is what happens to me when I don't have you."

"Don't you dare try to threaten me!"

"Threaten?" He laughed, or made some throaty, sickening approximation of a laugh. "Do I look like a man in a position to threaten you?"

She stomped her foot, and desire stabbed through him. "That's not what I meant and you know it." She pulled off her stylish hat and set it on one of Christopher's antiquities—half a broken column that he was currently using as a side table. Her hair tumbled loose as she turned to look at him, and he was quite certain he had never wanted to make love to her as much as he did in that moment: flushed, feminine and masculine all at once, quivering with emotion.

"Please?" He didn't know what he was asking for, but he was asking nonetheless. He wanted her like he wanted oxygen.

"Please *what*?" She was obviously frustrated with him.

"God, I have nothing more to give you than my name, my children—if we are lucky enough to have them. I beg you to be my true wife, to spend the rest of your life with me. I feel it in my heart that we are meant to be together."

Her nostrils flared. "I too feel it in my heart . . . I feel you in my heart." She tugged off one of the gloves and reached for him. As she caressed his cheek, the tension in his chest loosened for the first time since he'd walked out of Devonshire House.

"So you will give her up?"

She withdrew her hand as if he were some sort of hideous leper. "You are an extortionist! Would I ask you to give up your mother? Your sister? Everyone you hold dear?"

"Beatrix Farnsworth is not your family! She is your *lover*!"

Selina's eyes were brimming with fresh tears, but she did not shed them. "She *is* my family, and I will never give her up. You are too blind to see that I already *am* your true, devoted wife. That I love you—" Her voice cracked as if she were reluctant to admit it. "And yet that is not enough—not enough for *you*. What will happen when we have children? Will my very limited supply of love be cut in half yet again? Then into thirds and fourths? Will I be allowed to love our sons and daughters, or will that, too, threaten the love I have for you?"

He struggled to sit up straight in the bed, grateful that the pain in his head seemed to have improved somewhat. "You cannot be serious. You sleep in the same bed with her. You have sexual relations with her!"

"You have sexual relations with Christopher!"

"Your logic is preposterous. I don't *love* Christopher!"

She barked a cruel laugh. "And you think that is *more* honorable! To use your friend's body for some heartless carnal satisfaction? That is *better* in your mind than my loving, physical relationship with Beatrix?"

"No. Yes. *No!*" He shook his head in exasperated frustration. "The point is moot, because I have not had sexual relations with Christopher since you and I were married."

"Well, I'm sorry to hear it. That's your loss. Or maybe not, since you confess to having no real feelings for him—"

"You are twisting my words! I meant— I intend to honor the integrity of our marriage, that you can trust in my *fidelity*."

"And you can trust in mine, damn it. I promise I will never be with any man but you. Never!"

His nostrils flared. The sound of those words filled him with such desire and pride and then . . . frustration. "You should promise never to be with any *person* but me, damn it."

She pulled the glove back on and took a deep breath. "That I will not do." Hesitating and giving him a narrow look, she continued, "While we have been together these past few months, has it felt like you only received some fraction of my attention? Some shoddy portion of me?"

"No—"

"Do you want me as much as I want you right now?"

"Yes," he whispered.

"Then you, my lord, are a fool."

Selina picked up the top hat and was almost to the door when he said, "You have no respect for the rule of God."

She wheeled around and glared at him but did not walk back to the bed. "Don't you dare speak to me of the rule of *God*. The rule of God put me in a prison in Yorkshire with other *evil sinners* who masturbated or refused to marry a lecher twice her age, or didn't obey her parents' wishes when they called for silence after the neighbor's son raped her sister! That is your rule of God, *Lord Camburton*. I want no part of your rule of God. I love Beatrix. I love you. And even after all that, I will have room in my heart for all the children we might create—or might have already created." Her hand went protectively to her belly. "And since it seems *you* do not have room in *your* heart, I bid you good-night, sir."

"This can't bode well if you are leaving his side this quickly—with no alteration to your sartorial splendor . . . other than your hair." Christopher was resting languidly on the green velvet chaise near the fire. "Which is quite becoming with the top hat, I do declare."

She tossed the damnable hat onto a chair, and pushed his feet aside so she could sit at the other end of the chaise. "He's impossible."

"Is that news?" Christopher took a drink of his scotch and then passed her the tumbler.

"Thank you. I could use a sip." She took a sniff and then wrinkled her nose in disgust. "Perfect. Now I can't even have the pleasure of a stiff drink." She returned the glass untouched and leaned her back into the pillows behind her. "I shan't give up on him, damn it. He's clinging to some *notion* that I must abandon Beatrix if I'm to be his 'true' wife, whatever that means. He used words like 'integrity' and 'fidelity' and the '*rule of God.*'"

"I daresay it's not merely a *notion*. You are going up against centuries of religious doctrine and social law."

"It's all hypocrisy." She kept her voice level. "So if we were some typical tonish couple, and we married, and I gave him an heir and then he set up a lady love in town—or even if he visited you, discreetly of course—"

"Of course," Christopher agreed amiably.

"Then *that* would be in accordance with the social order?"

Christopher nodded slowly.

"But because I want to be open and honest and *true* from the outset—that makes me the rebel, the troublemaker . . . the sinner?"

Christopher shrugged. "Yes. I'd say that fairly sketches out the situation."

"But he is the Marquess of Camburton, damn it." She slammed her fist into her palm.

"And you the Marchioness of Camburton," Christopher added helpfully.

She sighed. "He is one of the richest, most powerful men of our time—and therefore arguably free of social constraints. Yet, still he persists with this nonsense."

"Come now. These are not merely social conventions as far as Archie is concerned. He is incredibly possessive, desperately in love with you, and despises competition of any sort. How can he possibly contend with Beatrix in any way other than to attempt to eliminate her from the field?"

Selina stared at her gloved hands. The male cut of the gray suede was far more comfortable than the tight-fitting narrow cut of her usual kid gloves. She stared at the excellent workmanship and contemplated the gloves for quite some time. "Men have designed this world to suit them."

"Better than designing the world in some *unsuitable* manner," Christopher joked.

She looked at him, and he set down his glass when he saw the depth of her seriousness. "Why can't he see that I will only grow to resent him if he forces me to part from Beatrix?" She shook her head. "Not that I ever would—or could—part from her. Why does he feel he must claim me like some territory, to stab a flag in me and declare me his?"

"Because that is what we were all taught to do, my dear. Especially Archie."

"He was not raised to—" Selina made to defend Vanessa and Nora, as if Christopher were implying that they were somehow to blame for raising Archie to be that type of man, but Christopher held up his hand.

"Hear me out. His sister, Georgiana, was always the wild one. Archie was the reliable one. And those were not just roles that were assigned to them, either. He *is* reliable. If you only knew the amount of research that is happening right now because of his anonymous generosity, the distribution of educational pamphlets throughout the country, the good charitable works that are taking place—all solely because of him. He is so damned good. You must know that."

"Yes, I know. He is very good."

"He loves you and you love him, and he doesn't understand anything beyond that. You confound him."

"I know." She looked thoughtfully toward the fire. "What do you suggest I do?"

Christopher narrowed his eyes. "I think Archie needs to be taken in hand once and for all."

Selina shivered at the possibilities.

"Ah. I see you've discovered that for yourself, have you?"

"Only playfully." She lowered her voice. "I feel a bit duplicitous conspiring against him in this way, but you make me want to plan something . . . extraordinary."

"That's the spirit." He leaned forward and set his drink on the table, then rested his forearms on his lap. "He's such a prisoner of convention; I think perhaps we should make our first skirmish in public. He is constitutionally incapable of misbehaving in front of a crowd of his peers."

"You are the devil, Christopher Joseph."

"You're welcome."

She closed the small distance between them and kissed him on the cheek. "He does love you, you know."

"I know."

"You heard all that?" She gestured with her chin toward the bedroom door.

Christopher thought for a few moments before he spoke. "Archie has never been able to own his feelings. Especially not feelings that go against every societal norm he has wanted to not only adhere to, but exemplify."

"I know that. But that's not who he is inside. He is openhearted and joyful. I know we can have this life I've dreamed of. The way he looked at me just now—he has so much love to give. We just need to make him see he is allowed to have it. All of it."

Christopher rubbed his hands together. "This will be a pleasure."

"You have a funny idea of pleasure."

His grin was contagious, and she smiled in return.

"Very well. Perhaps we all have a funny idea of pleasure. What do you have in mind?"

Christopher looked toward the bedroom and lowered his voice. "He's in no condition to do anything for a few more days, so we have some time to prepare."

After being so preoccupied with Archie's absence, on edge for many days, the bubbling up of happiness was unfamiliar. She reminded herself that Archie was safe and alive and, in time, all would be well. If she had to keep her relationship with Beatrix entirely separate, that was something she would have to reconcile, but she was not willing to give up her dream of a whole, integrated life just yet.

Christopher speculated aloud. "I'm thinking the opera... a private box . . . but partially visible . . . with the four of us? A new Colman farce is playing on Monday. Does Camburton still keep a box?"

"Yes, we went the first week we were here." She bit her lip. "I'm afraid he will try to bolt from the city and return to the estate. Are you sure you can keep him in town until then?"

Christopher smiled again. "How hard do you want me to try, Lady Camburton?"

"You are very, very bad, Mr. Joseph." Her cheeks heated at the prospect of Christopher restraining Archie. "As his wife, and with only his best interests at heart, mind you, I think you should use *all* the importunities at your disposal. I will send some of his clothes around. I'm certain he won't want to return to Mayfair if I am still in residence. And Reynolds is having endless fits about the state of the marquess's toilette in the absence of his valet." She looked around. "Are there any other apartments available? Perhaps he should take up residence here for now."

"Yes, I will see to it. That's probably what Archie will want as well. Far more discreet than a hotel, yet still in town to keep tabs on you, which I will convince him is the least he can do if he's going to fight to win your hand from the dastardly villainess, Miss Farnsworth."

She smiled at first, carried away with Christopher's charm and wit—how he turned all heartache into farce—then her face fell. "Oh, Christopher. Please tell me again we are doing right by Archie."

Christopher nearly growled. "He is the luckiest sot on the planet, and it's just a matter of knocking him around a bit until he realizes it."

She leaned over and kissed his cheek again quickly, then stood up. When she turned to go, Archie was standing—wobbling really—in the partially opened doorway to the bedroom.

"Are you going to make love to Christopher now as well?" Archie asked with venom.

She tucked her hair back up and put on the hat, then rested her hands on her hips and stared directly at Archie. Her first instinct was to run to him and weep—he looked so exhausted, so devastated, and his words stung like nettles—but she now saw that Christopher and Beatrix were right. Archie was the only one holding them all back from a life of freedom and happiness.

"You, my dear husband, are insane. I suggest you go back to bed until you are well."

Then she turned to Christopher and bowed her exit. Without looking back, she crossed to the front door and showed herself out. As soon as she released the knob, she heard the two men begin what she hoped would be a long and productive argument. She kept her head dipped down when two men passed by and bade her a gruff good-night, man to man. She grunted her reply.

One of Archie's more modest carriages was waiting for her in the forecourt, with Beatrix unseen within the dim compartment.

"Is he safe?" Bea asked as soon as the door was shut behind Selina.

"He is physically on the mend, but he is still a wreck in every other way. Christopher and I are hoping to wear him down."

On the ride home, she explained how they planned to go about it.

Chapter 16

"How dare you conspire with my wife?" Archie accused, his voice sounding too loud in his ears. It still felt awkward to be indoors after so many nights living rough—the dark-green brocade walls seemed to muffle his entire existence. "I need to get out of here."

Christopher stood up and refilled his glass. "Care for a drink?"

"No, I don't care for a drink, damn it. Answer me. Who do you think you are to meddle with Selina?"

Finishing with his preparations, Christopher set down the bottle and glass, then turned to face him. "You don't even know what you want, you fool." Christopher crossed the room slowly, with a predatory smile. "You say you want a little wife. A little country estate. A little science." By that point, Christopher was standing inches in front of him. "You are selling yourself short, Cambury." Before Archie could stop him, Christopher had his hand in Archie's disheveled hair and was tugging violently. "Do you hear me, man?"

He hissed in response.

Christopher's other hand slid down to Archie's cock, already hard and betraying every filthy desire that crossed his mind. "You want to be fucked by a man. By me, you dolt."

"No—" He tried to deny it, but his body thrust against Christopher's knowing hand.

"Yes!" Christopher leaned in and attacked his neck, not with a gentle nibble, but a hard, possessive bite. He soothed the red mark with the flat of his tongue and massaged Archie's cock. "Yes, damn it. Yes. You must learn to say yes. For yourself. I know when you say no, you so often mean yes, but it is time for *you* to say it, to own it."

"No," he whispered, as if the word itself could make it true, but he was beginning to weep; he wanted Christopher desperately. He'd missed him these past few months, but had set aside his desire, trying to convince himself it was a residue of his past, something that would fade over time.

"Say yes, Archie . . . to all of it. Say yes to Selina, who loves you with a profound, knowing passion . . ." Christopher worked his firm fingers around Archie's cock and teased his balls. He was physically weak and the nightshirt only came to his thighs so it was easy enough for Christopher to have full access to whatever part of his anatomy he wished.

But Archie fought him as best he could. "It's not right. In fact, it's terribly wrong!" He tried to shove Christopher's hands away, but he was feeble. "Not everything can be solved with an orgasm!" He withdrew from Christopher's reach and turned back toward the bedroom, but he was unsteady on his feet and his vision was blurry. At least this time it was from tears and not another fainting spell. He scraped the back of his hand across his eyes with rough impatience. When the bedroom door closed behind him, he hoped that meant he was alone. When Christopher's gentle touch landed on his shoulder, he stiffened. "I beg of you. Leave me be. If you care for me at all, you will not seduce me right now."

"I am not seducing you. I'm loving you." Christopher kissed the back of his neck, and a shiver shot down his spine.

"What does that even mean?" He gave up wiping the tears from his eyes, because they were flowing so freely. He leaned his forehead against the bedpost, where he was holding on for balance.

"Come to me." Christopher turned him gently into his arms and pulled his body into a firm, all-encompassing embrace. "You are not alone, you fool. That's all it means. We love you." Archie trembled and tried to tell himself it was the aftereffects of his illness of the past few days. Then Christopher cupped his cheek and stared into his eyes. "I love you, you idiot. Selina loves you." Slowly, with Christopher never taking his eyes from Archie's, he kissed him on the lips.

Archie had imagined this so many times, and then thrown away the image. Discarded it because it was impossible. A physical rout between them was somehow acceptable to his contorted sense of propriety. But loving Christopher? Kissing Christopher? Impossible.

But propriety evaporated in that moment. He needed this man's kiss; he'd never known how badly he needed it. He reached for Christopher's hair and grabbed hold.

"That's it. Hold on to me. I won't let you fall." Christopher was so tender, so thorough. His mouth was at moments gentle and then almost scolding, showing him what he'd been depriving himself of during all their years together.

It was utterly different from their previous couplings. He reached for Christopher's shirt and removed it with near reverence. He leaned down and kissed Christopher's nipple, toying with him, loving him. He'd never let himself—

"Oh God, I am awful—" He choked on emotion. "How have you stayed my friend? Why?"

Christopher caressed his cheek and smiled. "You're very easy on the eyes."

He laughed through his tears. "I suppose there is that to redeem me."

Taking off Archie's nightshirt—Christopher's nightshirt that Archie wore—Christopher murmured, "You are the kindest, gentlest, most honest person I have ever known." Christopher dropped the nightshirt on the floor and pressed their bodies together. "I would take any friendship you had to offer. But I think you are beginning to see you have far more to offer than you ever believed."

Archie looked into his friend's eyes, his lover's eyes. "I do love you. You know that? You've always known that, haven't you?"

Pressing his lips against Archie's, Christopher kissed him senseless for many minutes. Their tongues tangled and teased, the newness of this seemingly innocent act making them both giddy. "I want to kiss you for years," Archie whispered, touching Christopher's moist lips.

"And so you shall," Christopher agreed easily.

Archie's face fell, and he let his forehead rest on Christopher's solid shoulder. "What have I done? Should I not have married Selina?" He looked up again and tried to see an answer in Christopher's brilliant eyes. He saw only love, and that hint of humor that always shimmered through the man.

Christopher trailed his hands up and down Archie's back. "Do you love her any less now that you have declared yourself to me?"

He felt the accusation like a punch in his gut. "No. What is wrong with me?"

When Christopher laughed outright, his body shook against Archie's. He hugged Christopher close and kissed his neck, then, tentatively, initiated the next kiss. Archie simply held on, wanting that love and joy to somehow permeate his being as well. He wanted to show Christopher how much he loved and admired him, how much he had held back all these years. He turned them around and nudged Christopher onto the bed.

"Lie back . . ." Archie said softly.

Christopher obliged, and Archie finished undressing him, then crawled up the length of his naked body, covering him with his own. As their bodies warmed, from tip to toe, he reveled in every detail, every nuance of pleasure he'd always resolved to reduce or distill to some physical grunt. The feel of Christopher's chest against his, thigh against thigh, straining cock against cock. He rubbed and nestled himself against Christopher's lean, long body.

"I love you," he whispered again as he began to kiss his way down Christopher's ridged stomach. He licked along the edge of one particularly defined muscle that curved around Christopher's hip, and then continued, until he was resting between Christopher's spread legs.

He slid his cheek against the silky skin of Christopher's straining cock. "I can't believe I've never done this for you . . . with you . . ."

"Archie—" Christopher began to speak, then moaned in pleasure when Archie's mouth took him deep. He adored the feel of Christopher's fingers clenched in his hair, the taut pull of pressure and relief he sensed in that hold. Overcome with sensation, he was lost in the moment—found, perhaps. Free-floating joy overwhelmed him as he finally expressed himself wholly—physically and emotionally—with this man. *This person.* He'd adored him for so many years, but only let it show in some shabby approximation of love.

"Wait, I'm going to come—" Christopher pulled desperately at Archie's scalp, but Archie refused to relent. He wanted every ounce, every mysterious moment of what this meant to flow into his body. To accept Christopher into his body, willingly, openly.

"Archie . . ." It was almost a whisper, and then Christopher's hot seed hit the back of Archie's throat. The sensation was overwhelming and profound. He couldn't get enough, and he was almost desperate as he lapped at him and sucked and licked him clean.

"Come here," Christopher whispered, smoothing his fingers through Archie's hair and bringing him up to cradle in his arms. "Oh, my sweet man."

Archie clung to him, and felt comforted in a way he never could have been before.

"What have I done?" he asked later, when they were both in the bed under the light coverlet, still holding each other. The candles in the bedroom were guttering, but the fireplace was crackling and casting a warm glow. "Will she ever forgive me? I've been such a hypocrite. So lost."

Christopher squeezed him tighter. "You are magnificent. She loves you. Don't you see? Don't you feel how you can love her . . . and me? How she can love you . . . and Beatrix?"

He dipped his chin, embarrassed. "It seems quite obvious now, the possibilities I mean."

Christopher's laughter rumbled through his chest and into his palm, into his soul. "Limitless, eh?"

"Quite," he breathed contentedly, loving the feel of their bodies stretched long and languid up against one another, with no shame or denial. "So, what sort of trickery were you and Selina plotting before she left? I know that look of mischief in your eye. And hers." He kissed Christopher again because he could. Because he could, at last. "Tell me how and when I am to be reunited with my wife."

By Monday afternoon, Selina wasn't feeling quite so jovial and sure of herself. Christopher had sent word that he and Archie would be at the theater at the appointed time, but Archie had made no effort to contact her himself, and his absence was far more difficult to bear than she could have anticipated. She hadn't seen him in over a week, except for their brief skirmish at Christopher's; she missed him terribly.

Bea had tried to console her, first with words and then with tender caresses, and for the first time in their life together, Selina had asked her to stop. To stop being kind. To stop consoling. To stop touching her. She wanted Archie. Quite desperately. She still loved Beatrix, of course she did, and that would never change. But now that she had known the intensity of Archibald Cambury—the weight of him in her life—she felt off-kilter and deeply unhappy without him by her side. She was too light: not effervescent and joyful, but unmoored.

She'd gone to meet with her publisher the previous week, and he'd just written back that he was thrilled in every way with the new manuscript. Looking up from his letter that morning, she had turned out of habit to tell Archie. He was not there. The smallest things that crossed her path—a lonely thrush in the barren tree in the back garden, a little boy with a funny upturned nose—all of these she would have shared with him. In his absence, the little things seemed to be backing up inside her. She was worried she would forget a detail he would've enjoyed.

Archie was a physical creature, far more than a verbal one—he had never written her a line of poetry or even a brief note of affection—so she wasn't overly surprised not to have heard from him in writing. But God, how she longed for him, for the anchoring physicality of him, for the knowing look he would have given her when she described that lone bird crying out into the thin winter air. For the sweet, promising smile he would have shared when she described the features of that eager, ruddy-faced delivery boy—because the two of them would have a ruddy boy one day. Their boy.

That's what she wanted most of all: she wanted to tell him she was carrying his child. She hadn't had her courses since before their wedding; she now knew she was most definitely increasing. Not that she had planned on sharing such momentous news in a crowded box at the new Covent Garden Theatre, but she couldn't imagine spending even a moment with him without telling him the news. She was bursting in every way imaginable.

She'd been too frustrated and full of consternation when she'd seen him at Christopher's to speak of anything but how impossibly stubborn he was. Plus, any mention of a child would've only served to make him that much more possessive and intransigent about his *godly* demands.

That evening, she and Bea prepared for the theater with meticulous care. She wanted to be both modest and alluring. Archie adored her in any dress—or undress for that matter—but she wanted him to see her at her best, to be proud of her. To be glad he had married her.

Mary piled most of her unruly blonde hair on top of her head in a deceptively simple style, but she left a few curled strands dangling down the right side of her neck. She had never cottoned to the latest fashion of fussy curls hanging in front of her eyes—it was both distracting and unbecoming.

Beatrix was equally lovely. After being so peevish the past few days, Selina took a moment to stare at Bea while Mary coiled her hair into a loose Roman style, with a gold diadem a few inches back from her forehead. Her lips were dark red and slightly curved, her nose straight and proud. She was a classically beautiful woman, and the style suited her perfectly.

When Mary was finished, and asked if there was anything else either woman needed, Bea stood to leave the room. Selina held her back.

"Please tell the footman we will be down in ten minutes, Mary."

"Yes, my lady." Mary dipped her chin and shut the door behind her.

Selina kept her restraining hold on Bea's gloved forearm. Bea's muscles were taut and lovely from years at the piano. Loosening her grip slightly, Selina leaned in close and inhaled, never quite touching her. "I'm sorry, my love. I've been quite unkind these past few days."

Bea turned to look her in the eye. She was a few inches taller, and Selina's heart pounded when she looked up into Bea's eyes.

"May I kiss you?" Bea asked in a low voice.

"Please."

When Bea's lips touched hers, she pressed into her, out of habit and desperation and love. She didn't want to muss Bea's lovely hair or her beautiful dress, but Lord how she wanted her. She pushed her gently back to the settee, until Bea sat and exhaled.

"We are expected downstairs," Bea whispered.

Selina dipped to her knees, carefully adjusting her dress so as not to wrinkle the pristine silk skirt that Mary had spent time ironing and preparing for the evening out. "I've been so preoccupied, Bea. I need . . . I want . . ." She stuttered as she slowly pulled up the heavy copper velvet of Bea's gown. She stroked her palms along the silk of Bea's stockings. "I miss him, Bea. It makes me feel like a traitor. But I miss him."

"I know you do," Bea replied, placing her hand on Selina's cheek and caressing her way down the pale skin of her neck to the edge of her bodice. "It's fine to miss him, to want him."

"But I want you. I want you on my lips when I kiss him tonight." She dipped her head and kissed the inside of Bea's silken thigh, then looked up from her lower position. "I want him to know that you are part of me." She bent down and kissed her again, higher up her leg.

"Darling, you shouldn't—" Bea resisted.

Then Selina kissed Bea's pussy, interrupting thought and reason. She wanted her, a little taste of her for courage, before they were all thrown to the wolves of society and the ton and all those watching eyes, all those people who wanted a story, or clarity, or some sort of understanding about the Marquess of Camburton and his *unique* wife, and his wife's *friend* the pianist, and his *friend* the scientist. And how *strange* it all seemed.

She licked the familiar edge of Bea's cunny and shut her eyes. There was nothing *strange* about this, damn it. Beatrix was her home, her heart's home. At the moment, she felt like some porcelain doll, her hair coiffed to some rigid ideal, her dress crinkling in starched perfection, and her face pressed lewdly between Beatrix's legs. The two of them panted and groaned quietly until she dipped her tongue deep into Bea's center and Bea's hips tipped toward her and the suction and urgency of her lips brought Bea to a fast, brief climax.

Bea's fingers were ground into the edge of the couch, grasping the cushion. "Don't ever do that to me again." Bea's voice was rough, both satisfied and impatient all at once.

Selina pulled back and stood up slowly. "I am a selfish beast."

Bea looked up at her from the settee. She was flushed and happy and frustrated, and Selina felt something akin to pride at having elicited all that emotion.

"I want to touch you when you touch me . . . and that was terrible," Bea breathed. "To have you give me all that pleasure and instead of being able to clutch my fingers into your beautiful hair or press my lips against your lovely cheek I was frozen in some horrible approximation of unshared joy."

Selina pressed the flat of her hands along her bodice and then down over her hips. "We need to stay presentable. And I missed you."

Bea smiled up at her, took a deep breath, and then stood to face her. "I missed you too." Bea leaned in and kissed her, the lightest peck so as not to sully her appearance. "I shan't mess your cosmetics. You look lovely." They walked toward the door, arm in arm. "He loves you, my dear. And if I need to repair to the Continent for a few months, I shall do that—"

"No!"

"Shh. Let us go to the theater. Maybe he'll surprise you."

Selina had requested that the finest carriage be brought round to deliver them to Covent Garden. The gleaming red barouche with the marquess's crest awaited them as they stepped out onto Grosvenor Square. When they entered the compartment, she made a silent prayer that Archie and Christopher would be inside the carriage on their return trip a few hours hence.

"Soon." Beatrix read her thoughts and held her hand as they made their way slowly through the crowded streets of Mayfair toward the West End. When they approached the theater, the winter streets were clogged with carriages and pedestrians. Her heart pounded wildly and she kept thinking they should step out of the carriage and walk the rest of the way, but Bea kept her in place, soothing her with the familiar trace of her thumb on her knuckles. "Hold. We're almost there."

As they stepped out into the harsh light beneath the theatrical torches, she felt too exposed; she wanted to pull Bea close, to kiss her warm neck, but she remembered where they were.

"Keep walking, my dear," Bea whispered behind her.

She realized she'd turned motionless in the brittle air. The press of bustling people entering the theater created a human barrier to the winter wind, but even so the chill seemed to enter her bones. She looked across the jostling crowd into the lobby, and saw Archie in full evening dress. He was standing perfectly still—a steady rock in the sea of human movement all around him—and he stared at her through the glass doors with the piercing intensity of a ray of sunshine through a shard of crystal.

Chapter 17

rchie stared at his beautiful wife. Other men stared. She was pausing to check her hem or the hang of her reticule, and he was unable to breathe. Her hair, her skin, the trim fit of her bodice: he had never seen her looking more lovely, and the sight nearly bowled him over.

Christopher touched his elbow. "Stay standing, my friend."

"I wish you could hold me."

"Soon." Christopher's voice was low and passionate, while his face remained a casual mask of disinterest. "Soon I will hold you—your back against my bare chest—while your wife gives you all the pleasure you deserve."

Archie had a moment of worry that those around him would know what Christopher was saying, even though he knew his friend was a master of appearing nonchalant, no matter how depraved his words actually were.

"She's coming. They're coming."

Keeping his eyes on the front doors, he stared while Selina was distracted, and then he held his breath when she lifted her gaze directly to his. Her expression was incomprehensible at first, distant. Then her eyes caught fire—whether from love or anger he wasn't sure—but at least there was still something resembling passion inside her.

As Beatrix and Selina crossed the crowded lobby, several people intercepted them, and he could see they were congratulating Beatrix on her musical accomplishments and smiling at the lovely marchioness and congratulating her on her recent marriage. As the two women got closer to where he and Christopher were standing, he could hear the people around them referring to Selina as "the marchioness" and his heart hammered for how deeply he wanted her to be *his* marchioness in every sense of the word.

For the first time, he saw Beatrix clearly—as Selina's lover—and he forced himself to watch her. She was a tall, confident beauty. Her features were nearly severe, yet classically feminine. She'd done her dark chestnut hair in a style that served to solidify the comparison— once again, she looked like a Greek goddess. He admired her, the way she carried herself, the way she kept Selina safe and near as she moved through the crowd. Moreover, he was able to see why Selina admired her, which was far more important in any case.

Beatrix's head swiveled to him at that moment. He was close enough to hear the Romanian count praising her, throwing his hands aloft to indicate the depth of his appreciation for her recent performance in Bucharest. Beatrix kept her gaze on Archie, as if she were sizing him up. The foreigner kept yammering, and she nodded occasionally, so as not to alienate him, but eventually she dipped her chin to the other man. "I thank you again, but I believe we are headed to the Marquess of Camburton's box now."

The man turned to him and sketched an elegant bow. "How lucky the Marquess of Camburton is to be escorting two of the loveliest ladies in the theater." Then he bowed again to Selina and left the four of them to stare at one another in the crowded lobby.

"Lord Camburton." Beatrix dipped a curtsey, then looked at Christopher. Archie realized they had never been properly introduced at Devonshire House, and it would have been forward of her to call him by name, despite the shared intimacy that coursed between all four of them.

"Miss Farnsworth." He reached for her gloved hand and squeezed the tips of her long fingers. "Please allow me to present my very good friend, Mr. Christopher Joseph. Christopher, the renowned pianist, Miss Beatrix Farnsworth."

Christopher bowed and then took Bea's hand and kissed her knuckles through the fine kidskin. Archie was beyond imagining what lay in store for each of them individually, much less all of them together in a bed at one time. He was beyond imagining anything but the feel of his wife's skin beneath the pads of his tingling fingertips.

"Lady Camburton. You are looking very well."

Selina stared at him, her tongue peeking out slowly to moisten the edge of her lip. "Lord Camburton." She dipped a slight curtsey out of habit. "You are looking . . . quite splendid." The compliment spilled out in a breathy rush.

He felt his neck and cheeks flush in embarrassment. "May I escort you to our box?" He held out his forearm, and Selina stared at the familiar gesture. For a moment, he thought she was going to spurn him, but he stayed still and waited. "Please."

Her eyes flew to his, and then there was a press of people and Selina was shoved closer. He grabbed her around her middle to steady her, and the span of her waist in his hands set his mind afire.

"Yes. Yes. Always yes." Her lips were devilishly close to his ear, because of the crush around them. But when the crowd thinned, she pulled away again. Taking a deep breath, she took his hand from her waist, extended his arm as if he were a marionette, and placed her elegant hand on his forearm. "There. That is as it should be."

When she squeezed him through the fine silk of his navy-blue jacket, he wanted to fall to the marble floor and bury his face in the layers of her beautiful dress. They seemed to float through the crowd, Beatrix and Christopher following a few steps behind them.

"Have you—"

"Will you—"

They both began simultaneously, then smiled and fell silent again.

"You first," Selina said as they started to ascend the wide, sweeping staircase to the second level.

"Have you enjoyed your time in London?"

She'd been holding a piece of her dress a few inches above the ground so as not to trip on her way up the stairs, but his vapid question must have startled her. She released the fabric and nearly stumbled.

"Not in the least. Have *you*?" She sounded hurt, as if he were suggesting that he had somehow *enjoyed* wandering the streets of east London like a pauper.

They had reached the entrance to the box by then, so he did not answer what he supposed was a rhetorical question. He held back the curtain to let Selina pass, but she did not release him or move to enter.

"Archie?"

"Yes?" He was distracted, looking down the foyer and acknowledging an earl who had smiled in greeting. Christopher and Beatrix were nearly upon them.

"Look at me," Selina demanded.

He turned to face her, but it was incredibly difficult to hold her gaze. "It is very hard for me to look at you," he answered honestly, "when I want to rip that golden confection off your body and make love to you for the next five days."

Her eyes shone with answering pleasure. "Only five days, my lord?"

"Five months, my lady?"

"Five years?"

"Five decades?" he shot back easily, and then leaned in close. He had to kiss her, propriety be damned. For the first time in their acquaintance, he saw that he took her by surprise. Dipping quickly to press his lips against hers—ignoring the affronted gasp of a passing dowager duchess—he even teased his tongue between her lips and made a quick sweep into the warm welcome of her mouth.

He pulled away just as quickly and licked the inside of his upper lip. "Is that Beatrix on your lips?" he whispered, with a mix of joy and fear. His ego could only take so much. He wanted to give Selina everything in his power to give, even her freedom if that's what she was after, but the idea of letting her go made his chest constrict in pain.

"Yes."

"Do you love her?" He let the naked fear show in his words.

"Yes." But she reached up and touched his cheek to mollify him. "And I love *you*. And I've missed *you*. And I don't ever want to be parted from you again."

"Must we stay for the play?"

Selina laughed and patted his cheek. "Whatever will people say if the Marquess and Marchioness of Camburton leave the theater before the play has even begun?"

He stared into her eyes. "They will say the marquess is in love with his wife."

"Or they might suspect the marchioness is enceinte."

His breath hitched. "Are you?"

The way she gazed up at him filled every desperate inch of his aching heart with hope and joy. "Yes."

Beatrix and Christopher had arrived, and Archie turned to Christopher. "My wife does not wish to stay for the play after all. Shall we return to Camburton House and see to her comfort?" He looked to Beatrix as he asked that last, imploring her.

Beatrix smiled at Selina and then at him. And he realized how much of a fool he had been to see her as an adversary, or even worse, as an enemy. "I think that is a very fine idea, Lord Camburton. The marchioness has been quite agitated in your absence, and as you can see, she is in great need of relief."

Christopher coughed. "Out. Now. All of you."

The play was about to begin and the four of them, as if they were swimming upstream, hurried past the last stragglers who were racing to take their seats. A few minutes later they were seated in the spacious carriage, breathless with excitement and anticipation.

They were all together at last. Sitting through two hours of farce and wordplay would have been torture. The moment she'd spied Archie across the lobby, Selina could see he was hers—theirs—at last. She squeezed his hand. "Archie?"

"Yes?" He was staring at her again, and she loved the feel of that eager gaze.

"What have you decided?"

"I've decided I love you." He turned to look across the carriage at Christopher, and she watched in unexpected delight. "And I also love Christopher." Archie hung his head, as if waiting for the sword of an angry God to strike him dead—or her justifiable accusations of hypocrisy to let fly.

Instead, she lifted his chin and kissed him tenderly. "Congratulations."

"You don't mind?"

"Oh, darling!" She threw up her hands and then grabbed him to her, slamming her lips against his and taking what she'd missed all these past days—the rock-solid feel of him against her, on her, surrounding her, consuming her. She finished devouring him—for the moment—and pulled away a few inches from his mouth, yanking her gloves off with laughing impatience. "And may I kiss Beatrix in front of you? Or do you wish me to keep my love for her as a separate, private thing, apart from our marriage?"

When she sat away from him, awaiting his reply, he stared first at her, then at Beatrix. The wall of his defenses turned to sand. "I would like nothing more than for you to allow me the great privilege of seeing how you and Beatrix honor your love for one another."

She pressed the flat of her hand against his chest, and she could feel the frantic beat of his heart. "I still love you, Archie. You know that now?"

"Yes. I know that now." He was utterly solemn, and she realized this was far more of a vow than any he had made in that country church two months ago.

She couldn't keep from kissing him one more time. "You are my dream come true, my love. You are my dream." Then she turned to face Beatrix across the carriage. "Please come to me."

Bea smiled and moved from one side of the carriage to the other, dipping her head so she didn't bump against the roof.

Keeping her firm hold on Archie's hand, their fingers laced together, Selina reached up to Bea's cheek with the other. "Beatrix, my love . . ." Then she leaned in and kissed her. Her eyes slid shut, and Bea moaned into her. Archie's hand tightened slightly. She had never been more sure of who she was and what she deserved. She needed both of these people. She adored both of these people.

Archie began kissing the turn of her neck, where it met her shoulder. She whimpered into Bea's deepening kiss. The erotic play of Archie's lips, Bea's tongue, and Christopher's heated gaze sent all sorts of chills down her spine.

The carriage jolted to a halt in front of Camburton House, and she realized they had spent the entire ride in that effervescent bubble of kisses and light touches and discovery. Looking very much like four startled deer caught unawares in the forest, they began to laugh quietly as the footman opened the door to let them out. By the time they were at the front door, they were all laughing in great peals.

Heading straight for the staircase, she grabbed at her skirt and took the treads two at a time. Archie, Christopher, and Beatrix were close on her heels. She careened around the turn in the bannister, and Mary came flying out of her chamber. "Is everything all right, my lady? You're back so soon." Then Mary's face shifted from concern to embarrassed awareness. She curtseyed. "You won't be needing me, then."

"No!" Selina practically sang. "I'm ever so grateful for everything you did to make me presentable for this evening—" the other three had already entered the master suite ahead of her and she was walking backwards as she spoke to her maid "—but it seems it was going to be a terrible bore so we decided to return home for . . . a game of Whist. Now that the marquess has returned and we have a fourth."

Mary smiled and curtseyed again. "Yes, my lady." Then the maid turned, made her way briskly to the servants' stairs, and was gone.

Selina spun around and stepped into Archie's room. Her room. *Their room.* She shut the door behind her and watched as Christopher began to touch Archie. She marveled at the way he handled him, and how pleased Archie looked to be touched and almost roughened up in that way, especially while Selina and Beatrix watched.

"Archie," Christopher ordered, "say hello to your wife and her lover."

She realized all the shame was gone—all the forced compliance of their tryst in the laboratory, which had been delectable in its way: gone. This was something else altogether, something glorious. Archie's eyes shone with desire and eagerness, as they always had, but there was now a sheen of independence and self-acceptance that had never been there before.

"Hello, Selina. Hello, Beatrix." Such simple words, but said while another man's hands were roaming across Archie's hard abdomen, removing his immaculate blue jacket. Once the jacket was off, Archie reached his hands up behind him and laced them around the base of Christopher's neck. The posture was both relaxed and formal, as if Archie was presenting himself to her and Beatrix for their appraisal—as if he wanted them to look.

"Hello, Archie," she replied.

"Hello, Archie." Beatrix followed Christopher's lead and began undressing Selina, standing behind her and tracing the curve of Selina's breast, the flare of her hip.

Everything felt exquisitely *right*. "Kiss me," Selina whispered to Bea.

The first fiery touch of Bea's lips against her neck sent searing pleasure to her nipples and a rippling excitement between her legs. She kept her eyes locked on Archie's, searching his gaze for any hint of worry or resistance to what he was seeing. Bea moved slowly, those warm, wet kisses blazing a trail to her ear, where Bea proceeded to nip at her sensitive lobe.

Gasping at the piercing sensation, she kept watching Archie, watching the way his lips were slightly open and his cheeks were flushed. She glanced down to where Christopher had finished unbuttoning the fall of Archie's trousers and moaned when she saw Archie's hard cock spring free. She licked her lips when Christopher took hold of it with one knowing hand—so rough and sure—and her eyes flew back to Archie's. He was looking at her with so much hope and desire, and what appeared to be a hint of fear.

"This is me," he whispered. Christopher's hold around his bare waist tightened, keeping him safe, assuring him, but Christopher's steady pumping of Archie's cock never ceased.

"I love that this is you." Bea had loosened the upper half of Selina's gown, and she slowly lowered the sleeves and bodice to reveal her tight, aroused breasts. Bea's hands squeezed and kneaded her from behind. "This is me, Archie. Can you see me? Can you love me, knowing how much I love this? How much I love her?" Her hand reached up for Bea and, as if in a dream, she turned and brought Bea's mouth to hers.

The kiss was an inferno of need and desire and then pure simple love, Selina connecting with Bea in a way she never had—openly—without that lingering worry that Archie did not know the truth, that she had not been completely honest. This was what complete honesty felt like.

When she pulled away from the kiss, slow shallow breaths warm on her moist lips, she turned back to find Archie was right in front of her, with Christopher pressed close behind.

"Yes." Archie looked into her eyes, then leaned in and kissed her hard. "Yes," he repeated, "I love you like this." Then he turned his head slightly. "Welcome, Beatrix."

And Selina's heart fell to the center of the earth as he tilted his head and kissed Beatrix lightly on the lips. Her eyes closed as the seductive sound of Archie and Bea kissing, so near to her ear, right there at her shoulder, set her heart thudding.

"Thank you," Archie whispered into Bea's lips, and the words wound through to Selina's soul. She opened her eyes slowly to see Christopher looking at her with that devil-may-care half smile of his, while his hands roamed lazily up and down Archie's arms and shoulders.

"Are you happy, Lady Camburton?" he asked politely, as if they were in a public drawing room or at a ball, rather than half-naked and pressed together like the pages of a book.

"Ecstatic."

Archie smiled at her. "Turn around so I may finish with your gown."

When she obliged, she looked into Bea's eyes. "And are *you* happy, my love?"

In answer, Bea began removing the pins from Selina's hair. "I am. But I should be ever so much happier without all these confining clothes on."

"Are you sure?" All hint of playfulness was gone from her voice. She and Bea had spoken about this moment many times. Bea had never been with a man, and the last thing Selina wanted was for her to feel compelled to participate.

"Yes. Seeing you with him—being with you while you take him—loving you while he loves you—that will be one of the great joys of my life." Bea reached up and pulled the last hairpin out so Selina's blonde hair tumbled free. "I am quite sure."

Selina began undoing Bea's fastenings, fumbling with the stays and ribbons in her excitement—while Archie did the same for her, and Christopher did the same for him—until they were all naked and she was able to press herself against the curves and fire of Bea's supple body.

And then she simply groaned with joy and desire. Archie was naked against her back—the rough, familiar texture of hair and muscle and bone; Bea was at her front—smooth and lithe. Christopher was also there, encircling them all while providing the anchor and strength that fulfilled Archie's—finally admitted—needs.

She smiled dreamily, and Bea smiled in return. The four of them tumbled in an awkward pile onto the large bed, with laughter and touches and kisses and moans punctuating their fall. They pulled at the sheets, grabbed at each other, rolled, and squirmed. She was in an exquisite reverie, where all of her long-held fantasies were being brought to life.

Yet, there was nothing dreamlike about the very real details of their lovemaking: Bea's hand at her breast, Archie's mouth on her pussy, even Christopher's firm hold on her hip, all felt specific and necessary.

She closed her eyes in bliss, then felt a second mouth on her pussy—her head flew up off the pillow, and she saw Archie and Bea side by side between her wantonly spread legs. Christopher was holding her in place with both hands now, pressing her hips into the bed with immovable pressure.

And Archie was smiling, his eyes meeting hers while his mouth was on her, and then his mouth was battling playfully with Bea's mouth, and Christopher's hands were preventing Selina from rocking into the pleasure of it, until somehow that resistance forged a release that was even more spectacular than she could have imagined.

She cried out and arched her back and still their mouths sucked and licked and worked into her. While her body continued to quake, she gasped in amazement as Bea whispered something in Archie's ear, then Bea smiled up and nodded to Christopher. Before Selina realized what was happening, Archie was on his knees between her legs, lifting Selina's hips to suit him, and then thrusting into her. She was still so sensitive from the shattering orgasm she'd just experienced, but the pressure and thoroughness of Archie inside her set her muscles alight. Everything about him made her feel replete.

And then Bea's mouth was on her breast, making love to her and twisting her insides into something hot and malleable and desperate. She rode the pleasure, forcing herself to hold off her next release.

She breathed through the intensity of it and watched as Christopher positioned himself behind Archie and then tugged possessively on Archie's hair.

"You're ready, Archie?" Christopher growled, but it was more of a statement than a question. Archie *was* ready. At last. And then she felt the reverberating thrust as Christopher entered Archie from behind and Archie thrust into her again.

When she arched her back to withdraw from Archie, to get a moment to breathe, that only served to press her sensitive breasts harder into Bea's clever mouth; when she canted her hips in a vain attempt to pull from Bea, that only brought Archie deeper into her. It felt as if there were hands and mouths and lips and fingers everywhere. Her fingers finally found Bea's moist center in the flow of bodies, and she reveled in Bea's answering groan of pleasure against her breast.

"Come to me," Selina whispered, her voice already shredded from her cries of pleasure. When Bea didn't stop sucking on her breast, Selina dug her fingers into Bea's scalp and forced her mouth away. "Here, damn it." She pulled Bea's mouth to hers and kissed her, while her other hand worked Bea's pussy, circling her clit and then pressing two fingers into her swollen slit. "Come for me."

Chapter 18

Archie watched as Selina held Beatrix through her orgasm, Beatrix curled against Selina's side and burrowing her face into Selina's neck and shoulder while she shuddered. And Selina watched him watching. Selina held Bea with so much love and devotion, and *Yes*, Selina's look seemed to say, *through it all I can still belong to you.*

She gave him the smallest smile of intimate understanding, a tiny nod. And then he pressed deeper into her as Christopher pressed deeper into him. The pressure was nearly beyond bearing, and he turned slightly and let his head fall back against Christopher's solid shoulder.

"I'm going . . ." Selina whispered, her eyes saying more than her words. He felt the moment of pause, the infinite hesitation that always precipitated her release, and then she cried out again and her muscles pulled him deeper still, until he was following her into the furthest reaches of pleasure.

Christopher bit the straining, corded muscle at the turn of Archie's shoulder and held on to him like a primitive animal while he came into Archie's body. Archie had never experienced such an array of physical and emotional sensations. The human and the divine. The earth and the sky.

And Selina. Always Selina.

After that, the four of them were little more than a hapless bundle of limbs and breath and whispers piled atop his aristocratic bed. They all finally settled into the curves and planes of one another's bodies, and drowsed into blissful sleep.

When the weak winter sun peeked through a narrow opening in the velvet curtains several hours later, he opened his eyes to see Selina staring at him a few inches away. Christopher was asleep behind him—and probably would be until noon or later. Beatrix seemed to be sleeping soundly behind Selina, if the other woman's steady breathing was anything to go by.

"Happy new year, Lord Camburton." Selina's face was resting on her hands and he saw that Beatrix's hand was draped gracefully over Selina's hip.

"Happy new year, Lady Camburton."

"I missed you terribly. Please don't ever leave me again."

He reached up to her cheek and traced his thumb along the beautiful lines of her face. "I shall never leave you, my lovely wife." He kissed her briefly on the lips.

Then his eyes shifted to his right, indicating Christopher over his shoulder. "He sleeps until noon at the earliest."

"So does she." Selina grinned with conspiratorial glee. "Shall we go for a ride?"

"Yes." He was as excited as a child about to play the truant, then his face fell. "Is it safe? For the babe?" He reached his hand under the covers and let his palm rest over the slight swell of her lower belly.

She put her hand over his, then laced her delicate fingers into his stronger ones. "This child comes from us, so I suspect he will be as stubborn and willful and vital as we are."

"Still . . ." He couldn't hide his worry.

"Very well, let us ride in your curricle."

He smiled and squeezed her hand in his. "Excellent."

They slid out of bed without disturbing Christopher or Bea, and quickly changed into warm clothes. Selina helped him with his cravat, and he helped Selina with her riding habit. They went down the grand staircase hand-in-hand, then crossed the front hall and turned toward the back of the mansion.

When they reached the stables, he rigged up the matching bays himself, telling the sleepy groomsman he was free to go back to bed. Confused, but grateful, the man returned to his room.

When Archie finished with the traces and the harnesses, he offered his hand to assist Selina onto the high seat. "My lady?"

She took his hand and held it, but before stepping up, she turned to him. "Thank you for loving me."

A warm flood of emotion bloomed in his chest and then spread out to his fingertips and toes. "Thank you for showing me how."

Explore more of the
Regency Reimagined universe at
riptidepublishing.com/titles/universe/regency-reimagined

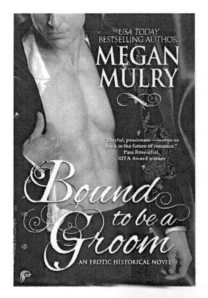

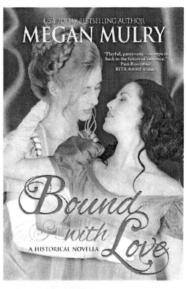

Dear Reader,

Thank you for reading Megan Mulry's *Bound With Honor*!

We know your time is precious and you have many, many entertainment options, so it means a lot that you've chosen to spend your time reading. We really hope you enjoyed it.

We'd be honored if you'd consider posting a review—good or bad—on sites like **Amazon, Barnes & Noble, Kobo, Goodreads, Twitter, Facebook, Tumblr,** and your blog or website. We'd also be honored if you told your friends and family about this book. Word of mouth is a book's lifeblood!

For more information on upcoming releases, author interviews, blog tours, contests, giveaways, and more, please sign up for our weekly, spam-free newsletter and visit us around the web:

Newsletter: tinyurl.com/RiptideSignup
Twitter: twitter.com/RiptideBooks
Facebook: facebook.com/RiptidePublishing
Goodreads: tinyurl.com/RiptideOnGoodreads
Tumblr: riptidepublishing.tumblr.com

Thank you so much for Reading the Rainbow!

RiptidePublishing.com

Acknowledgments

There are so many people to thank for bringing these stories to life. *Bound with Honor* is the final installment in the Regency Reimagined world, all of which began way back when with *Bound to Be a Bride* in early 2012. At the time, I thought the books would be about three Spanish heroes who were trying to sail to the New World. They got waylaid, obviously.

Stories tend to take on a life of their own and that's precisely what happened here. As I was writing and researching these books, I became increasingly fascinated with polyamory and sexual power dynamics and gender fluidity and *everything*, until suddenly these books became the repositories for all my nascent enthusiasms.

So without further ado, thank you to *all* the readers, writers, editors, and fellow twitter pervs who came along for this wild ride (and the stick-figure four-ways): Janet Webb, Miranda Neville, Anne Calhoun, Mira Lyn Kelly, Pam Rosenthal, Sarah Frantz Lyons, Delphine Dryden, Sarah MacLean, Jeffe Kennedy, Julia Broadbooks, Lexi Ryan, Magdalen Braden, Alex Whitehall, Chris Muldoon, Rachel Haimowitz, Andrea LeClair, Amelia Vaughn, Kelly Miller, Adara O'Hare, Alexandra Haughton, Amy Jo Cousins, Peg Mulry, Kathy Fay, Hope Kelly, Tamsen Parker, Alexis Hall, Jennifer RNN, CJ Lemire, Bobbi Dumas, Stephanie Wrightsman, Sassy Outwater, Mermaid Sharon, RealAng00, Jodie Griffin, Petra Grayson, Christine Maria Rose, Isobel Carr, Jenn LeBlanc, Michele Harvey, Saschakeet, Elisabeth Lane, Eloisa James, Lisa Hendrix, J. Huisinga, Kiersten Hallie Krum, Cathy Pegau, Sara Harlequin Junkie, Lori Alpert, Sasha Harinanan, Heidi Cullinan, Landra Graf, Maya Rodale, Shari Slade, Shelley Ann Clark, Liz Blue, Emily Jane Hubbard, Deidre Meyrick, Adam Peck, Rachel Kramer Bussel, and Ken Elias.

I also want to thank all the bloggers and publications that supported these anachronistic romps: Heroes & Heartbreakers,

Publishers Weekly, AustenStudent, 3 Chicks After Dark, Goodreads Ménage Reading Group, Marienela, Love Bites and Silk, Harlequin Junkie, Romance Novel News, Prism Book Alliance, Erotic Enchantments, My Book Addiction and More, Joyfully Jay, The Romance Evangelist, Creative Deeds Reads, Herding Cats & Burning Soup, and Romancing the Book.

And a very shiny, silky, breathlessly panting thank you to L.C. Chase for making the delectable Riptide covers, with wonderful photography from Novel Expressions!

ALSO BY Megan Mulry

Regency Reimagined series
Bound to Be a Bride
Bound to Be a Groom
Bound with Love
Bound with Passion

Contemporary
A Royal Pain
If the Shoe Fits
In Love Again
R is for Rebel
Roulette

Historical
The Wallflowers

ABOUT THE  Author

Megan Mulry writes sexy, stylish, romantic fiction. Her first book, *A Royal Pain*, was an NPR Best Book of 2012 and *USA Today* bestseller. Before discovering her passion for romance novels, she worked in magazine publishing and finance. After many years in New York, Boston, London, and Chicago, she now lives with her family in Florida.

Website: meganmulry.com
Goodreads: bit.ly/1boncLy
Facebook: facebook.com/meganmulry
Pinterest: www.pinterest.com/meganmulrybooks
Twitter: twitter.com/MeganMulry
Email: megan@meganmulry.com

Enjoy more stories like
Bound with Honor at
RiptidePublishing.com!

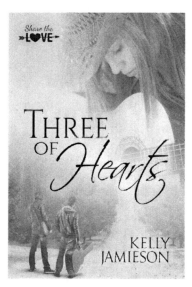

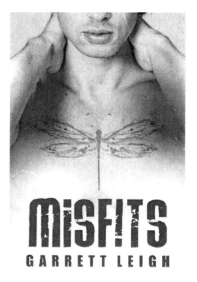

Three of Hearts
ISBN: 978-1-62649-255-4

Misfits
ISBN: 978-1-62649-247-9

Earn Bonus Bucks!

Earn 1 Bonus Buck for each dollar you spend. Find out how at
RiptidePublishing.com/news/bonus-bucks.

Win Free Ebooks for a Year!

Pre-order coming soon titles directly through our site and you'll
receive one entry into a drawing to win free books for a year! Get
the details at RiptidePublishing.com/contests.

CPSIA information can be obtained at www.ICGtesting.com
Printed in the USA
LVOW08s0105190815

450694LV00004B/265/P